The
BOOK
of
DAYS

FRANCESCA
KAY

Swift

SWIFT PRESS

First published in Great Britain by Swift Press 2024

1 3 5 7 9 10 8 6 4 2

Typeset by Tetragon, London
Printed in England by CPI Group (UK) Ltd, Croydon, CRO 4YY

A CIP catalogue record for this book is available from the British Library

ISBN: 9781800753495
eISBN: 9781800753501

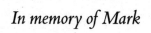

In memory of Mark

The tenth day of the month of April

Caught on the daylight that comes glancing through the clear glass of the windows on the south wall, the stone dust dances, drifts away and invisibly falls. Stone-taste in the mouth, a breath of dust and bone. New light from the east where there was dark before, and dust on light-beam dancing, dancing to the music of mallets striking stone, a ringing and a rhythm. Jack the elder and Jack the younger taking turns and swinging forward, pulling back, and the stone dust rising as the old wall shudders and yields. A scatter of bright paint across the floor.

A ceremony this, the knocking through, that should have witnesses besides a pair of Jacks, the mason Simm and me. It marks the start of something new. But in the village they are afraid of newness and convinced that when the wall is breached, the roof will fall in too. Even the priest and the churchwarden are keeping at a distance for fear of shattered skulls. They should have greater trust in Simm. He may be saying his prayers this minute to the patron saint of masons but he has also driven iron bars into the stones above the intended rupture and made temporary buttresses from tree trunks; we will be quite safe. Although he was surprised to see me, he did not turn me away and simply warned me to beware of flying chips of stone. Yes, I will be, I remember that a young lad lost an eye last year to a nail that came arrowing straight at him from a piece of timber. Today, the men have bound lengths of cloth about their mouths and noses, and they squint cautiously beneath their caps.

If it were fresh stone that they worked, Simm would call the tune. He is the master musician of the band, the one who hears most clearly the inner note of every new block, who tests it, tapping gently with a chisel, listening, tapping again, ear cocked for the stone's response. Stone speaks; it says to him: strike here, this is the place for the first cut, here will I break open for you, clean as chalk, clean as the bark of a beech tree lately felled. I have heard Simm whisper to a stone. And seen him tasting one; he tells the provenance of stone by tongue as well as eye, and by his sense of smell. When it is freshly cut, he says, limestone gives off a charnel scent, an autumn air of earth and dying leaves, as if it held within it a remembrance of a time before its form was solid.

But it is not new stone that makes this dust, it is stone that is part of a wall so old that no one knows how long it may have stood here. Yesterday, on Easter Sunday, there was an altar by this wall on which a bank of tapers burned, as they have always burned for untold years, and today the fragments of that altar are stacked up on a barrow. And in the wall itself, where Lazarus once was, for centuries emerging from his tomb still swaddled in his grave-clothes, there is now a widening hole. To make things new, we must destroy, my lord my husband said; but the new will bring great glory.

Jack and Jack work fast. Between the inner face and the outer wall a narrow gap is filled with rubble and crumbled mortar. Jack the elder reaches in and pulls out a length of bone.

Sheep's bone, Simm says without looking. Throw it on the barrow.

He has a wooden template, the outline of an arch, a graceful shape like a wishbone or like the tips of fingers meeting, which he is holding at the ready. There is still a way to go but now the hole is wide enough to admit a slender person. Little Jack looks enquiringly at the mason.

Yes, why not, Simm says, and Jack crawls through to the far side, one leg first, then folded body, the other leg hauled after. Framed by jagged stone he reappears, his broad grin signalling success.

May I see too?

Simm shakes his head. You will break your ankle on the unsteady pile.

But Jack says he can make a sort of ledge for me from the tumbled stone and help me to jump down. She is but a thin creature, he says to Simm in a whisper that is not as quiet as he thinks. He scrambles back and offers his hand and I take it before Simm can stop me.

Climbing in is as easy as crossing a stile, but as soon as I am there, I feel trapped. The chapel is only half-built; it has a make-shift roof of rushes, the spaces left for windows want mullions and glass, and nothing stops the light from streaming in. But it is still a prison. Women *are* enclosed by men, in chantries and in tombs. I have a sudden fear that these four walls are drawing closer. Damp and mud-smell now, and Jack's sweat, the leather of his jerkin and the stone dust, and pools of chilly water on the ground, for winter, having freely played through the scant thatch and the empty windows, has only just retreated, and there has been much rain. I shut my eyes and try to imagine the place when it is finished, to see the traceries of stone, to hear the chanting that it is made for, but I cannot; I must go back into the full light of the sun.

❧

How is it that the seasons turn so fast? Here is a conjuring overnight of green – or white and green – new leaves and cherry blossom, wood anemones and hawthorn in drifts of pure whiteness, as if these green days could not quite surrender their memories of snow.

I should return to the house, now that I have seen what is happening in the church, but it is too hard to forsake this world of light for the stale air of a sickroom. I shall go to the river instead, there is no one here to see me and I will not be long. Such depths of sadness there have been in these past months, and such dark days that I almost stopped believing in the existence of the sun. Weeks of snow, with storms to follow, and then a Lenten spell of pewter skies and rain so fierce it flooded fields, made rivers of the furrows and tadpoles of the seed. Linen, clothing, paper, straw, everything was sodden, and men were fearing for the grain and the waterlogged feet of cattle. Everywhere the sickly bloom of mould. And then it changed. As if the skies had wept their fill, the rains stopped suddenly and left behind this well-washed world of colour.

Simm predicted yesterday that this fine weather would hold at least a week and therefore the building work could recommence. I was not so sure this morning. At dawn, a mist lay thickly on the water meadow or, more exactly, hung above it, like a cloud that is tired of holding itself high but wary of sinking to the ground, lest it be enveloped by the dew. However, Simm was right, and now that mist has disappeared, burned away by sunshine. This April day is already hot as June, and it is good to walk alone through the long grass and the world's awakening to water that is likewise welcoming the sun's return and reflecting it in a million discs of gold.

Here the willows, like the thorn trees, are misted in soft green and it is quiet but for the chatter of ducks preoccupied with nests, and the soliloquy of water. No, soliloquy is not the right word, the river does not talk to itself, it converses with its banks and the stones that it flows over. Listen to its voice change when it meets a clutch of roots and must eddy round it, or when it combs through a skein of weed.

When I walk by myself I talk to myself aloud. It is the only way I know of knowing what I think. How else to trap elusive thought but in a net of words? Although there is no call for thought when walking by the river; it conduces to the stilling of the mind. In the continual movement of the water, the dapple and the patterns that it makes of light, in the quicksilver flash of a fish so swift that it might have been imagined had it not left a testament in ripples, it is possible to lose oneself. The river has its own purpose and is indifferent to mine.

I am ever hopeful of the kingfisher, that heart-lifting dart of flame and sapphire-blue. He is in hiding, though, this morning – and why should he be generous with his jewel colours? – but there is a heron, standing so stock-still on the riverbank that at first I mistake it for a dead branch lodged above the water. And, strangely, the bird remains there, unafraid, until I come so close to it that I can see each feather of its schoolman's cap, its cruel beak and the yellow roundel of its eye. For a while we contemplate each other, bird and woman, until it tires of me and takes slow, meditative, ungainly flight downstream. Yes, and its departure tells me that it is time to go back through the grass-scent and the cuckooflowers to the churchyard and the shadow of the yew tree, and from there to the darkness of the house.

༝

The hangings are drawn back around the bed but the one window is closed and the air lies flat and heavy. He is leaning against pillows, red and gold embroidered, a gaudiness that by contrast turns his skin to parchment. His daughter Agnes sits beside him on a stool.

Do they make progress? he says to me in greeting.

They do. There is an opening almost as wide as a door now, in the north wall. I stepped through it.

And the roof is sound?

It is.

Good. And the Easter sepulchre?

It is broken. The mason Simm could not remove it in one piece but he thinks the stone can be reused. What should he tell the people of the parish? They love that altar.

We will put something finer in its place and the people will be happy. Ask the mason to come to me this afternoon. If this weather stays and the carpenters make haste, he can send for the stone-carvers from Tewkesbury. They are working with my chosen imager at present and he might make the journey with them. If he does, so much the better.

The weather is fair indeed. Will you rise and go to dinner today? Hugh is expected home.

Yes, I will.

Despite the warmth of the room, he is wrapped in furs, silver hair entwined with sable. I go to him and put my hand against his forehead, where I ought to put my lips instead. His skin is dry and scaly.

I am reading to my lord my father, Agnes says, unnecessarily, as she is holding a book open on her lap. She does not say, because she dare not, that I am an unwelcome interruption.

You are a clever girl, I tell her.

Titus, quiet until now, starts rattling the chain that ties him to a bedpost, and jabbering in that urgent way of his. Hush, Agnes commands, but he persists. He must think us very foolish that we do not understand him, however hard he strives to share his meaning. If he could talk in human tongue, would he speak of fetters? There is something deep in the brown pools of his eyes, but he also has sharp yellow teeth and spiteful little fingers. I do not think he is a fit companion in a sickroom, and I say so.

He is company for my father, Agnes protests.

A different accusation left unsaid. I let the matter drop.

I feel for Agnes. Her father's sole surviving child, motherless since she was eight and finding the transition from girl to woman hard. Some girls slip into womanhood with ease but Agnes is all angles, awkward, stringy-haired and obdurate, and she suffers outbreaks of red pustules on her cheeks and chin. There might be remedy for those if mention of them were permitted, but it is not. Agnes is a proud girl and keeps her cares to herself. I wish it were otherwise, I wish we could be closer. She wrenches my heart. Motherless children, childless mothers, that's the way of the world.

Agnes walked before me at my wedding to her father, bearing a gilded branch of rosemary. Twelve gold coins he gave me then, laid out on his shield, and a golden ring. Women are chattels that men dispose of: my father sold, my husband bought, his first wife by that time almost three years in her grave.

꙳

It is eleven before noon and he is coming down the spiral staircase to the hall, with his servant Lambert by his side. One hand on the stone banister, the other clutching Lambert's lifted forearm. Step by single step, with great deliberation, slowly, slowly, slowly. Small children and the elderly do that same careful placing of both feet but he might reasonably have hoped for more time between those stages. Time is accelerating for him, winding his years onto its remorseless spool too fast, while for the rest of us it seems to be more lenient. I begin to see why the founding of the chantry is so urgent.

We who are already gathered, with our hands washed, observe this slow descent. When he gets to his place he lets go of Lambert. He can stand on his own still, supporting himself with both hands on the edge of the table. His nails are overlong, yellow on the bleached white cloth. Lambert fetches him the bowl of water.

The priest, Sir Joselin, having waited, takes his own place too, and so do we, remaining in silence for his mumbled grace: benedic, Domine nobis et donis tuis quae de tua largitate sumus sumpturi, et concede ut illis salubriter nutriti tibi debitum obsequium praestare valeamus, per Jesum Christum Dominum et Servatorem Nostrum.

Amen, we say. Sir Joselin, irrevocably wedded to the old ways, hurries through the words, impatient for his food. Everyone is hungry. My husband is served first.

On either side of him we sit, his wife and daughter, and we both watch every spoonful as he lifts it stiffly to his mouth. His hand trembles but he does not spill his broth. Agnes eats almost as little as her father does; although Lent is over, she has forsworn meat because, she says, it tastes of blood. All she has on her plate today is bread and herring.

Sitting next to Agnes, Hugh, newly returned from his visit to Oxford, asks if the roof of the church still holds, without a wall beneath it. Did Saint Stephen save it? Does it float? I wish I could have been here to see that wall knocked down!

It holds, my lord my husband answers, and smiles at Hugh, his dear nephew.

Never mind Saint Stephen, my lord's cousin Marmion says. The credit is all Simm's. Although we may have need of that saint yet, for don't forget he is also the patron saint of headaches. And of coffin-makers.

Hush, his wife, Dame Joan, reproaches him.

In the pause that follows, my mind-sight drifts to an image of a pitched roof and a steeple floating in the air, while far below a congregation gazes upwards in amazement, seeing sky where they expected rafters. Why not anticipate a miracle when it comes to the making of a chapel? There is a church in Rome that was built to the precise design of Our Lady. She came to the donor in a dream one August night and told him the place where she wanted it to be, and when he went there in the morning he found the outline of a church in freshly fallen snow. Only think of that: how the people must have marvelled at the sight, the sere and yellow grasses of high summer starred with snowflakes, the lovely coldness of them on their thirsty tongues. Mater castissima, our Lady of the Snows. Could there be a church made all of ice?

I am still thinking about snow when my attention is snatched back by a now-familiar argument between Marmion and my lord my husband.

Whatever you believe, the truth is that the church does not
befit us as it stands, my lord says. I should have razed it to the
ground, perhaps, and begun afresh. But in any case, walls have
been pulled down before and new ones built, as anyone can tell
from the traces that remain there. Have you never noted that
ghost of an old arch and a window blocked up long ago?

The fault lies not in the destruction of the old but in the
ambition of the new, Marmion disputes. This is no time to be
building church or chapel, it were better to put your superfluity
of gold into granaries and barns. Are memories so short these
days?

No, but the times are quieter now and the greediest of the
wolves is dead. I will have my chantry built, and no man will
stop me. Besides, I do nothing that contravenes the law.

When he arrives, my brother will tell us how things are – they
hear all the news at Lincoln's Inn, Hugh says happily. I think he
will be here within the week. Is the new priest travelling with
him, did someone say?

At the mention of the new priest, all eyes turn towards the
old one, but Sir Joselin says nothing and shows nothing of what
he feels. He simply chews his steady way through his slab of
pasty, doggedly and heedless of the fact that the rest of us have
finished eating. O Joselin, sweet man, with grease stains on the
black stuff of your gown, the relics of past meals, and drifts of
white flakes on your shoulders. We all fall silent too, except for
Titus, who is scratching around in the straw, playing daredevil
with the dogs. And still Sir Joselin eats, without haste and without a single glance about him.

It was Hugh, my lord's nephew, who showed me the ancient picture that is almost completely hidden in a corner of Yatt's field, beyond the village, by the quarry. My first summer here, on a hot day before the harvest; I remember that we skirted the tall grain and came upon some stones by a tangle of briar and hazel, like the remnants of a wall, and a few broken red clay tiles. Hugh, knowing where to look, knelt to pull away a mat of grass and hedging and uncovered a picture made of little squares of different-coloured stones. The face of a man, wide-eyed, dark-browed, with the sun behind him, or a wheel with spokes of gold. Who put it there, and why – who knows? Hugh said that there would certainly be more to see if we went on digging, look, here is what could be a horse's ear, probably the man was only part of a much larger picture, buried now beneath the earth. One day, he said, we will come back and search. Yes, perhaps we will. Meanwhile, I sometimes think about that man, mysterious and beautiful, with the curling hair across his forehead, resting there below his coverlet of grass. So many years he must have lain there, longer than mortal memory can stretch, seldom visited, almost entirely forgotten. And yet, who is he, that solitary man blazing out of darkness, who is he if not a god?

The nineteenth day of the month of April

A s swiftly as it came, the warmth of last week has now left and this morning there was sleet. Having been trapped in the house all day I fled outside near dusk, to walk along the walls of the demesne, and the clouds were still low-lying and deep-dark. But then, above the bank of cloud, a sudden glow of setting sun. I was at the locked gate, looking through it at the near field, and I saw how the light fell on the new leaves of the purple beech, so that they seemed transparent and they shone.

Simm and his men make headway in the teeth of constant rain, and at mass times hang up an oiled cloth to shield the faithful from the wind. Whenever I can, I go to the church to admire what is new. Such considering, measuring, assessing, shaping; trammels, templates, springing line and span. Twenty-six voussoirs for the arched doorway and every one of them requiring to be strictly cut and dressed, the facing edges combed. Stone has a grain and a bed, Simm says; it remembers how it lay when in the quarry and it must be set into a wall in the same way. For Simm, stone is a living thing. He was stung by the decision to import the master stone-carvers from Tewkesbury, protesting that he and his men already had the necessary art. But when my lord husband dreamt of this work, in his mind's eye he saw perfection; mere craftsmanship will not suffice. Limestone rubble might have done for old walls but the new stone must be immaculately dressed, smooth as butter in a mould. Instead of a plain wooden ceiling, there is to be stone tracery as delicate as

the pinions of a bird or the skeleton of a leaf. This chantry and
the other works that he has ordered are to be his monument, his
lasting gift, and I think they may also be his penance.

Village mason though he may be, Simm is possessed of great
skill, and it is a beautiful thing to watch him and his men at work.
They slid those twenty-six cut blocks of stone, each larger than
a child's head, precisely into place, and now the arch is perfect,
looking almost seamless, as if the stones were fused together or
had forever been one curving piece, like a rib bone or the bent
bough of a tree. And indeed the slender shafts that frame the
doorway do look like a gracile cluster of newly sprouted birch
trees, braceleted by hoops of honeycomb-gold stone.

While Simm's men are finishing the doorway, the carpenters
are working on the roof of the new chapel. Their beams will be
concealed by the stone-carvers' vault when all is done, but even
so they cut and plane the green oak as carefully as they would
if the end results were going to be on show. Until I looked, I
did not know how much there is unseen or hidden in this place:
rafters, the inner faces of outer walls, the finger-width of space
behind the column of the stairs to the rood loft, the layers of
ancient floor, and bones in their forgotten graves. What will
they make of my lord's chantry, those who step in through this
arched doorway in centuries to come? As little as we who dwell
here now do of the long departed who built the church's tower
and walled up the entrance that was there before and which has
left its scar? Or of the legions of the nameless, beneath successive
sheets of clay? Is there any consolation in the knowledge that my
lord and I will be remembered in this building if it withstands
the years, the storms, the wilfulness of kings, although we be
translated into stone? I am not certain of that. I pleaded for my

baby to be buried in the soft earth of the churchyard, where grass and flowers would grow and she would feel the touch of rain and sun, not here beneath the beaten floor with the other children. And I prevailed. Still, I must hope that the promise of stony immortality gives my husband comfort. I am afraid that some will say these works of his have been inspired by vanity, but I do believe it is his faith that moves him.

The last day of the month of April

Cow-dancing day, and to the world of white and green has come a wash of blue, a fall of sky onto the ground beneath the new leaves of the beech trees in the woods, a lake where last week there was grass. When I was walking there this morning, having escaped the house unseen, I wondered why we cloister God in stone and not in that sky-colour, with the blackbird's song. Is it because he himself demanded that a tabernacle should be built for him, and its pillars overlaid with gold? Perhaps, and perhaps because no sinner ever won remission by putting up a church that had the sky for vault and woodland trees for walls. These blue flowers obey no man; they come to no one's bidding and they die in their own season, their beauty while they live a careless rapture.

The cattle are in raptures too, released this morning from their byres for the first time since late autumn, kicking up their heels in the pasture as skittishly as young maids dancing, giddy with fresh grass and the warmth of sunshine on their backs.

Tomorrow is the first of May, and the stone-carvers are here from Tewkesbury, with the image-maker. At supper in the upstairs chamber, Hugh, teasing Agnes, said: so, cousin, shall you wash your face at dawn with morning dew? May Day dew makes women beautiful, you know. Agnes is already beautiful, I said, but she was cross and blushing, and we swiftly changed the subject.

Other girls will surely rise early in the morning or stay out all night long, for May Day dew has magic power and purifies the skin. Older women too maybe, in memory of beauty. In my father's house, the women also gathered dew on other spring and summer mornings, going to the fields if there had been no rain the night before and spreading out a linen cloth, which afterwards they would wring out, saving the resulting droplets in a glass, to be distilled. May-morning dew is finest though, and the best is collected from the hawthorn. If I could, if I were not kept to the house by rank and by my husband's illness, I would go with them. I would like to be by the river at sunrise, where the grass grows tall enough to hide a woman and the dew would fall cool upon my arms, my face, my breasts.

Some claim May Day dew engenders diamonds, Hugh said. But that cannot be true.

A drop of dew, a world of dew, as fleeting as the blossom of wild cherry or a newborn baby's breath.

In the month of May, a Tuesday

A Rogation Day, and a light rain falling as we process behind the cross and banner with Sir Joselin, along the fields, around the boundaries of the parish. Cadd the warden loudly rings a bell. Priest and borrowed cantors sing the litany of saints, and we who follow them respond: ora pro nobis, pray for us.

Sancta Maria
Sancta Virgo virginum
Sancte Michael
Sancte Gabriel
Sancte Raphael
Omnes sancti Angeli et Archangeli
Sancte Ioseph
Sancte Thoma
Sancta Lucia
Sancta Agnes
Sancta Caecilia
Sancta Maria Magdalena
Omnes sanctae Virgines et Viduae

Pray for us.

Bell and book to scare away the wicked fiends that would harm the wheat; prayers to make the air clean and the sun to shine; prayers against lightning, hail and tempest; prayers to spare men and beasts from sickness; orate pro nobis, pray for us. Green the barley still, and the tender corn, ramsons by the

damp hedges, and the briar rose. The entire bounds we beat, and
the men and women and children of this place have walked the
same ways, sung these same words, heard the same prayers each
year of their lives, season after season.

Ab omni malo, a morte perpetua, libera nos Domine, O
Lord, deliver us.

Once, when I was a little girl, I made a long journey with my
mother and my brother to the country where she came from,
to the west. This was a short while before she died. Her father,
my grandfather, was still living then; we stayed with him in
his great stone keep, a place that I remember for unending
staircases so strait that grown men must ascend them sideways,
and windows without glass that were even narrower, set deep
in stone embrasures and giving so restricted a view over the
land beyond that to me it always seemed to be split into thin
segments.

Abutting the walls of this castle of my grandfather's was a
church so old in parts that some said it had been built by the
people who lived there before the present race of men. Strange
people they must have been, if what was said was true, small
and very cunning. The church was quite unlike the great abbey
church in the town my father ruled or even ours here, in the
village. Every church that I had seen in my life till then had been
constructed to soar skywards, at least in intention, but this one
was squat and round, more like a wasps' nest than a house of
God, and it teemed with carvings in stone. Almost every inch
of it was covered: the outer doorway, the shafts and jambs of

the thick columns that held up its curving roof, the font, the shallow chancel arch.

It was entrancing to a child. There were men and there were beasts: tumblers, jugglers, wrestlers and dancers, men playing pipes and viols, hares, rabbits, birds, dogs, a sow suckling her farrow. And there were creatures known to no one living in this land: scaly things, a fish with legs, winged things with quills and haunches, a lion-headed man. Over the doorway, which was so low that even my mother stooped to enter, was the round face of a laughing man with leaves and tendrils sprouting from his head and curling beard. And, most extraordinary of all, close by him, a mermaid with a bifurcated tail. A mermaid caught unaware by the carver in the act of dressing, it would seem, for half her hair was neatly plaited and the other half tumbling loose. Her breasts were bare. In her raised left hand she held a mirror, in her right a comb. Like her hair, her fish-scaled tail was parted equally in two, with both halves curving upwards in a half-circle round her, forming an escutcheon, the finny ends flowing into the doorway's upper arch. Between the two forks of her tail, her woman's parts unfurled and open, displaying the little bud of flesh within.

In the month of May: the day following the beating of the bounds

Titus has bitten Susan my maidservant, in spite of yesterday's incantations against evil. She was straightening my lord's sheets while I was out of the room when the creature jumped up from the floor as quick as a flea and sank his pointy teeth into the soft part of her arm above the elbow. Poor Susan, it is an unpleasant wound. I am suing for Titus to be banished from the upper chambers, like the dogs, for it is unfair to expect Susan to put up with him any longer, but Agnes says that if he is, she will have to sleep in the hall with him, for she will not be separated from her darling. Besides, there is no need for the maids to enter her father's chamber as long she is there to tend him, together with faithful Lambert – who is not afraid of little Titus – and in any case he will be cured soon. It is but a matter of time.

I hope that she is right. Doctor Moreton comes every week from Banbury with leeches, purges and new tinctures, which he claims are doing their work but, before our eyes, the man is losing his power to move. It is as though thick clay crept through his veins instead of blood. In the warm week of April, he could walk in the garden, but since then he has kept to the house, and often to his chamber, night and day.

A root of herb bennet boiled in wine preserves against poisoning, plague and venomous bites, according to Dame Joan.

In the month of May: Ascension Day

Bell-ringing in the church again and a great stir and bustle in the house, for Roland my lord's nephew has come, with another young man, a friend of his from Lincoln's Inn, but not the expected chantry priest, whose whereabouts are unknown. The two arrived this afternoon in a swirl and jangle of hooves and harness, having ridden fast from Watlington as if they had urgent business, although it appears that they do not, and are here merely because they have nowhere else to be. Strange how some people agitate the air around them. Roland is one such: he can be sitting in silence in a corner of a room and still compel attention; he is impossible to ignore. It is as if some invisible thing clung always to his shoulder, shivering its unseen wings. All eyes turn to him wherever he goes and yet he himself seems heedless of his own effect. He absorbs the regard of others as a storm cloud does the sun.

Hugh is touchingly pleased to see his brother, and Roland's appearance has also lifted my lord my husband's spirits. I know that my lord is fond of both young men, these sons of his dead sister, but Hugh is familiar, a part and parcel of the household, having been here since his mother died. Roland, however, who is five years older, was a boy at Paul's at the time, and later a scholar in Cambridge, and afterwards returned to live in London. Consequently, when he visits, he is a novelty and he brings to this secluded place a welcome breath of the outside world. He has acquaintances at Court, he has travelled across the sea to faraway cities – Paris and Geneva – he has studied law; he can converse with his uncle on terms that no one else can, in this house. He resembles him as well, they share the same dark eyes and unusual height.

I too am glad that Roland is here, but I do not love him as I love his brother. There is no sweeter-natured person on this earth. Hugh has something of a child's directness and clarity of gaze, and he has deep wells of kindness. If he possessed as much gold as there are leaves on a pear tree, he would give it all away to anyone in need. When I came here, as the new wife of my lord, Hugh was but a boy, and yet even at his age he sensed how hard it was for me to conform to a house with long-established ways, to a man so much older and a bereft stepchild, and all without companion of my own, except for one maidservant. It was Hugh alone who strove to turn this strange place into home. He showed me everything – the house, the garden, the village, the fields, the meadows and the woods, the riverbank – until he thought I knew my way well enough to feel that I belonged here, to some degree at least. We still walk the demesne together, when we can. Dear, round-faced, gentle Hugh who, like my own lost brother, knows the names of flowers and stars and birds, and hears the songs of the fields.

Roland, though, is for the new. And, unlike his brother, he is not blue-eyed and plumpish but as gaunt and beaky as the heron. There are shadows beneath his cheekbones and his hair is black as night. He is a beautiful young man. His friend is called Henry Martyn, and so far he has said nothing but for that demanded by politeness. I have never seen a grown man so pale of hair and skin. He is as white as a garment washed in lye and left out in the sun to bleach. Thistledown hair, eyelashes as fair as strands of spider's web and eyes a milk-whey shade of grey. When they stand side by side, Roland and Henry look like a painted allegory of darkness against light, although in life they are not in the least opposed but evidently think alike on every matter.

In the month of May: the day
after the feast of the Ascension

At the church a whispering parliament is in progress. Now that the doorway is nearly finished, the supports removed and the rafters all in place, it is time to start upon the vault, the tomb pit and the porch. Simm is in command by general agreement, as he is the mason of the house, even though he has had reluctantly to cede the finer work to strangers. When I get there, I find him drawing over the painting on the north wall of the chancel with a stick of chalk. Jack the elder, the man called Dickon and others of the men whose names I do not know are clustering about him, somewhat abashed by this unaccustomed trespass beyond the rood screen, giving their opinions but keeping their voices low. The three stone-carvers, brothers or cousins I think, from their likeness to each other – stocky, dark men – are keeping their distance and their counsel. Sir Joselin, whose holy space is thus invaded, is nowhere to be seen and nor is the imager, as far as I can tell, although, having had work at Gloucester, he travelled here together with the carvers. Unlike them, he is to have his lodging in the house, for he is a man of standing, but I was in the blue-hazed woods when he arrived and have not seen him yet. Agnes says he comes from Italy.

The far side of this wall once faced the elements, but now that a part of it has been adopted as one wall of the chantry, its weather-beaten stone will soon be coated in thick plaster. Or, rather, the little left of it, for much will be torn down to give those of us to be buried here a clear view of God's altar. This entails the destruction of the picture that is here.

From year to year wall paintings fade and are renewed but this one, protected from the touch of passing hands by its location, is older than the rest and may never have been repainted. It shows the Last Supper. Candle-grime has partially obscured it and the painter was not especially skilled – some of the disciples look more like Titus than the usual run of men and the hand in which Our Saviour holds the cup of his own blood could be mistaken for a paw – but the villagers revere it. Still, the nave is not the parish's domain and in any case there will be fresh painting in its place. Other images have been despoiled more cruelly in the past. Saint Thomas, much beloved, who was once depicted on the square of wall beside the door, had his face scratched out by edict years before I came here. He is still here in a way, featureless and ghostly, his halo a faint arc of gold, for no one has had the heart to paint him out entirely. He had his own altar then, but that was outlawed too. Things change; we have to recognise that; the world will not stay still. What we must hope is that the new is better and stronger than the old.

Simm's chalky line comes to a point that cuts through the neck of the Holy Ghost, who hovers above the head of Our Lord in the form of a dove. I can save the angels, he says.

Unobserved by me and Simm, Hugh and Roland have entered the church, with Henry Martyn. Hugh, having heard what Simm was saying, tells him not to be concerned about preserving any of the paintings, as they will all be made again when the new plasterwork is dry. While they are talking, Roland and Henry prowl about; this is Henry's first visit to the church. As ever,

Master Martyn, snow-white as the dove, is frugal with his words, but I note how closely he inspects the images and the figures on the rood screen. Henry is a watchful man.

Roland, seeing the new works for the first time, is also quiet but has a clouded air. Something is troubling him but he does not voice it, he simply runs his fingers up and down a pillar as if he were testing it for dust.

Hugh, coming away from Simm, explains to Henry that his uncle's intention is to render this the most glorious church in the whole of the county and therefore fully worthy of the inestimable treasure that it already holds. Come look, he says.

Taking Henry by the hand, Hugh leads him to the altar of Saint Margaret on the north wall of the church, to admire the silver-gilt casket that rests upon it. It contains a fragment of her girdle, Hugh says, and it behoves you to kneel. Henry bends one knee, looks briefly at the casket, nods his thanks to Hugh and turns to leave the church. Roland follows him, and so does Hugh after a minute, I suppose to resume their tour of the demesne.

When they have gone and shut the door behind them, I pause before that altar too. The saint is pictured on the wall above it, at the instant of emerging from the fearful dragon's gut. As she came forth unharmed and without pain, so women pray that they will be delivered. Although now it is forbidden of course to burn lights on that or any other altar, or to make offerings to the saints, women still do what they have always done, and kneel before her there. In the silence of an empty church, they pray to her, and she looks down upon them with pity in her eyes. Her painted belly is well smudged by the mouths that have kissed it and the fingers that have rubbed it in hope, or in thanksgiving, or despair. Often there will be a silver bead or a small coin left for her in secret. And sometimes Joselin can be seen carrying something wrapped in silk, going stealthily to aid a woman in childbirth. As he came to me. He undid the chain that secures the casket to the wall, brought it to where I laboured, unlocked the casket then, with the key that he wears always, and touched my belly with the scrap of hemp that Margaret was wearing around her waist when she was swallowed. Exi infans, Christus te vocat, Joselin prayed. And the child obeyed.

In the month of May, a Tuesday

The stone-carvers of Tewkesbury have magic in their fingers. They speak to us in drawings instead of words. With my scant understanding of these matters, I cannot see how the ceiling that they propose to build is possible: can stone be made to float? They have come, shyly, to my lord my husband's chamber, ushered there by the mason Simm. The chief of them, John Isak, holds a paper that he unrolls to show a wonderfully intricate design, a harmony of curving and connecting lines, like a pattern of lace, or flowering cow parsley when seen from underneath, and this, he says, they are able to render in the fine pale stone quarried close to here, at Taynton. In spite of himself, Simm is impressed, although he tries not to show it and complains that this fanciful stonework has no real purpose. It is not proof against the weather and so requires an ordinary roof above it. John Isak does not disagree, he simply shrugs.

It serves the same purpose as prayer, my husband says, and he gives the carvers his commission. They show him their proposed designs for the window mullions too. My lord's cousin and steward Marmion will draw up the necessary contracts.

In the month of May: Whit Sunday

The seventh Sunday after Easter. At mass this morning Sir Joselin told the story again: of the people who had locked themselves into a room, terribly afraid of persecution, of the sound that came from heaven like a rushing wind, of the tongues of fire that touched each person there, of the gift the Holy Ghost bestowed on them so that they could speak of the wonderful works of God in every language known to men. Parthi et Medi et Elamitae et qui habitant Mesopotamiam et Iudaeam et Cappadociam Pontum et Asiam Frygiam et Pamphiliam Aegyptum et partes Lybiae quae est circa Cyrenen et advenae romani… well, that was a gift indeed, when it is hard enough to say what you want to say in the tongue that you learned at your mother's knee.

White Sunday, white-winged spirit, breath of God. At Paul's Cross in London, a trapdoor in the ceiling slides open at the high mass on this Sunday and a flock of doves descends upon the worshippers below. After the snowy doves, a shower of white flower petals, and that is a sight that I should love to see.

Here we had just one little dove and that, poor thing, too timid to fly when Joselin let it go. It stayed shivering between his palms until he set it back into its basket. Afterwards, I recounted this to my lord my husband and he said that Simm must make a trapdoor in our church's roof above the chancel; what they can do at Paul's Cross, so can we. Next year we shall have our cloud of doves.

Perhaps. We'll see. White petals and white feathers drifting slowly down through incense-heavy air, falling softly on our bent heads and on the earth that weighs the babies down, while Joselin sings in his croaking voice:

Veni, Sancte Spiritus,
et emitte caelitus
lucis tuae radium.
Veni, pater pauperum,
veni, dator munerum,
veni, lumen cordium.
Consolator optime,
dulcis hospes animae,
dulce refrigerium.

❧

Before I met him, I had an image of the image-maker in my mind, but he is nothing like it. His name is Piero da Fiesole. The young men found him comical when he first appeared, and indeed he could seem so, being somewhat dwarfish, with a head as smooth and bald as an egg and a rotund belly. An accident at birth has left him limping and lopsided. But his hands are elegant, his eyes as bright and beady as a robin's, and he smiles often. There is something in his look that suggests a lively interest in the world and I like the way he speaks – fast and flowingly, leaving at the ends of words a singing tail. A long time ago, the king chose him to make a dead queen's tomb, and he still has the design prepared, but for reasons that have not been explained, the work has been delayed. Where does she lie meanwhile, I want to know, and what of the others, the headless ones, will they also be remembered? Piero has no answers. He is only lately returned from a stay in Italy and now hears nothing of the king's affairs.

Today he has announced his intention to begin with some detailed drawings of my lord husband, as his is the main figure. It was the custom once, he says, to set images on tombs that were merely types of men and women, each as like the next as green peas in a pod and able to be ordered from a workshop in the same way as a chair or table. These effigies conformed less to the person in the tomb than the clothes they died in, which had at least been tailored to them. Once the first was made, many copies followed, and it took no special art to carve them. That is not his way at all. His pride is in cutting alabaster to a fine likeness with such skill that one would think the dead still breathed.

But what then of my mother? Agnes asked him. She was with me when Piero came to the hall to speak to us for the first time, and Cousin Marmion's wife Joan was there as well. I caught the note in Agnes's voice but did not fully understand her question. Joan did. You have her picture, she told Agnes, in your locket with the pearls. But it is only small, Agnes protested, sounding near to tears. It will be enough, Piero said.

Dame Joan keeps things from me now, as she keeps the household keys that she received when Agnes's mother died. I don't care that she has those keys – the servants and the cooks are used to her – but I could wish for more openness sometimes.

I told Piero that my lord husband could not rise at all today, having had a troubled night, but Piero said that for his purposes that was to the good. Recumbent is how he will be, on his bier. If he were already dead, Piero would take an exact model of his face by means of a mask made by pouring molten wax upon it, and indeed it is possible to do this to the living, using clay, but it is not an easy thing to undergo. Hollow straw must be inserted in the nostrils to let the subject breathe. Moreover, the eyes perforce stay closed. No, to make a likeness of the living it is better to begin with pen and paper.

Agnes and I led Piero da Fiesole to my husband's chamber after dinner, the three of us in solemn procession on the spiral stairs. Agnes cradled Titus in her arms and the image-maker carried a wooden box and a beautiful surepel made of leaf-green leather tooled with gold. I touched the binding when he was not looking and felt how soft it was. I had not known there could be such a lovely thing, in so bright a colour.

The sickroom reek met us at the door but Master Piero bustled in with as much haste and cheer as if he were entering the throne room of the king. He bowed low in greeting. My lord husband seemed paler and wearier than ever but also interested in the new visitor. When he returned the image-maker's greeting, his voice was strong.

And then another sort of ceremony began. Having asked permission, Master Piero drew the hangings round the bed as far back as they would go, saying that he needed light. He removed the heap of cushions that my lord leant against and helped him to lie back with only one thin pillow beneath his head. He walked slowly round and round the bed, head cocked, apparently considering. He asked Agnes and me to take our seats in the corner of the chamber and keep quiet, while he pulled up a table and a stool beside the bed. He sat, remaining still for several minutes with his eyes shut and his face raised to the ceiling before abruptly becoming purposeful again and undoing the clasps of the box that he had placed upon the table. Being hinged, the box opened like a book into two halves and had within it a folding wooden

board that gave an inclined surface, like a little desk. Beneath the
board were the materials of his trade. He selected from them a
tool resembling a pair of compasses or pincers and a thin leather
tape with markings on it, showed both to my lord husband, and
then described what he was going to do.

Firstly, while his eye was fresh, he would make a rapid drawing. Next, with the tape, he would take the measurements: the
circumference of the head, the length of the body, the length of
the arms from shoulder to elbow, from elbow to wrist, the width
of the hands, the length from wrist to tip of middle finger. Using
the compasses, he would ascertain the height of the forehead,
the span of the jaw, the length of the nose, the distance between
the eyes and between the eyes and chin. Finally, he would make
precise drawings of every feature. While he was drawing, the
noble lord need not stay awake but should rest, or even sleep if
he so wished, provided he stayed lying on his back. For his part,
although he was generally fond of conversation, Piero liked to
work in silence.

Luckily, Titus had already fallen asleep on Agnes's lap. She
and I watched Master Piero's pen move assuredly and rapidly over
the first of the sheets of paper that he had taken out of his green
binder, but from where we sat we could not see his drawing.
Then we watched him measuring the man who lay completely
still before him. Head to foot, shoulder to shoulder, eyebrow
to cheekbone. I could not hear whether my husband breathed.

How might it feel to be the mask-maker, the one sequestered
in the chamber of the newly dead, dripping hot wax over the
cool face of the fresh corpse in the way Piero had described,
watching it set, peeling it off as a child peels the scab off a scraped
knee? Where the wax had been, pale hairless flesh. Does the wax

pluck off the dead man's beard, do the dark hairs fur the mask as bristles do a butchered pig's skin? Does the warmth of the wax last for a while, reheating flesh as if death had been undone for a brief span? The mask-maker and the dead left in solitude together for the one to make of the other the necessary art in silence, before the mourners return and the women come with winding sheets to lay out the body. I thanked heaven then that for now my lord my husband lived.

The sheet of paper turned for space to make more drawings. Verso. Death is not reversed. Agnes and I, unsighted, listened to Piero's pen scratch, the small snorting sounds he made and the crackle of wood burning down to ashes in the grate. Awakened by the heat after its winter sleep, a butterfly beat its wings against a windowpane, beat and beat again, vainly seeking egress. A frantic clattering against glass, as if by a minute drummer; flash of vermilion, white dashed on velvet wings; how confounding for a butterfly to meet a thing that looks like air but is mysteriously solid.

It will die if we do not let it out, Agnes said, breaking her vow of silence. Titus woke at the sound of her voice and strained towards the beating wings. Master Piero, as if also released from the intensity that had bound him while he drew, pushed back his stool – scrape of wood on wood – and Agnes, emboldened, rose to cross the room. I followed. On the sheet of paper in front of the imager, my lord husband's eyes and ears and lips exactly, his chin, the bony place where his hand and his wrist meet. Yes, my husband exactly, Agnes's father, but as if he were a broken vase and each fragment separated. A dismembered man.

He was not asleep. Piero spoke to him then. In your robes or in full armour, sir? he asked. An unnecessary question. I could have given him the answer. In death the man will want to be what he was in life: a victor, a conqueror, and strong in saecula saeculorum. It must be very hard for him to bear his frailty now.

But if you are in armour, how will I see your face? Agnes demanded of her father.

Master Piero smiled. Excellent question, he told her. But you must not worry. His visor will be raised.

And please to make my hands upraised and joined in prayer, her father ordered.

❧

Hands joined. Fingers touching. Legs touching, the hard weight of his body above mine. His breath in my mouth. Nothing spoken, no words ever, neither in the darkness nor in the morning light. Night deed. Night duty. Want it or not, it is the only way: the contact of flesh on flesh and bone on bone and breath on breath; to bring forth flesh of my flesh, bone of my bone, heart of my own heart, there is no other way.

For three years I lay beside him every night. No words in the beginning, when there was pain, and no words later, but bodies speak to one another, if only haltingly, and slowly learn the other's tongue. I lay beside him for all the months of my baby's growing; while he slept, I felt the child kicking at my ribs and dancing in my womb. My chrisom child, who lived as lightly as a mayfly and left no dint upon the surface of the earth. But since Candlemas my child's father has been too ill to share his bed, he drifts in and out of sleep, he says, scarcely knowing whether he dreams or wakes. Perhaps I would go to him if he wished, if he were to ask me, but it is his servant Lambert whom he chooses to stay near him every night, sleeping on a pallet by the door and listening for his call.

Inwardly I picture him tonight, lying still and silent in the dark, with his eyes wide open. I too am wide awake, in the room I share with Agnes and the maid, and thinking of his tomb. Through the unshuttered window comes the stark light of the moon, reminder of the speed at which the wheel of nights is turning, how quickly the crescent waxes and the gibbous wanes.

On the first day of the month of June

The sun woke me this morning and now the day is warm. Sancta Maria, pray for me, pray thy son for us.

It was bitter cold the day my lord my husband asked Sir Joselin, Cadd the churchwarden, Simm the mason, Cousin Marmion and me to attend him in the church. The day after All Souls. I was surprised to be summoned; he had never discussed his affairs with me and I knew nothing of them. Although we had been married for over a year, he was still in many ways a stranger to me, and remains so. I do not know if there is anybody living in whom he would confide, apart from his confessor, and that a matter of obligation not of choice. Was he always so reserved or did he once laugh and jest and speak his mind like other men? I wish I had an answer. To me his heart is cloudier than water at the bottom of a well.

Did he know that he was ill? If he did, he gave no sign of it. Anyone who chanced to see him that November afternoon would have thought him at the peak of strength. He was grey-haired long before he married me, and his old age was nearer than his youth, but he was still a full head taller than the generality of men and as powerful as the taut string of a bow. I think that the seeds of sickness were sprouting in him already by then, but surreptitiously, so that they troubled him less than a stutter of the heartbeat or a fleeting shadow in the corner of an eye. Who can say how sickness comes or how it goes? And if anyone could say what matters apart from disorders of the body may have weighed upon my lord my husband's mind that day, it is not I. He is like a pillar of stone that will not yield, however hard it's pushed. A pillar in a salt land, endlessly alone. And more so now, even as his strength is ebbing away.

Our breath misting on the air and Marmion muttering to himself about fireplaces being more valuable than fonts. Darkness already skulking in the far corners of the church. My husband stood on the chancel step like a preacher, with the rest of us huddled and shivering before him, and he spoke with a fervour I had never heard in his voice before. It was as if he were describing a thing seen in a vision or commanded by an angel, rather than a real place. He said that shallow graves beneath the earth on which we stood, or in the yard beyond, had been enough for his forefathers, but he would have more visible and lasting commemoration for himself and his descendants. A tomb of solid marble. And a chapel in which to house it. And endowments and a chantry priest paid to sing requiems for his soul until the final syllable of time.

But that marble tomb was not the end of his ambition. He flung out his arms as if to take the whole church into his cruciform embrace. Look, he said, look how dully lit, how impoverished it is, and when the wind blows it comes knifing through the door. We shall not only have a chantry chapel but also a porch for shelter without and, within, new woodwork and tiles on the chancel floor instead of mud. New vestments and new frontals. A set of funerary vestments, for these Sir Joselin sorely lacks. No longer will there be masses for the dead in common violet, but a chasuble, fanon, stole and cope in velvet of the deepest black. And there will be windows. Windows where there were none before and new glass in the windows that exist. No more the plain glass or the yellowed horn but sapphire glass, and ruby, emerald, such that the light that shines in through it will bejewel those who kneel here while they live and those who lie here later. Ad maiorem gloria dei, imagine it: a place of glory, fiat lux!

I saw what he saw: a place ablaze with light and brightness, newness, white stone, images and gemstones, silver, gleaming gold. I saw it through his eyes. I heard it in his voice. But that was many months ago, and much has intervened to dim this vision. The vigour that surged through my lord my husband on that day has mostly seeped away like wine out of a leaking barrel, and other things got in the way: foul weather, an accident that laid the mason low throughout last summer, the imposition of yet another tax by our war-thirsty king. And, overshadowing all for me, a death. There is a solid reminder though, in a model carved by Simm. Impatient to see his imagined works made substance, my lord immediately began to draw up plans and seek out craftsmen but, being no architect himself, his drawings were never exact enough to serve as patterns. Therefore Simm, after diligent listening, translated his wishes into cherrywood. The model looks like something a child would dream of – a lovely house for poppets, small enough to hold in two cupped hands – but it is perfectly faithful to the church and the plans in miniature, although it is roofless. It shows the chantry and how it will abut the church, how it will open to the chancel, where the east window will go, and the new entrance that the porch will form. If Simm had shaped it roughly, it would have sufficed to guide the workmen, but instead he chose to make it very carefully, smoothing and polishing and carving little wooden arches, pews and a pulpit for it. My husband keeps it by him in his chamber, and when I see him stroking the fine wood with his fingers, I pray that it is not the closest he will come to seeing his intent accomplished.

And today I begin to think that those prayers have found their mark. Simm's men are making swift progress after the long interval of winter. For months the chantry stood half-built, looking like nothing so much as a sheepfold, but now it is joined to the church as a suckling lamb is to its mother, the stone-carvers are busy, and walls are rising on the foundations of the porch. The masons have already knocked a hole through the east wall for a window. It is not midsummer yet; by the grace of God there will be weeks of fair weather ahead, and if the work continues at this pace, it will be finished before the onset of next winter. Perhaps that will be soon enough.

Marmion complains about all this renewing, buying, commissioning and building but, at least for the time being, he does not hold the purse strings. Disease afflicts my husband's limbs but not his intellect, and from his distant bed he can oversee the work that has preoccupied him for so many months, with Marmion as his deputy and Hugh and me as eyes and ears. However, Marmion is my lord's close cousin and his trusted steward, long used to taking charge during his absences abroad, and it is always wise to hear him out. I don't know why he so strongly disapproves of this whole business. It could be that his ear is close to the ground. These are troubled times and the world is turning faster than a weathervane in a gale. What was truth one year is heresy the next, and erstwhile saints are scraped out of the prayer books. Here in this parish, the decree that forbade devotions to the saints and lighting candles anywhere but on the sepulchre and rood caused great distress. We have been buffeted by crosswinds, like birds tossed in a storm, barely having any say over our direction, and no one truly knowing right from wrong. Some claim they do, but if their belief is someone else's falsehood, where is the Solomon who decides?

On that icy November day, the priest Sir Joselin received my lord my husband's passionate speech without comment. Cadd the warden also kept his thoughts to himself at the time but later he told Marmion that there were small stirrings of discontent within the parish. In the main, people were thankful for the promise of bright glass and coloured tiles, but there would always be a few who held those things to be ungodly. Even in this village, where most men hold to the faith of their fathers, there were one or two who had been lured by foreign voices calling for reform. Or, perhaps it would be truer to say, had been convinced by these dissenters that the new ways would release them from the burden of penances and fasting and having to pay for lights upon the rood. Perhaps those men formed so small a band as to be of no importance. Much more widespread was concern about trespass and ownership. By right, the body of the church, the nave, belonged not the lord but to the people, and the people would not yield a single foot of it to him. Nobody – whatever their persuasion – would let the church become a rich man's tomb.

Marmion showed Cadd the model Simm had carved and assured him that there would be no encroachment on the nave. And that has held true, by the letter of the law. But no one warned the parishioners then that they would lose their Easter sepulchre and the Last Supper that they loved. I must assume that my lord my husband knows them well enough to be certain they will take his new works to their hearts and so forget the old, for otherwise he would not have set out upon such costly and extensive work. But, speaking for myself, I am not sure that the storms are over. The old ways or the new; one man's will or the law of ages; new images or no images at all? It seems to me that the winds are howling still.

❧

Susan's wound is healing well and she is out of danger, by grace of the blessed herb and Doctor Moreton's lancet. If she had died, Titus would have had to die, for animals that have poisoned human flesh are no longer to be trusted and cannot be kept within a house. Agnes, I am sure, would have fought off his intending slayer with her bare hands, for she loves that creature as a woman does a child.

In the month of June, a Monday

It is my turn to have my likeness taken by Piero before he leaves for London in the morning. Must I lie prone? I ask.

No need. Please take this seat here by the window.

He and I are alone in the upper chamber; the window is wide open to this fine morning; there is birdsong and a breeze and the small sound of the imager's pen scratching on his paper, little else. He does not talk. The silence is beguiling. I know that he is observing me with a hawk's attention, noting every eyelash, but in a strange way his dispassionate gaze puts me at my ease. I might as well be the block of alabaster that he will cut me from eventually, and I do not feel judged. What I have noticed about Piero da Fiesole in our brief acquaintance is an ampleness of spirit. He is curious about many things and his eyes are sharp, but the countenance he turns upon the world is amused and generous.

After a while he takes up his measuring tool and comes closer to me. Permission? he asks. His touch is gentle, he holds my chin to tilt my head towards him and he bids me put my hands together at the level of my heart.

More drawing. I am drifting into dream. A sudden burst of laughter from the garden reaches me as if from far away and I do not want this time to end, but I know it must. The imager had placed himself between me and the window; when he rises from his stool I can see past him to the garden, where Agnes is playing a skipping game with Titus, watched by Henry Martyn. She is tossing her hair and laughing gaily for Henry's benefit – like an orphaned duckling she is cleaving to the first man she has seen. The warm air is soft and gentle on my face.

Do you like to wear your usual headdress? Piero asks.

I am unsure what he means. Does this headdress please me? No, he wants to know what I should like to wear upon my tomb.

So, could your hair float loose? he says. Or is that too virginal? A simple chaplet, gilded? But as you will be a widow, I suggest a veil. I will make it flow like finest silk and you will not believe its folds are stone. If you have a favourite gown, bring it out so I can see how it is cut and drapes. I have copied your rings and your beads and I have your hands exactly, both raised and in repose. Will you clasp my lord your husband's? Ah no, you will not, for his are to be joined together, I forgot.

May I see the drawings?

Yes, but please to remember that they are not finished.

I am there, on the paper, as I have never seen myself before; my face, my features, not as in a glass but through another's eyes. He has drawn my wrist. It is mine, I am myself, and yet I am a stranger. Without intending to, I touch my fingers to my lips, my cheekbones and the bridge of my nose as if to test the flesh against the likeness; and the likeness holds. It is truthful, I admit, although I did not know my mouth was set so hard or my aspect was so melancholy. I had thought my sadness hidden. No one else has remarked upon it. How could this stranger read my face so closely and catch a look in my eyes that I do not want anyone to see? With nothing but a few strokes of a pencil?

Are you happy with it?

I think you have extraordinary skill.

Thank you. It will be a very great pleasure to make the figure of a woman as beautiful as you. He begins to gather up his tools.

Would you show me the whole design? I ask.

Gladly, if I could. But my lord has asked me to submit it to him first, before showing it to any other.

But I would like to know how you will show my daughter. Your daughter?

My baby daughter, who was born at Christmas and then died.

He says something in his own tongue that I do not understand, and then he says, in English: I am sorry. Nobody told me that one of the dead children was yours. But, please do not be concerned. All the babies will be angels, you will see.

But my child lived. Although it was only for three days, she lived. And she was perfect. She was beautiful. She was herself, a human being, unlike any other. You promised that you would make us as we are – as we were – in life.

Piero nods. Angeli, he says.

※

Not once has my lord my husband said our baby's name to me since the day she died.

※

As neither my lord nor Sir Joselin were at dinner later that day, Dame Joan felt free to grumble. This chantry priest, whoever he is, where is he to lodge? Am I to put him with the gentlemen? With my lord's own nephews, Hugh and Roland? Or the servants? When my cousin said that this person was coming – and where was he dredged up, I'd like to know? – he cannot have given any thought to the practicalities. Joselin will pretend he has no room to spare but why he must keep an entire chamber empty, I really could not say. After all, he used to house his curate.

In all likelihood he will house this one, Roland said. He will have a curate's duties, will he not? Joselin should be glad of his company and help, now that he is getting old.

Joselin will never admit to needing help, Joan said. Instead he will complain that, by bringing in a young man, my lord your uncle is scheming to replace him. And will the young man do the duties of a curate?

What else is he to do? He cannot sing for the repose of souls all day.

He is to teach me music, Agnes said, and we all turned to look at her, smug in her sole possession of this knowledge. He is schooled in music. Also, he is not a priest in the same way that Sir Joselin is, he is a monk. That is to say he was, at Reading, before the abbey there was closed.

He will be equally as costly though, said Marmion. I hope we shall not live to rue his hire.

Where is he now? I asked Agnes. Is he still in Reading?

No, in Spain, I think. Or is it France? A distant country, anyway, that's what my father said. He has been living abroad. But perhaps he is already on his way back to England now. We expect him soon.

He will have quite a journey then, said Joan. I pray he won't be shipwrecked!

The chatter continues but I am distracted by this faceless monk in my mind's eye, black-cowled on the deck of a ship, water all around him, an infinity of blue. What is the sea like? I long to know. Imagine voyaging across unbounded and unfathomed depths, your ship so small in that vast emptiness, that wilderness of salt and sky. My brother did that once, eight years ago. Come to me across the water, Jesus called to Peter in the storm.

Hugh might have been thinking some of the same things, for he asked Roland if he had been afraid when he sailed to France. No, not at all, said Roland, the winds were light and the ship was sound and so there was no cause for fear, either on the voyage out or on the return journey.

I have been in a storm at sea, Piero said. And I assure you it was fearful. The waters rose far higher than this house. I was certain I would drown. I had to hold on to a rope so tightly that it galled my hands, I have the scars still, look. You would not believe how loud it was, the water and the wind.

What happened?

I lived, as you can see. The tempest passed after many hours and the ship stayed upright although it had been bucking in the waves like an untamed horse. The decks awash. Since that day I am afraid of going by sea but, alas, there is no other way to Italy. I pray for a bridge!

Did you pray in the storm? Hugh asked.

Do you need to ask? Every man on deck prayed, even the infidels.

A wall of water higher than a house. Cold salt water roaring and the raging wind. Does it take long to drown? I am shivering on this warm day, but why I cannot say. Come to me upon the water, through the wild storm.

So do you know his name then? Joan is asking Agnes.

William Clare, she answers.

The eighth day of the month of June:
the feast of Corpus Christi

A miracle has happened. First light, and the household had collected as usual in the hall when my lord my husband suddenly appeared at the foot of the spiral stairs. Lambert was close behind him, but my lord was standing upright and unaided, as white as a pillar of salt. I will take my part in the procession, he announced. We stared at him in great surprise, saying nothing, until Marmion voiced what everybody thought: but can you walk? Yes, my husband said. Not far, not yet, but certainly to the gates and some more steps thereafter.

Agnes ran to kiss his hands. Doctor Moreton was right, she said, and I told you so. You of little faith! He promised that my lord my father would be well, and look now, here he is!

Was it the beneficial effect of summer? Dame Joan asked. Perhaps the heat has thawed your aching bones?

In London, Roland told me once, a thousand priests process at Corpus Christi, bearing crosses and lit candles. It's a river of light that flows through the city's streets, its banks embroidered banners, its source a gold and crystal shrine. Here, in this parish, the shrine is gilded wood and we have only one priest for now, yet he is followed in procession by the children of the village, and they carry candles. Their way is strewn with woodruff, lavender and roses; marked at the door of every dwelling by clean cloths or coverlets in place of silken flags.

My lord accepted a coddled egg with his bread and ale at breakfast, more than he has eaten at one meal in many days. Even I began to think then that he could be cured. Hugh told Joan that it was not sunshine but prayer that wrought the change, and he must be right. Yes, we say our prayers in the morning and in the evening, on waking and on sleeping, singly and together, and do they rise like incense straight to heaven? Sir Joselin says they do. And when I prayed for my infant daughter? Ah, but fiat voluntas tua, let thy will be done.

I had presumed that Lambert would have to carry his master at least part of the way, but no, he walked, slowly, stiffly and in evident pain, with Lambert at his elbow but otherwise alone. We reached the gates in time to hear the handbells and to see Joselin coming from the church, with the men of the guild behind him bearing the house of God. Four boys walk with them, to hold a canopy over the shrine in case of rain, but they are redundant; it is hours short of noon and yet the sun beats down upon the priest and the procession, and the bowed heads of all who kneel as they pass.

Hoc est enim corpus meum; in that wooden box the body of God. A morsel of bread that is not bread but is the flesh of Jesus, which is not what it looks like, tastes like, what it is, but a thing entirely other. Hoc est enim corpus meum, spell and invocation: words that Sir Joselin pronounces every single day, and every day this transformation.

※

In the church, Simm is fretting over matters of interment. His complaint is that the foreign image-maker has not provided enough instruction as to width and weight and depth. And nobody else can tell him how the tomb is to be built. How then should he proceed to make the tomb pit? The dead who are already buried in the church – by which he means the lord's kin and the ancients, for nowadays every other Christian soul is in the yard – are just beneath the ground, their noses barely inches from our feet, and by the by, it's a blessing indeed that none lie where the tomb will go, as far as he can tell. But if they do, will they be reburied somewhere else? In the tomb as well? The old ways he can understand. But when this new creation is in place, how will the dead get in? It's one thing digging up an earthen floor, but what if a floor is tiled? Can tiles be dug up and relaid? Will they not break? What is he expected to do? He has hardly seen hide or hair of the imager since the man arrived; a five-minute visit to the church was all this foreigner seemed to feel the need for, barely time to exchange greetings, let alone to explain what he and his alabastermen required by way of preparation for the tomb.

Hugh, who had come with me to the church, asked if Master Piero had supplied any details on paper. Only these, said Simm, unrolling a thin scroll to show the drawings on it.

Hugh took the paper from him and studied it. I am no builder but that does look extravagantly large, he said.

That's what I said. But this is what Piero ordered. He said that we must dig a pit in the ground, that the footing and three of the sides are to be made with set stone, very strong, the north side open, with an arch to bear the weight that is to fall on it from above. And the pit to be eight foot long, five foot wide and three foot deep, for the burial therein of several bodies.

So then, is that not instruction enough? What he is wants is a sort of cave or vault beneath the ground, upon which he will build. A little stone-walled room.

That's as may be, but I want to be sure of these measurements before we begin to make a great hole in the ground. How many is several bodies? And would those bodies be in shrouds or coffins?

We'll ask Master Piero to come to you before he leaves us.

One of the stone-carvers happens to pass by then, and Simm recruits him into the consultation. He cannot help. Although he and his brothers have lately been at Gloucester with Piero, and before that in Oxford at the old cardinal's college, they do their own work and he does his. But the master is careful, he says. He knows his craft. Nodding to us, he backs away from this interruption and disappears to the workshop that the stone-carvers set up when they arrived, as far away as they could get from Simm's lodge, beyond the sheds and stables.

They chose that place, I suppose, for its distance from the great dust and clamour in the church. The Tewkesbury men seem more like scribes than masons, they often work in silence, and indeed the patterns they are carving are so fine that they might be wielding quills instead of chisels. Every single piece of their miraculous vault has individually to be shaped, each as delicate and detailed as a moth-wing.

※

Agnes cannot but be much distressed by all this business of death, but she does not say so. Going in search of Piero for Simm's benefit, I find her with him, in her father's chamber. Piero spends much time there: perhaps the ordinary bond between craftsman and patron has in this case turned to friendship, for it certainly appears that the two men have interests in common.

They are talking of Jerusalem today. Piero, cradling Simm's little wooden church in his hands, is telling of the model he once saw of the church in which Our Saviour lay for three days in the grave. Ebony inlaid with mother-of-pearl and silver; he saw it in Verona, it was a marvellous piece of work.

In life, as I remember, that church is somewhat cramped and dimly lit, my lord husband said.

But it must be truly wonderful to be there, to place your hand upon the tomb?

Yes. The empty tomb.

Warmth must have restorative power; my husband is sitting erect on a chair and looking well. Or is it daylight that heals? Of late he has been so much in the dark. I never knew that he had travelled in the Holy Lands; why did he not say before? When did he go, and did he go alone, across the wild seas and over the high mountains; why is there so much about him that I do not know?

Today his eyes are bright. In breaking down a wall of the church, he says to Piero, the altar that the parish used at Easter has been lost. What do you say that I should put in its place?

Piero jumps up from his stool, he is so eager. By great good fortune, I have exactly what you need, he says. A dead Christ in immaculate marble. I brought the stone from Italy six years ago for a commission I was given then by the Prior of the Knights at Clerkenwell – it was one of my first commissions, when I came to London. I had almost finished it when they closed down the priory and the poor man died.

Executed with the rest?

No, but they say his heart broke the day he heard that his priory would be destroyed. I made his tomb. The Christ is in

THE BOOK OF DAYS

my shop, waiting for a buyer. It only needs a little work to fit it for your purpose.

🙟

Angeli, he said. There is an angel in the church already, informing the Virgin Mary that she will bear a child. Quomodo fiat istud, how shall that be? she asks, virum non cognosco. That angel's wings are stretched behind him, as if he were ready any second to take flight, as if he did not want to feel the dust of earth beneath his feet for any longer than it took to deliver his astounding message. In this small picture, Mary has her head bowed and her hands tight crossed to guard her belly, and her cloak spills round her in a lake of blue. What happened then, in the minutes that followed? Did she feel a shiver in her womb? Did she watch the angel turn upon his heel, stretch out his wings still further and soar upwards? Did she try to call him back? Perhaps he accidentally let one feather fall, a feather longer than any bird's, in unearthly shades of fire and gold, and she kept it as a plaything for her baby.

The feast day of Saint Barnabas

Light at dawn and light at dusk and today the scent of grass; salve Saint Barnabas and thanks be for the grace of sunshine on the meadows where the workers are making hay, and their women and children with them. Their voices reach the house. Word has come from London that the king has made peace with France, or signed a treaty anyway, if that is the same thing. Deo gratias, if fewer young men will bleed to death on foreign battlefields. And less milking for war money will be welcomed in the village, where tempers have been lately tried, not least by my lord's appropriation of the better part of Edgings field. Marmion says that the lord is putting his affairs in order, and no one dares to add the words that ring so loudly in their heads.

As reward for labour, my lord my husband has offered the cottiers a sheep, which they will roast tonight, when the first grass is stacked. They will be bone-weary then and burnished by a long day's sun, and later by the firelight, dimmed by summer brightness, that with the moonlight conquers night. There'll be ale and the rare grease of rich meat on their lips, there'll be music playing, songs and dancing. It is quiet in this house.

Late in the night of the day after the Feast of Barnabas

Susan told us this morning that in the revelry last night nobody noticed Mobey's child was ill. All the little ones were in the barn, rolling around like puppies, pinching scraps, while the elders were happily at their cakes and ale. It was not until time for bed that Mobey picked up the child, a girl not two years old, and felt how hot she was, fiery hot, as though she had swallowed burning coal. And now Mobey fears his wife is sickening too. Everyone is shunning them for fear of contagion.

Dear Joan, stout of heart and constitution, rises as ever to the challenge. Poor souls, she says, they need some of my brew. In the village, Joan is famous for her bitter infusion of marigold, sorrel, dragonwort and feverfew, which has saved many from the pestilence, with the help of God.

On an impulse I said, I will take it to them.

Joan was astonished. You? But it's not six months since you were brought to bed, and have you now forgot what happened? How you ailed for such a long time later?

But I am perfectly well now, I said.

Joan is used to being the chief performer of charitable works, and I perplexed myself by demanding to take her place. Why did I do that? To assert my own position? Or to court death? I don't know. Must every action need a reason? She remained doubtful but could not gainsay me and only made me promise to carry a posy of sweet marjoram and lavender against the noxious odours.

When she had bustled away to her still-room and we were left alone, Agnes looked furiously at me. What an odd fancy to take into your head, she said. You had better not go anywhere near my lord my father until you are sure you have not caught the fever too.

⚜

It is close to midnight. Her head hangs heavy on my shoulder, her hair is damp and matted, but she is not dying, she is asleep. The fever is no longer raging. Her mother, though, is in the grip of it and shivering under coverlets; too weak to rise, she has vomited where she lies upon the rushes. Her lips are dry and cracked and her breath foul-smelling, but she has swallowed a little of Joan's concoction mixed with wine and let me wipe her face with a cloth wrung out in rosemary water. The poor woman is bearing her sickness bravely and making no complaint; only asking after her daughter and sighing with relief on being told that she is out of danger.

When I arrived at the cottage, the child was awake and crying. I lifted her onto my hip and carried her about while I tried to tend to her mother, and the carrying soothed her, for she slept, but she wakes and cries again if I put her down on the floor. So I will stay a while, holding her on my lap, letting her sleep, for sleep is her best cure. She spat Joan's remedy straight out, it is too bitter for her, but when she is properly awake I will give her pure water from the well.

I was afraid to hold a child again. Those bones of the skull as frangible as eggshell, the hands and feet impossibly small. When they were closed, her eyelids were streaked with the thinnest filaments of blue, like the petals of marsh violets, but this child is older than my daughter was, more solid, and it is not fear or pain I feel now but something nearer pleasure. When I picked her up she yielded her whole weight to me, she was so trusting, and now she sleeps peacefully, this vinegary-smelling, mud-streaked little girl with tangled reddish curls.

Is she the reason I took Joan's place and came here? It is a long time since I was in the village; I have been keeping to the churchyard, the riverbank and the woods. This afternoon, women came to the doors of their cottages to watch me as I walked down North Street, but no one spoke.

I am in danger of becoming a ghost in my own life.

The child shall have my spray of flowers and sweet herbs to play with, when she wakes.

In the month of June, a Wednesday

Today the Tewkesbury men have finished the traceries in the new windows of the chapel and east wall of the church. Simm's men made the sills and lintels, the incomers the mullions, and each of these branch into two curved bars in such a way that every line flows into the lancet-heads, forming arches within arches and within them circles and leaf-shapes. In the hands of these carvers stone seems as supple as willow and as likely to sprout green. So now the windows are ready for the painters of glass, who are expected here before midsummer. Their designs, which they call vidimus, were sent ahead, and are in a locked chest, with the other secret plans and drawings that my lord my husband is amassing.

In the month of June, a Friday

Today the church is crowded with scents, of incense and fresh rushes, plaster, stone, new wood and molten lead. And of the bodies of men who are hard at work in mighty heat. It is packed with noises too: sawing, sanding, hammering and, above all, voices; a Babel of instructions, warnings, arguments and jokes. The silent stone-carvers have returned to Tewkesbury for a while but in their stead are carpenters, carvers of wood and now glassmakers, who are soldering lead cames for their panes. There are three of them, sent from their master's workshop in Southwark, which is a borough near London. The master made the designs that were submitted to my husband; these three will shape the glass to them and fit it to the stonework of the windows. They are to glaze some of the old windows in the church first, leaving the new ones in the chapel until later. Some of the glass is plain and some painted or coloured. Marmion says that the glassmakers use a wheel tipped with diamonds to cut it. And that they paint it with powdered lead and copper filings, gum arabic and their own piss. If you want an earthly miracle it's this, he says: turning piss to pictures.

The wood-carvers are making a new rood screen and a pulpit, which will have on its four sides the four Gospel writers and their winged emblems: eagle, angel, ox and lion. My lord husband had also ordered them to carve new figures for the loft but Sir Joselin sued successfully to keep the old rood and the saints, which he himself had rescued years ago from Godstow Abbey, when it was suppressed. So they will stay: the pain-wracked body of Christ upon the cross, a crown of thorns about his head, nails through his hands and feet, to right and left his mother and Saint John. Age has worn them and worms have eaten them but nothing has lessened their hallowed power, and it is said that when darkness falls, and the only light comes from the candles flickering on the rood beam, the two saints lift their eyes towards the dying man they love.

And so the work goes on and the sun still shines and every day it melts a little of the stiffness in my husband's limbs. He is able to leave the house again and walk around the garden, but he has not been to the church.

⁂

> *Matthew, Mark, Luke and John,*
> *The bed be blest that I lie on.*
> *Four corners to my bed,*
> *Four angels round my head;*
> *One to watch, and one to pray,*
> *And two to bear my soul away.*

The twenty-third day of June

Saint John's fire lights the dusk tonight, the village streets, the corners of the fields. Blazing bones, and a wheel of flame rolled down the hill towards the river, flinging sparks into the sky. Fireflies, dying into embers, witches' night, midsummer's eve, if you watch and wait in a church all night, you'll see the apparitions of those that shall be buried there in the year ahead. One by one they'll pass before you, saying nothing. So, should I go? Maybe, and on my way I'll gather fern seed and walk invisible thereafter, wherever and when I wish.

There is feasting in the village again, and all the doorways garlanded with green birch, fennel, orpine and Saint John's wort; lanterns and bright torches burn by them too. Saint John's wort bleeds scarlet from its stem; hide a sprig of it beneath your pillow to scare the Devil away. Despite the lateness of the hour, it is still warm.

Roland and Henry Martyn are to leave for London in the morning. Agnes, I fear, will be sad when Henry goes. She says nothing but she lacks the guile to hide her new-hatched feelings. Love preoccupies young girls. And women too? What Henry Martyn may feel for Agnes is anybody's guess; mine is that he pays attention to her out of courtesy alone. He has been here for more than a month now, and yet I know him no better than the day he came. Never was there a man with such tight shutters on his soul.

Midsummer's eve. Maids stick sprigs of orpine two by two in the cracks of beams and joists: one for themselves, the other for their sweethearts, and if in the morning the flowers lean towards each other, their love will prosper and endure. But if one of those two sprigs should wither in the night, it signifies that either man or maid will die. I hope that Agnes has not been out today, gathering flowers in secret.

Tonight the veil between the worlds is cobweb-thin. A baby can be stolen from a crib and a soulless changeling left in lieu, to greet the mother with blank eyes. A man who seems to be composed of flesh and bone can turn into a shadow.

※

Agnes's mother's name was Agnes too. She bore five children and four died; the last of them would not be parted from her. She travailed for days, said Joan, but even Blessed Margaret failed to save her. Surely the saint would have tried her best to intercede for one who lived a blameless life, but heaven's ways are not our ways; they are not for us to question. Poor Agnes's cries that terrible time would have moved the very fiends in hell to pity. She was saintlike herself, and that is how they perceived her in the village. If there were anyone who ailed or was in need, Lady Agnes would be right there, by their side. Oh, how she was loved. Oh, how great the sorrow when she left this world. Oh, how she is missed.

She was a widow when she married my lord, but childless and still, I think, quite young. She brought her dead husband's estates with her as dowry. Land begets land, it seems; the more you have the more it grows. Just don't ask what those who start with none can do to get a portion.

John, Richard, Edith, Agnes, Creature. Only little Agnes left, out of all the five. I pray for you, dead children. It was a mercy,

Joan told me, that Sir Joselin arrived in time – he had been in Wales – to christen little Creature, who then being half in Agnes's womb was still of sex unknown. Afterwards, they saw she was a girl. She lies with her mother and her sister and her brothers in the church. A little heap of bones, no larger than a bird's.

John and Edith also died in infancy, but Richard outlived his mother by some months. Agnes must remember him, though she never says so. No one speaks these children's names now, in this house. If their father mourns them, it is in the silence of his heart.

Their mother was a rare beauty, Joan says. Golden hair and eyes like stars. She looked like the angel that she was, no wonder the Almighty claimed her.

Midsummer's Day

Every day is hotter than the last. The sun god is stoking his furnace and the world below is wilting. Summer's bright greens are already dulled now and grown harder, the white cow parsley gone to seed and blackbirds no longer singing.

Constantly I dream of the sea, of infinities of water. When I was a child, I used to swim; I learned to trust the water and surrender to a river's gentle pull. I wish I were in water now, in that river's green embrace, with its cool flow on my burning skin.

The third day of the month of July

What summer sickness struck me down on the day after Saint John's day, I do not know. It was not the fever of Mobey's child, nor was it grave, but in a household fearful of plagues and contagion, it was more than enough to have me banished to a closet. Susan looked after my needs, and brave Joan came with oil of hypericum and purges, but otherwise I was alone in quarantine for seven days. I could have freed myself but dared not risk infecting anybody else, especially not my lord my husband. Joan told me that in any case he had suffered a relapse, and Doctor Moreton had advised him to keep to his bed until he recovered his strength. Maladies such as this have peaks and troughs, he said, according to Joan, but in the end they find a level. The doctor never gives this malady a name – perhaps it does not have one.

When Joan pronounced me fit to be in company again, I went directly from the house to the grave. The gillyflowers I had left there on midsummer's eve would be sadly withered by now, so on my way I gathered field roses to replace them.

It was late, almost supper time, there was no one in the churchyard and no sign of anyone nearby. I knelt and prayed a while, and gave her my white flowers, and then I thought I would like to see what progress had been made inside the church. Since I was last there, the walls of the porch had grown waist-high, and Simm's men had left a plank as walkway.

I unlatched the door and at once was dazzled by a fountaining of colour across the floor. Reds and greens and yellows brighter than poppies, kingcups, lime leaves; blues more brilliant even than the dragonfly's or kingfisher's; colours brighter than the jewels in the crown of any king. But if their origins were sapphires, emeralds and rubies, these stones had been melted into airy thinness and magicked into light.

Then I turned to look upwards, and the dancing colours were no longer disembodied light but resolved into a bright assembly so vigorous and forceful that I felt myself swept up into it, caught upon its eddy like a feather in the wind. There, at its centre, was the Lord seated on a rainbow, with the sword of vengeance flashing in one hand and a lily in the other, the yellow sun behind him and the earth, glowing red, as his footstool. His blue-cloaked mother on his left, the beloved disciple on his right in green and scarlet, and a multitude of saints and angels all around. Haloes a blaze of gold. But, immediately below the Son of Man in glory, the winged archangel with a balance, weighing souls. In one pan, the good soul, robed in white, kneels trustingly, with hands clasped and an angel ready to receive her by her side; the wicked soul squirms naked in the other, like a toad in boiling water, while a devil with a crest and monstrous talons grasps him tightly by his wrist.

The dead are bursting from their tombs still trailing shrouds and, with them, the living, as bare upon the last day as on the day of birth, but they will be divided, as a shepherd separates the sheep from the goats. For the saved there are angels to escort them to Saint Peter with his keys to heaven's gates; for the rest there are devils, scaly, green or red, with heads like nightmare dogs or snakes and grinning mouths and jagged teeth. There are pitchforks, there are flames. The fires of hell will not be quenched and the damned will not escape them, weep and gnash their teeth though they may. Their worm will never die. There is the rich man begging Lazarus, who once was poor, to soothe the torment of his thirst with a finger dipped in water. But he cries in vain, for none in heaven can pass to hell and none in hell will cross the gulf to heaven.

Fire and flame and light and sky, clash of cries and trumpets. The lily and the sword. The archangel wears a sheathed sword and the doublet and hose of an ordinary man, but his wings are like a butterfly's, veined and marked with glowing eyes; the devils' claws are sharp. I was spinning, flying in this glassy scene, and gasping, burning too, for none can tell the hour or day when he shall come to judge the quick and the dead, and I am powerless because alone, for there will be no one to pray for me when I am gone, and in that last court there is no appeal.

And there came a sudden sound, a man's voice, a stir beyond the rood screen and then a figure casting a long shadow, and the span of his wings was wider than an eagle's.

※

He carried you to Cadd's house, Joan said, bustling to my bedside in the morning. All the way. He did not know who you were or where else he could take you. Joselin was out. Cadd's was the nearest house. It was folly, I must say, to rush out after a week abed, having eaten almost nothing. No wonder you were giddy and light-headed. I believe you may be suffering from a suffocation of the mother – do you need rue to bring on your courses? You had better stay in bed again today and I will bring you almond milk.

I am quite well, I said. I am hungry. Who was it who carried me?

William. The chantry priest or curate or whatever he may be. That one. He came yesterday. He said he had been singing his first mass at the altar in the church and, being done, was about to leave when he saw you fall. What a blessing he was there, or else you might have lain there on the floor all night. What a blessing that you did not hit your head! Or did you? You do seem a bit addled, but I can see no bruising.

I don't know. I don't remember. Nothing hurts. I would like to dress now and come down to breakfast with you all.

Against my better judgement, Joan said crossly.

⁂

But he was not there in the hall. Sooner or later I would have to greet the man who had lifted my unconscious body and held it in his arms. I would have to thank him, but not yet. How long did I lie there beneath his scrutiny, exposed? I remembered my amazement faced by the Doom, I remembered the winged figure at the rood screen, but then nothing until I opened my eyes in Cadd's house and his wife was giving me a drink of ale. I did not think to ask then how I got there.

At breakfast, Agnes said: William Clare is come and I am to have a virginal for my daily lessons in music. Do you suppose Titus could learn to play it too?

Birds can learn tunes and also words, Hugh said, but monkeys cannot sing.

No, but they do dance, and they have nimble fingers.

Ask William then, said Marmion. I suppose he will do

whatever he is ordered. Poor man! Little did he think that he was hired to teach music to a monkey and a lass! A flounder out of the frying pan and straight into the fire, I say!

But he was not, protested Hugh.

Well, what then? To sing requiems for souls still living in a chapel not yet built?

Almost built.

That's true enough. And almost dead?

⁂

The heat increases. Later in the morning in my lord husband's shuttered chamber, the air had almost turned to steam, no longer element invisible but palpable material, and difficult to breathe. I watched his chest rising and falling with the effort, beneath the green coverlet.

You have been ill, he said.

Yes, and I heard that you too have been confined to bed. I am sorry that I could not come to see you. Joan forbade me to.

She told me that you suffered some sort of falling fit.

I fainted. It was nothing. I should not have gone out in the heat. I am quite recovered now. But you?

I have lost all sensation in my legs, he said. The doctor promises that it will return. I hope that he is right.

Then, for the first time ever, I read fear in his eyes. It flickered only for an instant before he set his face again, but it was there, and it undid something in me. All these months he has maintained that a cure is but a matter of time and no one in his household has allowed the possibility of doubt. We have parroted what the doctor says, nodding and smiling – yes, all

75

will be well – because we dare not confront our fears or his. As the keystone of this house for more years than most of us who depend on him have lived, weakness in him endangers us. Long ago he built his own wall round his heart but it was the rest of us who shored it up, mortared him firmly into place, and now would rather deny him fear than admit our fear of his.

I was as afraid of the depths of his fear as anybody else. But I did see, and will never unsee, that fleeting look in his eyes, and I longed to wrap my arms around him, to soothe him with the fond words that mothers murmur to fevered children, to tell him that if he were dying, I would be with him and he would not die alone. I climbed onto the bed and reached for his hand, but he kept his arms under the covers and I could only stroke his shoulder through the silk.

We must keep faith with Doctor Moreton, he said after a spell of silence broken only by his laboured breath. He has recommended daily bloodletting to restore a liquid flow into the limbs, and I will be able to walk again within a day or two.

Of course you will. Of course you will feel better when the weather is less hot.

Do the men at the church complain?

Everyone complains. They say it is unnatural, that the cattle are dying and the grain will be parched before it is tall enough to harvest. They want only to crawl into the shade like dogs and lie there, panting. But Simm keeps his men hard at work, and much has been accomplished in the past few weeks.

Hugh says that the new west window is a masterly piece of work.

Indeed it is. The colours are astonishing. I know that when you see it, you will be very pleased.

But then I saw in my mind's eye those scaly devils digging their claws into the damned and dragging them down into the fiery pit, and I felt glad that he was spared the full image for a while. O Richard, silent, suffering man. What was it that seared your soul so deeply that you must make such great atonement in glass and wood and stone? Do you confess to Joselin? Will you have time for that?

※

At dusk I saw a barn owl in the garden. It flew by me on silent wings, with no warning of approach: a sudden, startling whiteness, a shiver, a disturbance of the air.

In the month of July, the feast day of Saint Thomas

Through the thin walls of the upper chamber comes the sound of Agnes at her music lesson. She has only just begun to learn the virginal and she stumbles over the keys, striking some too hard and fumbling notes, so that what we hear is not music yet. But when he plays, teaching her by example, he draws out of the plain-looking wooden box that was lately delivered to Agnes sounds that I have never heard before and cannot find the words for; sounds both gay and grave at one and the same time, airy as the wind in willow leaves, earthy as bare feet dancing on the floor. This is music made of equal parts of tears and laughter, and I don't know how that can be. A form of magic? He seems to be a quiet man, even a little solitary, a man who would prefer a cloister to a crowd, and yet he has that music in him?

In the month of July, a Monday

A dragon is breathing its hot breath across the land, scorching the grasses, turning skies to brass. Soon we shall be dwelling in a desert. Roland and Henry Martyn have returned to help harvest the first of the grain. Why both of them together? Joan wanted to know. One would think that they were wedded. Has Master Henry nowhere else to go? But Agnes is happy, I suppose.

The sixteenth day of July

Saint Swithun's Day has been and gone: we must endure many more days now of raging sun. Fever is falling from the air and nothing will quench my burning thirst. I dream of ice and snow. Now is the season for falconers to take young hawks from their eyries. Until the birds are manned their eyes are seeled with a fine thread drawn through each eyelid: where once they lived in a world of light and saw with marvellous acuity, now they are at once cast into utter blackness.

❧

Word of the sickness has evidently reached my father; he has written to ask about my lord my husband's health. He hopes that whatever may happen, my dower will be safe, despite the new statutes of law. Am I sure that there is no entail? Alas, he bemoans, that you have not borne an heir, and now it is too late. Alas for the loss even of a daughter.

I have not considered what my future holds. Looking into it now is like looking into starless skies on winter nights or balancing on uncertain ground at the edge of a fathomless pit. What am I, barely a wife, barely trusted to carry herbs to fevered children, merely another burden on the household, if I cannot be a mother?

My father's castle is larger than the house where I live today, but in it there is no room for me. He has a wife and six children by her; the eldest and the youngest three are sons.

In the month of July, a Thursday

Tilers were here, and now there are bright pictures on the chancel floor: fleurs-de-lys, gryphons, knights on horseback, my lord my husband's coat of arms, and interlaced initials R&A. The tilers took squares of clay, stamped them with pattern blocks made of applewood, glazed them green and yellow, and fired them in their kilns. They were cheerful men, proud of their craft and eager to describe it; when I saw part of my own initial separate on a shard – a reject from the firing – they gave it to me as a keepsake. An A for Agnes or for me? For both of us?

Stepping into the church will be like stepping into a box of jewels when all is done. Not an inch but will be filled with line and colour. Now though, until the time comes, the great square of the tomb pit is conspicuously dark by contrast with the brightness of the tiles. A deep gash of bare earth that awaits its load. Marmion does not know when we may expect Piero to return. Soon, he thinks. But cutting so much stone must be a lengthy task for any image-maker.

Today is Margaret's feast. It is forbidden to keep it, under the new rules, but the people do, of course, with Sir Joselin's help. If he has ever troubled to study the new laws, he disregards them in the main. He said a mass this morning in Margaret's honour, and there were candles burning at her altar. It was a morrow-mass, at dawn, and the day was fairly fresh then, the cool of night not quite yet banished by the fiery sun. All the women of the village who are expecting children, or hoping that they will, came bearing flowers with red petals – roses, poppies, campion – symbolising blood, and Joselin invoked the saint for them: kind virgin, present on behalf of thy devoted handmaidens their earnest prayers to Almighty God, thou who art the benign assister of women in travail.

William Clare's true singing voice, augmenting Joselin's croak, has woven a new strand into our worship, enriching it, as an embroiderer sews gold thread into plain woollen cloth. I close my eyes to hear him.

Henry Martyn attended the mass, to my surprise, and afterwards, at dinner, asked if the parish was not afraid of lighting candles to a saint to whom devotion is proscribed.

We have always honoured Margaret, and our mothers before us, Joan protested. It does no harm, said my lord's nephew, Hugh. My father says that the king has bethought himself again of what is right and is cured of his newfanglery, said Agnes. Her cousin Roland frowned at her and raised his hand in warning: be very careful, Agnes, what you say. Why? she asked. We are amongst family and friends.

A silence followed. As the reeds in the meadow whispered the secret of Midas's ears to passing winds, so the faintest talk of heresy may reach the Court, if it concerns the king. Even to think a treasonous thought is courting danger. Did the king not promise to wreak vengeance on the loose-tongued and destroy their wives and children?

Cousin, you misunderstood your father, Hugh said. I am sure that he commends the king for steadfast faith.

But Joselin laughed. My own conscience will always rule me, he said, half under his breath but meaning to be heard. William Clare said nothing. I saw him glance from face to face around the table in his quiet, clear-eyed way, and for some reason the apostle Peter and his three denials before cock's crow came to mind.

※

In London last week a woman was burned at the stake, a heretic, they say. Her name was Anne. Before she was burned she was broken on the rack, and she had to be carried to the fire because she could not walk. I think of her having to hear the roar of flame, to smell the smell of her own scorched hair, her pain beyond words, beyond imagining, beyond bearing, and I pray the smoke was merciful and stopped her breath before her marrow roasted.

※

I was in the village today and I saw the child who had been ill playing with some others near the ditch at Nether End. Mobey's little girl. Her mother died, Joan told me. The child looked happy enough, making her mud pie; she is perhaps too young to comprehend her loss. She did not recognise me. Who attends to her now, I wondered. Does Mobey do so alone? What happens when he is at work in the fields? Someone has combed the hair that was so damp and matted when I held her. Those reddish-golden curls.

In the month of July, a Sunday

Last night I could not sleep, I was too hot, there was no air and so I rose before daybreak, put on my cloak, crept from the house so stealthily that not even the dogs woke, and walked out to the meadows. Dew-soaked grass beneath my feet, the willows resolving into leaf and distinct green but the far trees on the hillside undifferentiated in near-darkness, not yet brushed by light. Mother-of pearl glow, veined with faintest rose and dove-grey, to the east. And then I saw the fox. She stole out of the obscure woods onto the slope below, and she was as white as snow. For the length only of an indrawn breath she stayed stock-still there, her head lifted, a white ghost on the hillside, and then, as quietly as she came, she disappeared.

The first day of the month of August

L ammas Day, and the first wheat has been gathered in, but
only just in time. Yesterday began, as every day this past
fortnight and more, cloudless and brazen, but the skies grew
darker and more leaden as it wore on, and yet it stayed so hot
that the dogs were gasping. A little before the supper hour, as
the fieldsmen were binding the last of the day's sheaves, it was
as black as night. And then the sky was suddenly splintered by a
blinding flash of lightning, pursued almost at once by a terrible
roll of thunder, and the rain began to pour. Except that it was
not rain, for that falls drop by drop, and this was water in full
spate, as if the world had been upended, the heavens become
seas and the thin skin between the two had ruptured. More rain
fell in an hour, I swear, than did throughout the waterlogged
weeks of Lent. Agnes, Joan and I watched from the window of
the upper chamber as the storm raged and the ground below
us churned and frothed, with each successive drench of water
digging deeper furrows in the earth, beheading flowers and
crushing plants.

Susan said this morning that great hailstones shaped like skulls
fell on the neighbouring village of Stoke during the night. They
were exactly like skulls, with hollows where there had been
eyes and grinning open mouths. The people are very afraid.
Everywhere is flooded, the fishpond has overflowed and the fish
themselves are swimming through the meadow. When the water
retreats they will all die on the drying grass. Not even the oldest

in the village can remember such a storm before, and everybody knows this is an omen. It is too soon to tell if the second crop of grain is lost but probably it will be, and the people will go hungry. Several cottages are ruined.

The rain has stopped for the time being, but the sky is still dangerously dark and last night's lightning struck the purple beech. A black gash now scars its trunk and Marmion predicts that it will die.

⁂

At dinner, Roland said that this village prattle of signs and portents was nothing but fiddlesticks and flimflam. But do you not believe that the Lord God and his holy saints make the wind and weather? Agnes asked. In the village they are saying that the storm was punishment.

For what?

For some dreadful evil that is not yet known.

Joan said that if he were here, which he cannot be because his house is flooded, Sir Joselin would argue that it was a sin to banish all the saints of harvest-time. We always used to keep the feasts of Martin, Mary Magdalene and Anne, she said. And that of dear Saint Thomas! When I was a girl, we had a fair on the day of the translation of his bones. I have ribbons still that I got there. But now he has been scraped out of our prayer books. Was that not cause enough for commination?

Hush, wife, said Marmion. You talk flimflam too.

Yes, Joan said quite comfortably, no doubt I do.

We cannot reach the village from this house because the path is a muddy streambed, under water for a hundred yards. Simm, likewise, is marooned, and no one knows if there is damage to the church. William Clare is trying to salvage what is left after last night's flooding in the house that he now shares with Joselin, at the old priest's invitation. Joselin has taken William to his heart.

I am nothing to William, nor he to me, and yet I feel his absence from the table.

The third day of the month of August

The storm of two nights ago has not cleared the air at all; still we droop and languish, moving slowly through the hours like aged carp in clouded water. When the church could be reached, it was found that the winds had torn off several roof tiles and water had poured through the still-unglazed east window, but no great harm was done. However, as Simm's men have all been called to the fields for harvest, and for the same reason the Tewkesbury stone-carvers have gone home too, there will be scant work done in the church from now till Michaelmas. Only the glassmakers have stayed; there are no fields in Southwark. Now they are hard at work on the new window, which they promise will match the west for splendour, and then they will begin on the windows to the south. Cadd the warden has been fussing over the profligate waste of the crown glass that was there before, and whether filling every window with deep colours will rob the church of daylight, but Marmion says the glassmakers will surely find a way to let light in.

My lord husband has regained a slight degree of feeling in his limbs, as Doctor Moreton promised that he would. On the doctor's last visit he said the patient must not lie supine all day because that renders him weaker than he should be, and moreover he has developed sores upon his back, and therefore Lambert lifts him out of bed in the mornings, like a child. Well, I presume he does; Lambert's ministrations are rightfully a private matter between him and the master he has served since he was a child.

He came to this house out of nowhere, Joan told me; he landed at the back door like an abandoned fledgling fallen from its nest and, because he was mute, no one knows who his parents were or what had happened to him. That was thirty years ago, or thereabouts, my lord's father was alive then, and they took him in. Marmion remembers it. They guessed he was a gypsy's brat, cast out or left behind because he could not talk. He still cannot, but he can hear and he is certainly no want-wit. Indeed, he seems to understand more clearly than some talking people do. And he is strong, which is a blessing, given that he has to lift, support and settle a man who, when he stood straight, was the tallest of them all.

⚜

Roland and Hugh have gone to Windsor on business of my husband's, leaving their friend Henry Martyn here. Who Henry is and where he comes from is a mystery to me. All I know is that he was born and raised at Whitechapel in London and his parents are dead. Joan believes he is the bastard son of a noble lord but I suspect that to be a false rumour. He and Roland were pupils together at Lincoln's Inn.

With the brothers away, Henry is too much alone with Agnes in my view, although Joan disagrees. She says that he is sport for her in an otherwise dull household and that young girls must play at love before they love in earnest. Or are wed. It's like practising how to be a mother on a kitten or a poppet.

I wonder if Dame Joan, mother of sons, wife for years to Marmion, remembers her first love as I remember mine. He was secretary to my father for a while, his eyes as blue as speedwell, and if he saw me at all it was only as a little girl. But my feelings for him were a woman's. I thought of him all day and dreamt of him at night, in bed I pressed my fingers to my lips to practise kissing. I loitered outside rooms in which he could have been, to catch a glimpse of him should he emerge; I waited by the castle gates for hours on end, in case he should ride by. If he spoke a passing word to me, I read a whole world of meaning in it. I was sure that he loved me as I loved him and would say so when he could. But, swallow-like, he was gone all of a sudden at the end of my tenth summer and I never heard of him again.

Henry is nine years older than Agnes, and whether he looks on her as a child or a woman cannot be told from his demeanour. He gives nothing away. But she blushes when she greets him, she pouts and flutters her eyelids, she whispers his name in the night-time when she thinks I am asleep.

When grown women laugh at lovelorn girls and tease them, do they forget that they too burned in secret once and might yet burn again?

In the month of *August*, a Friday

Dog days. The world that was green is yellow now, a world of stubble and dry grass. The hillsides look like the flanks of brindled hounds.

I went to the church this morning, early, for the first time since the storm. William Clare was there, kneeling in the chancel. I did not see him when I came in, otherwise I would not have entered and disturbed him. By the time I did, it was too late. Apart from him the place was empty, although Agnes and Henry, who had been walking with me, were not far behind.

William startled when he heard me and rose to his feet.

I am sorry, I said.

Why should you be?

For interrupting you at prayer.

You haven't.

I came nearer to where he was, by the new-made tomb pit, and he came to stand there too. It was so much wider than one man. Still the smell of fresh-dug earth, that graveyard smell.

They say that it will be a magnificent tomb, said William Clare.

Well, Master Piero, the imager, is famous for his skill.

We shall have to pray that such a monument will lessen the trials of the dead.

Do you believe it will?

I don't know, and what I have just said I would retract. But I do believe that it may console the living who mourn, and that is justification enough if anyone should question why it is made so large and bold.

I think they do question, in the village.

Some, perhaps.

People don't like change.

No, but when change happens, they forget what went before. In years to come, the people of the village will think the tomb stood here forever, like the font.

It's so wide, I said.

It does seem so. But surely you have seen the finished drawings?

No, my lord husband keeps them to himself. Unless he shared them with Sir Joselin?

Sir Joselin has not said so.

I looked up at William Clare. His eyes were dark and deep. The tombs of the dead are the hearts of the living, I said, beneath my breath. But I was heard.

Yes, he said, perhaps they should be, but hearts are not as lasting as cut stone.

Agnes came in then, with Henry Martyn, and with Titus, unleashed, at her heels. Ah, there you are, she said to me. We thought that you had run away back to the river. Good morning, Sir William. I have practised my notes already, before breakfast.

Titus, skittering around the church, stopped at the glassmakers' workbench, stretched up on his hind legs to see what might be there and toppled a pot of mastic. O little knave, said Agnes fondly, you were lucky that it spilled upon the clay, for otherwise you might have had a beating. Come here, sweet rogue! The creature bounded to her and jumped into the pit. All four of us watched it scrabbling at the bricks. He's making ready for when he rests there, Agnes said.

What, Titus?

Yes. Maestro Piero is making a likeness of him for the tomb. My lord my father will have a dog at his feet, for that is the noble custom, but my mother will have Titus below hers.

Your mother?

My lady mother Agnes.

Was Titus hers?

Yes, she had him as a baby, my lord my father's gift.

Your mother on the tomb? I asked, foolishly confused.

Bien sûr!

Then you have seen the master's design? William asked her.

Not in its entirety, but my lord my father has described it. And he says that you, Sir William, are to compose a mass for my dead mother.

Am I?

Has he not asked you yet? He surely will.

Piero said there would be angels, I protested. Angels but not monkeys.

Why not both? Henry said. The more the merrier: angels, monkeys, dogs—

Agnes interrupted. Sir William, do you hold that creatures have no souls?

It is the teaching of the Church that only persons have immortal souls.

Then the Church is wrong. You need only look into Titus's eyes to see the soul beneath them. And anyway, if animals were soulless, why place them on tombs?

In olden days, Henry said, kings were buried with their treasure. Their gold, their weaponry, their hounds and horses and, I daresay, their wives.

But the wives still living? Agnes cried.

So I have been told.

The glassmakers were arriving, and so we left the church and walked back to the house together, as it was time for Agnes's music lesson. There was no more talk of tombs. In my heart I pondered what Agnes had said, but I was still confused.

> O father O father go dig my grave
> Dig it both deep and narrow
> For my true love was buried today
> And I will die tomorrow.

In the month of August, a Sunday

Today, the feast of the Transfiguration and the blessing of the first fruits; in the hall this morning a great basket full of cherries, glowing red as rubies, red as burning coals. William Clare preached at mass, for the first time in my hearing. He is God, he said, and God hath no man ever seen. Through the veil of his flesh such beams he cast, as behind those clouds they might know there was a sun; as that way only could he be made visible to the eyes of flesh, which otherwise could not behold him.

My lord my husband rose for dinner. Such pride he has that he will not be carried, even now after the last turn in his illness, but instead he walked painfully, stiffly down the spiral stairs and lowered himself into his chair. Sir Joselin was there, with the rest of the household, and my husband asked him how he found the new works to the church. He said only that he would reserve his judgement until they were completed but that the people of the parish were very pleased by the west window.

The east window will be finished today or tomorrow, Marmion said.

It is right that they bear sacred images, Joselin said. Books for the unlettered, Scripture for laymen. Though I could wish you had not caused the removal of the Last Supper in the chancel.

But we will replace it, my lord my husband said. And much more.

Really? Henry Martyn interjected. Then you go against the fashion. Plain walls are the coming thing, or walls with holy words inscribed on them.

All eyes turned to Henry, surprised at his boldness. Yes, words can be a delight to look on, said Agnes hastily. As in my primer with the scene of Jesus as a little baby in the first letter of the opening page.

In the alphabet of the Armenians, letters take the form of birds, said William Clare.

Roland and Hugh have come back from Windsor. It appears that the business they were sent on has been successfully concluded; they brought lawyers' letters with them, all these letters sealed, according to Hugh. He told me that Roland had seen the lawyers on his own. At Windsor they also met the Earl of Cumberland, who offered Hugh a post as secretary in his household. Hugh is to go there after Twelfth Night, when the earl has returned from a voyage to Aragon. I do know that Hugh must have an occupation and a livelihood, but I will miss him sorely when he goes and am glad the parting will not be for months to come.

The brothers and Henry Martyn were talking in the garden after dark. I overheard them in mid-conversation through the open window of the upstairs room. It was Roland's new horse that they discussed, a beautiful, shiny morel. They spoke of speed and girth. Then Roland said: that young priest looks like my horse, that William. With his long nose and those great big eyes, and the lock of hair forever falling on his forehead.

Henry laughed. Yes, and batting thick eyelashes. But I say that he is more like a donkey. He must be, as he is a cleric. Asses. They all are, these creeping, prating priests.

Be quiet! ordered Hugh and Roland with one voice. You do not know who could be listening, Roland added.

I do not care. I have said nothing not openly said elsewhere. Roland, you know that. All those fat priests with their caskets full of pigs' bones and phials of holy water that might as well be piss. If I were to piss in their stoops, no one could tell the difference.

You imperil your soul by speaking like this, Hugh said in a shocked voice. Are you not afraid?

Hugh, you are a sweet boy and the brother of the man I love, but you are a fool.

Enough! said Roland. For my part, I like Sir William. He holds his peace, which is a good thing in any man. But, if he seldom speaks, he certainly sings! What a voice!

True, said Henry. And it was quite a feat to turn the raga-muffins of the village so swiftly into songbirds.

Henry, what did you mean by pigs' bones? Hugh asked.

Think on it, Hugh! If all the bones attributed to any single saint were assembled into a body, that body would have a hundred arms and a thousand toes. Not to mention an inconvenient quantity of foreskins.

That is not true. Yes, there may be instances of fraud or error, but not many and not here, not in our church.

No, not in your church. But not so very far away from here, at Hailes? Where the abbot himself confessed that the phial of holy blood which the pilgrims flocked to see came not from Jesus but a farmyard duck?

Come, said Roland, it's getting late.

A duck, said Henry. Quack, quack, quack! Have you never heard of those priests who strap lighted candles onto the backs of crabs and send them scuttling round churchyards on All-Hallows Eve to trick ignorant men into believing that they see the souls of the dead?

Dis manibus, Roland said.

⁂

Darkness brings no relief. At midnight it is scarcely cooler than midday. There is not the barest whisper of a breeze. The sleeping world suspends its breath, apart from Susan and Agnes who snuffle in antiphonal chorus, and Titus who chitters in his cage. I am so hot. The foxes of the night have surrendered to the heat and hide panting in their dens, the owl spreads its wings into a fan and stays silent on its perch beneath a thatch of drooping leaves. I am so hot. Sweat trickles through my hair and seeps between my breasts, between my legs. A night for snakes, not furred or feathered things, or women.

The curtains of this bed enclose me like a tomb. Agnes insists on drawing them, for otherwise, she says, she cannot feel safe. She likes tight spaces, is a seeker-out of small corners and even now, in this bake-oven of a room, she has pulled the coverlet close about her. Susan is luckier, in her uncurtained truckle. Lucky to be lying without another sweating body by her.

When I was a child, I slept alone. When I was a wife – I am still a wife – I slept beside my husband in a bed with a canopy of coffered wood and a carved headboard. More box than bed? Or coffin. Thick curtains of embroidered wool. Feathers encased in silk. A coverlet of green patterned with white lilies. He sleeps in that bed still. If he sleeps at all. It may be that he lies wakeful through the dark hours, feeling his own body turning slowly into his tomb.

He used to lie on his back, a quiet sleeper, not a snorer, hardly moving. Sometimes I would wake and, sensing his wakefulness, picture his eyes wide open in the dark. Two people lying next to one another still as statues; we seldom spoke. I was always afraid of disturbing him if he slept and I did not. There is a special terror in lying sleepless next to someone whose temper is unyielding – or did I impose that fear on myself?

On hot nights he would not draw the curtains closed, there being no one else in that bedchamber. Moonlight on the silken lilies. Tonight there is no moon. We did the deeds of the night in silence always; I wonder, does he think of them? In a body that is petrifying, what potency remains? Does desire still stir in him?

I have not asked, but I am sure that Agnes and her brothers and sisters were conceived in that same bed. The weight of coupled bodies sinking into feathers. Did Agnes's mother die there too, did she want to be carried back to it after the stillbirth, to spend the last day of her life in her marriage bed?

My daughter was born in a little room made ready for the purpose, a cloth hung over the window to keep out the light, a constant fire glowing in the grate. Christmas Eve; quiet, warm and dark. The midwife's hands anointed with wild thyme and oil of musk. A bed of straw to soak up blood and water. Lady's bedstraw grows golden in the meadows in the summer, honey-scented sweet.

Lavender aids restful sleep. Joan distilled oil of lavender last month, dry flower heads steeped in sunlight. There are phials of it on the shelf in the still-room, but the room is locked and she keeps the key. I will be awake all night, I am so hot. If I dared, I would creep out of the house, but I am afraid to walk alone in the moonless dark. Agnes turns in her sleep and says something, but I cannot make out the words.

Pigs' bones. I think of frightened crabs with wax dripping on their shells. But if you were to see flames darting between graves in the dead of night, you too would be afraid. Queen Artemisia of Caria drank the ashes of her husband Mausolus and made of herself a living tomb.

I wish that dawn would come. At first light I will rise and go down to the river. Before the sun can burn it off, there will be dew upon the grass; pale, wet leaves, cool water.

Does he lie awake now in his high four-poster bed, staring up into the dark? Could I go to him? Could I step soundlessly over his servant Lambert, sleeping like a faithful dog outside his door, and climb into that bed beside him? Would he want me still?

Sed tantum dic verbo, but only say the word.

In the month of August, a Thursday

Something extraordinary came to the house this afternoon, and it came unheralded. Piero's journeyman, who brought it here with an apprentice, said that his master had sent a letter stating that the Easter work was finished and asking for instructions but, if he did, it must have gone astray. The first the household heard of it was the rumble of heavy wheels on cobblestones. Not knowing where else to go, the carter had driven it directly into the courtyard of the house.

On the bed of the cart a rounded shape, like a tree trunk or a body, wrapped in cloth. Marmion was there, and Hugh. Marmion told the carter to go straight to the church but as the man was turning his horses about, I thought of my lord my husband. Wait, I cried. If my husband's pride would not allow him to be carried to the church, or driven to it like this cartload, he could at least walk into his own courtyard and see the work he had commissioned.

Hugh ran to fetch him. He came, leaning on Lambert for support, and his daughter with him, just as the journeyman was unfastening the last of the ropes that bound his freight to the cart. Then he slowly drew back the waxed cloth, as a counterpane is pulled off a sleeping body. We saw a head, resting on the raised end of a bier, still with its crown of thorns. It tilted towards us, the eyes closed, the lips parted, the long curling hair matted with dried blood. A body thin and outstretched, scabbed and crusted knees a little bent. It lay on a crumpled cloth of deepest purple that I took to be a blood-soaked shroud until I saw it was a cloak.

I could have sworn that this man lived. Or had lived and only died a day or so ago. A tall man, as tall as my lord my husband. An infinitely suffering man, pain written on his face, in the arch of his spine, in the tension of a ribcage sorely wounded, on his bleeding, broken feet. His left arm was tight by his side and his right bent over his body, his fingers curving slightly as if to shield the wound that the Roman lance had made. Tangled in the folds of his cloak was a scroll with words carved on it: VSQVE AD MORTEM: MORTEM AVTEM CRVCIS.

We stared at him in silence. Hugh knelt. Even Marmion found nothing to say. Out of stone Piero had made flesh that lived and had endured an agony beyond imagination. I came closer and put out a finger to touch him but then found that I dared not; I knew that what I would encounter would not be cold stone but the unnatural coldness of a beloved person lately dead.

After a while, Marmion ordered the carter away. There's no sense in unloading it here, he said. Piero's envoy said that he would need some men with a barrow and a pulley to help him move the monument into place, as it was very heavy. Much debate ensued until a serving man was called who knew that Simm was near at hand. Marmion said that he should also bring Sir Joselin to the church, as he too would want a say in the positioning. And William Clare, I added.

When the cart had thundered off with Hugh and Agnes following, I turned to my lord my husband who until then had not said a word.

Is it what you wanted? I asked him.

It is very fine, but there is no consolation in it, he replied.

The twenty-fourth day of the month of August

Saint Bartholomew
brings the cold dew...

Thatʼs true – the few poppies that survived the cropping of the fields have faded, blackberries are ripening in the hedgerows and the water-mint that is growing by the river releases a strong and lovely scent when it is crushed. The sun continues to burn brightly and the daylight air is thick as honey, and yet even now in the harvest-height of August, autumn whispers softly. After dark, a chillness falls, and every day the dark comes a little sooner.

Joan scolds the young men for swimming in the evenings. August can be a melancholy month, she says, engendering fevers that cannot be cured. You should not go to your beds still damp, she warns them, but they pay little heed to her and I envy them their freedom.

⁂

There was an infant here this morning, in the garden, the baby son of one of the serving maids. Not yet a fortnight old, his proud mother eager to display him. The women of the household gathered round her and admired him but, because I heard him crying while I was yet indoors, I did not join them. That newborn cry, still so piercing to my ears, still a knife blade to my womb.

Joan said afterwards that he was a darling little thing. I know that, as I saw him for myself, from the upstairs window, held in the arms of William Clare. As the priest was walking past the group of women on his way from the house, the new mother naturally seized the chance of a blessing on her baby. I heard her call to William, I saw her hold out her child to him and I saw the sign of the cross that he made upon its head. Then he took the child from her and cradled it a while, crooning words that I could not hear, and the sunlight touched the baby's filmy hair.

In the month of September, a Saturday

The yellow world is green again but a tired green, not the green of spring. A turning green that anticipates the russets and the gold. All day long the drone of flies and sated wasps, at dusk the caw of rooks, but the swifts have flown and without their flourishes and their high calls, the skies are empty. When there is rain, the river receives it gratefully, as does the earth. Warm rain on parched ground, a smell as sweet as incense.

I went to see Sir Joselin in the church. We were alone. The dead Christ lay on his bier in the chancel near the altar, where one day soon he will be joined by a second, matching tomb. I told the old priest what my husband had said about the want of consolation in the statue. He was silent for some time and I thought about all the secrets he keeps stoppered tightly in him. He surely knows my lord my husband better than anyone else on earth, but not even the rack would drag his or anybody else's confidences out of Joselin. Silence, even in company, holds no fear for him. The consolation is here, he said after a while, and he pointed to the new east window, which at present only lacks the last few panes of pale blue glass needed for the sky.

Within a deep embrasure, there stands Our Lord, with his left foot planted on the stone lid of a tomb. He is naked but for a purple cloak draped over his shoulder, across his hips and his raised knee. Drops of blood seep from the gash in his right side. He is a king, crowned with a golden halo, a banner bearing the sign of the cross held aloft in his right hand. Before him, sleeping soldiers sprawling on the grass, in armour, chain mail and helmets, oblivious to the miracle happening above them, their pikes and swords still in their hands but rendered wholly useless. That tomb is in our churchyard. It is the low tower of our church that you can see in the background, our yew tree and, in the distance, the slope of the hill above our valley. It is dawn, the eastern sky is starting to turn blue, still lightly streaked with rose.

Ego sum resurrectio et vita. Qui credit in me, etiam si mortuus fuerit, vivet, Joselin said.

Yes, I said, so we are taught. But I can only hope that if my husband sees this window, he will read that message in it.

I did not say to Joselin that it was the isolation of this Christ that struck me most, this solitary man in a world still sleeping deeply. How did he feel when he woke on the third day and found himself alone in his dark tomb? Did he hope that when he succeeded in pushing the heavy stone lid of his sarcophagus aside and climbing out, he would find someone waiting there who was awake and loved him? Well, I know that he is God and God has foreknowledge instead of expectation. Omniscience is very far from hope. But even so. He was a grievously wounded man who died and then came back to life on a cold early morning when the only other creatures there were guards who stayed asleep through the sound of stone sliding over stone. Ah, the desolation of the dead, lonely and silent in their tombs.

The seventeenth day of September

Apple-scented air. Pearmain, Costard, Pomewater, Codlin, Jennetting, Catshead, Nonpareil. Fruits best gathered when the moon is full and the weather is fine, as it is now, on Saint Lambert's Day. Who gave our Lambert his name, I wonder? As he can neither write nor speak, he cannot have said what he was called when he came into this household. Perhaps he has another name, his own, by which he was known when he was born and now perforce keeps locked away with his other memories of childhood. Perhaps he longs to hear it spoken now. I asked my lord my husband if he remembered the renaming of Lambert, but he did not. He did not think that it was on this same saint's day that the boy was found, three-quarters starved, asleep on the kitchen doorstep.

Unbroken days of sunshine in September are a cordial sent by heaven to fortify the people and the land against the coming winter. We cannot store heat in us, as if it were wheat in a barn, and must make the most of it now. It is working like a spell on my husband. His legs are less rigid than they were two weeks ago and for the first time since midsummer's eve he can walk as far as the garden. This time has a dreamlike feel, a time that is not of an ordinary season, a time suspended between the last of the grain harvest and the winter sowing, a time of leaves becoming gold and ripe fruit falling from the trees. In this household it also marks the end of Roland's long vacation. At Michaelmas he will go back to Lincoln's Inn, taking Henry Martyn with him, I suppose.

❧

To sundew that was gathered in summer, add cinnamon, ginger, cloves, fine sugar, red rose petals and dates without their stones. Steep in aqua composita for twenty days precisely. Then, if you have it, add some gold leaf too. Rosa solis, it's one way to cage a little of the summer in a glass. A poor way, yes, but what else is there to do? Hold the bottle up to the light and catch the glow of sun in the depths of winter. Gleam of sunlight and fire also in the jars of quince and crab-apple jelly that Joan keeps in her still-room; they were in my mother's too, my memories of childhood, those scented liquids that were cloudy in the pan but then miraculously clear, as bright and shining as panes of coloured glass.

In the month of September, a Monday

L acking my rosary beads, I went to my bedchamber this morning before dinner. As I neared the closed door I heard laughter and a man's voice, and for a heart-stopping second I thought the voice was William Clare's. At the threshold, I could tell that it was Henry's laughter and that he was in the room with Agnes. Even so, I badly wanted to step away. He should not be there, of course he should not, with Agnes on her own, and my duty was to turn him out. Something made me hesitate; perhaps a fear of what I might see, or a deep reluctance to brave Henry's smirking face. He has a way of pressing his lips together and lowering his eyelids as if he were concealing his pleasure at his cleverness, and his disdain for the rest of the foolish world.

As I listened, I perceived that they did not sound hushed or furtive. I straightened my shoulders and pushed open the door. Henry was sprawling on the bed but Agnes was kneeling on the floor beside an open casket, trying with one hand to keep Titus from breaking free of her grasp and with the other to tie the strings of a little white cap beneath his chin. The monkey was wearing a white nightgown. Henry at once slid off the bed, with the grace to look ashamed. Agnes, however, seemed delighted to share the discovery she had made, and before I could open my mouth, she said: look! I found it in the loft. Did you put it there?

No, I have never seen it before.

It was exquisite – about three foot long, richly gilded and decorated with pictures on the lid and all four sides. At first I thought it was an elaborate coffin, a coffin made for a child, but when I looked more closely I could see that the painted scenes were of a wedding. There was a bride with loose flowing hair, in a leaf-patterned gown of cloth of gold, an arch of rosemary above her. A bridegroom and his attendants mounted on white horses, lutenists and drummers, children waving branches of red blossom. On the inside of the lid there were flying cherubs, and initials entwined: R&A. And within the chest, a pile of folded clothes. Impossibly small clothes: white, embroidered, lacy.

I supposed that it was yours, Agnes said, and I was sure that you would not be too annoyed with me for dressing Titus in your baby's garments. I only meant to borrow them for a short while, but would you look at the little darling, how quaint he is!

They are not mine, I said. Where did you find that casket?

It was under some sackcloth in a corner, behind those wormy bedposts that no one uses any more.

What were you doing in the loft?

Playing a game with Henry, Agnes said. A game of hide and seek. I was looking for a place where Titus and I could hide and he would never find us!

Henry, not meeting my eye, was busying himself with holding Titus who, maddened by the restraint of strings and knots, was ripping at the white gown with his teeth.

Agnes, do take it off him before it tears beyond mending, I said. And Henry, you must leave this instant. You should not be in here.

He does no harm, protested Agnes. But Henry sidled out and left her to fold the clothes away with me.

So, the casket must be my mother's then? she asked. And the clothes my own? To think that I was ever small enough to

wear this gown and this pretty cap! Shall I take them now, for
Titus? Or no, on second thoughts, should I keep them for the
day when I have children?

Much better that, I said, than let the creature slash them all
to shreds.

Not that he would, she retorted, walking off with wriggling
Titus cradled in her arms.

When she had gone, I lifted the casket and tipped the soft
contents out onto my bed. A scent of orris root and cloves rose
from that little cloud of whiteness, of hopes renewed, hope
lost, happiness and sorrow. In a way, I was relieved that I had
not known of this hidden store, that no one had ever told me
of it or wrapped my daughter in these ghost-garments, these
swaddling clothes that too soon turned into shrouds. But still
they made me cry. O Agnes, mother of Agnes, mother of John,
Richard, Edith, Creature, forgive me for my want of compassion,
forgive me that this was the first time I truly grieved for your
daughter and for you.

At dinner, less than an hour later, Agnes did not say anything
about the painted chest and the infant clothes, and I knew she was
hoping I'd keep quiet too, for else her father would have asked
how she had found them. For safety's sake she filled the time
with chatter about a dream that she had had the night before,
a dream in which she had been lost in a field of tall corn until a
talking crow showed her the way out. As I listened, I thought
how little I understood her, in spite of having lived with her
these past three years, sharing a bed with her, eating every meal

of every day with her, spending almost every hour together. I long to understand her and to love her – the only daughter that I can have, a child in need of loving. But Agnes is like an unevenly weighted arrow that flies true and straight at first but strikes wide of the mark, or a leaf caught in an autumn gale; impossible to tell where it will fall. Things that should please her often cause her discontent, and yet she seems quite blithe in the midst of all this talk of sickness, tombs and death. Perhaps I misread her. Perhaps she is hiding her anguish. And here is a question: how to interpret someone whose feelings are written in a foreign alphabet.

The crow was speaking French, Agnes said.

The last day of the month of September

It is now past Michaelmas: the rents are paid, the tithes collected, the swine are rooting for beechnuts in the woods, we have eaten the goose, and Simm's men are back at work. The stone-carvers also. The church and the chapel are almost done, laus Deo; three things remain: the vaulted ceiling, the paintings and the tomb. None of these ask much more time. Simm is already preparing the new walls with a white ground made from water, sand and lime, and the Tewkesbury men say that they will be finished by the feast of Luke. The painters will begin their work when the ground and all the stonework are completed. No one has heard from Piero da Fiesole for many weeks but he surely must come soon. Roland and Henry are gone.

My lord my husband is no better but certainly no worse. He rises before noon, comes down to dinner and can even walk a few steps in the garden before he must make his way back to his chamber for the remainder of the day. Time and again, Hugh or Marmion or Joan will urge him to make the most of the lastingly warm weather and go to the church by cart while the ways are passable but adamantly he refuses. On my own feet or not at all, he insists as always.

This morning, when we were walking by the river and debating this stubbornness, Hugh said he could not understand why his uncle would persist in denying himself the pleasure of seeing the new windows. Was that not cutting off his nose to spite his face?

Yes perhaps, I said, and pride comes into it, but I think he is putting his faith into a cure. He truly believes he will recover his health and all will be well again. He may be right. Can strength of will purge a body of disease? I pray it can, but if he is deceiving himself – or we are leaving him to be deceived – the truth when it comes will be cruel.

It is natural to fear death and therefore to shun the thought of it, Hugh said. Every mortal creature must.

Do you suppose Sir Joselin does?

You think that a man of real faith must welcome death for the promise that it brings? Well, maybe he does, but anticipating eternity with joy can't take away all fear of the journey to be made before you get there.

That's true, I thought to myself. The stony places of the wilderness, the salt land where no one lives, parched wastelands unbridged.

I believe only saints and martyrs go straight to heaven, Hugh said. And saints cannot know that they are saints until they're dead.

William Clare's new choir of village children sang an anthem of his composing at the mass of Michael and All Angels. Factum est silentium in caelo, dum committeret bellum draco cum Michaele Archangelo. There was silence in heaven while the dragon fought, but the dragon did not prevail.

This man must possess the powers of an angel to make the music that he does. Or the powers of Orpheus, who made flowers bloom when he played his lute, and drew the wild things out of the woods of Thrace to hear him. Even the sea was still when Orpheus played, even the winds ceased howling. And there was silence in heaven too, while Michael and the host of angels listened.

❧

Into the night, lying in bed with her back to me, Agnes quietly weeps. I touch her shoulder, hoping that she will turn to me and allow a comforting embrace, but she shrugs my hand away. I remember those tears so copious they soak your pillow, flood the shells of your ears and stop your breath; so much salty water streaming from your nose and eyes that you think you will be rendered as flat and dry as a frog trapped in an empty pail. I know that trying to silence those heaving sobs hurts the muscles of your belly.

Poor little Agnes. What can I say? That there will be other men and better men than Henry? That the heart she thinks is broken is just a little bruised? She will not believe me, and if I were her, I would not believe it either. Empty words, empty promises of consolation. One day she'll learn that the daughters of rich men can seldom choose when and where to love, but at the moment all she knows is that her life will have no meaning and she no happiness at all with Henry Martyn away in London and small hope of his return.

No doubt Agnes will be contracted in marriage soon with a man of suitable estate, as her mother was, and I too in my turn. When a woman's heart is not in her own gift, it is safer to keep it intact and cold than to offer it to one who cannot hold it. Henry is nobody and Agnes is her father's last surviving child. He will never consent to their marriage.

And when her father is gone? That's a different question. Grim comfort it would be for Agnes that her hope is in his death. Three things she loves, and only three: her father, Titus and Henry Martyn; exchanging one for the other would come at a high cost.

There was once a queen for whom a king rebuilt a tower. She was borne through its main gate on her way to coronation dressed in cloth of gold and satin, but she walked through a postern on her journey to the scaffold, and her white falcons watched. That queen had a daughter who still lives, and now must bend her knee in reverence to her father and her king. How can she love the man who killed her mother? Was she forced to look on when a second queen laid her head upon a block? We bow to those who dispose our lives, we who have no power.

In the month of October, a Monday

The first frost this morning, a thin skim of whiteness on the fields. The beech woods have turned gold. Agnes refused to leave her bed and would eat no breakfast. When William Clare came for her music lesson, Joan told him why. Poor elf-shot child! she said. But her heart will mend in a day or two, for that's the way with calf-love, and meanwhile I will dose her with my cordial against melancholy that has never been known to fail. Even so, I think it best to stop the music lessons until she is more herself.

But William said that music could complement and fortify Joan's cure, and that if we would permit him, he would go up to the chamber where Agnes lay and persuade her to come out.

Evidently he succeeded, for soon afterwards I heard the sound of the virginal; she was practising her scales. And later the music of a dance, a pavane I think, played perfectly by him, a liquid spilling of clear notes underpinned by a steadier beat and on the turn suspended for a fraction of a moment, like an indrawn breath, like the moment when a dancer holds her hand out to a man, the moment before he takes it and they come together. Then the same piece played more stumblingly by Agnes. Whenever she faltered and mistook the notes, she stopped and he would play them for her; over and over again the same bars, this music that sounds to me like a marriage of tears and happiness, a plucking of the heartstrings that is unendurable and yet so much desired. I thought of William's fingers on the black and white bone keys. I remembered dancing, a man in step beside me, the warmth of him, his breath, his body, his strong hand in mine.

❧

By the river a scatter of white where a swan has shed its feathers; the wind in the alders sounds like rain.

In the month of October

Yesterday afternoon there was a great excitement in the village, Joan told us at dinner, the cause of it a wanderer or vagrant who called himself a preacher. Joan happened to be passing near the water pump with Susan when he was setting up his pulpit, and naturally they stopped to listen. A wild-looking man indeed he was, bald or shaven-headed, with goggling eyes and a spittery way of speaking; crazed, or worse, an evangelical, most people said. But some of those who came to jeer him on their way from their work then stayed to hear him, and it certainly appeared that his rantings struck a chord. Goodge the wheelwright and his sons were there, nodding their heads up and down in agreement like a triad of puppets. The churchwarden Cadd was standing by but did nothing to stop him.

Woe to those who go a-whoring after idols, the man declaimed. By the idolatry of the few, God's wrath is kindled against the many, and the consequence will be a rain of fire and brimstone on all heads. And woe to the fools who spend their hard-earned pence on prayers and offerings and candles for the dead. Since even as he hung upon the cross, Jesus foreknew the few who would be saved and the multitude who would be damned, what profit can there be in praying for their souls? The goats are separated from the sheep already, and their ways predestined from the instant of their birth.

At this point in Joan's report, everybody at the table turned to look at my lord my husband. This is nothing but the old familiar Lollardry, he said, and both Marmion and I remember what befell those who spread such heresy before, not so many years ago and not so far from here. Sir Joselin too, you must recall it clearly? Burned alive at Amersham and their own daughters made to light the pyres themselves. Cousin Joan, I am surprised you gave this scoundrel credence by paying him attention.

My Lord, I did not. Hearing is not believing.

That's as may be, but the man should have been hounded from the village straight away, not granted an audience.

Dame Joan is right, said Joselin to general surprise. Hearing is not believing, and the greater danger lies in trying to stop men's ears. Words that are suppressed beguile, while words spoken aloud can be judged for what they are – falsehood or truth.

Yes, but can the common man tell the two apart?

The spirit of truth is always clear to those who listen carefully.

But its message isn't always welcome, Marmion said.

If the truth were welcome, a king would have no need of an Act that turns an honest word against him into a weapon against its speaker, Hugh added hotly, and with one voice all around the table instantly said: hush.

Steering the talk to less dangerous ground, Marmion remarked that whatever they may have made of the so-called preacher, most people in the village were delighted by the enrichment of the church. The new glass is the envy of other parishes for miles around, he said, and everyone is glad of the shelter of the porch.

Yes, and even more than that they adore the image of the dead Lord in particular, Agnes said. Every time I go to the church, I find someone on their knees before it and there are always candles burning there in secret, even though it is not Easter.

She is right, I thought. And let us pray that no one mistakes that statue for an idol, when the intention was simply to replace a broken altar. Set within the alabaster bier is a hollowed heart space, there to hold Good Friday's host and, when it does, the stone will truly be a tomb. Christ himself will be buried there, and a vigil kept until he rises from the grave.

It is true that the painted windows are a general source of wonder. To be in the church is to find oneself caught between walls of floating colour, in a blaze between east and west and in the middle way between damnation and redemption, death and everlasting life. With the arc of the sun as it moves across the sky the colours fade and brighten, yet even in this near-winter season there is never a minute without a dark-jewel glow of blue and red and green and yellow. But, speaking for myself, it is the more modest windows in the south wall that please me best. When there was no window to the east, and the narrow windows of the north wall had panes of cattle-horn, the crown-glazed windows to the south were daylight's only means of entry, and I was worried that it would get lost in the furnace of bright colour. I need not have been. Marmion was right: our artists in glass have found an ingenious way to let it in.

The Last Supper of Our Lord fills the wide central window; the agony he suffered in the garden on the day before is to the right of it and, to the left, three stark crosses on a hill. Three images, three panels like an altarpiece, Wednesday, Thursday, Friday; three days in the life of God. In the death of God. The detail is spare. Gethsemane is a garden that could be ours: a small slope with an ascending spiral path set in interlacing beds of gillyflowers, lavender, violets and thyme. A young man prays there with his hands clasped while his friends sleep the sleep of the dead amidst the flowers, and far away, on the horizon, a solitary angel raises its right hand as if to bless, to greet or to console the grieving man. The hill is like the hill that rises to the west of the village, beech, oak and ash trees on its slope. And the room in which Jesus and the twelve disciples eat their meal of bread and lamb is the hall of an ordinary house, furnished with a long, low table covered in white cloth. Behind the table and the thirteen people seated round it is a window that spans the whole length of the room, a window with panes of clear glass, a window within a window through which daylight streams, open to the sky. And there is pale sky above the garden, behind the hill; pure light against the crosses and the flowers.

As in the Resurrection window, these glaziers have fused our land with the Holy Land, brought past and present together. Their mastery steals my breath. They have made the light that shines upon the sacred hands that bless the bread, the light that shines on us.

Their work is done. In one of the two narrow windows on the north wall they have placed our own Saint Margaret, golden-haired and robed in green, circled by the dragon's scarlet wings like a rosebud by its calyx; an echo of the old, revered wall painting at her altar. In the second, Saint Christopher, knee-deep in rushing water, carrying a baby pick-a-back, a baby so lifelike that it catches at my heart. The saint holds his staff with one hand and the baby's ankle with the other, keeping it safely balanced, but the baby, for greater protection, has his fat fingers tightly knitted through the old man's hair.

The four-light windows of the new chapel are taller and more graceful than the old windows and mainly glazed in clear glass – diamond-shaped panes in lead framed by slender mullions.

Only where the mouldings intersect at the heads of the panes is there any painting: the initials R&A alternating with a pattern of vine leaves and, at the apex, my lord my husband's shield. I am grateful for that plain glass, open to the eastern light, receptive of the dawn.

William Clare was not at dinner. He often chooses to stay in the village and eat bread and cheese with the fieldmen, rather than dining at the house. Joan says this is a sign of madness. I wonder what he would have said to the raving preacher, had he been there to hear him yesterday. That the Lord God is merciful and gracious, perhaps. That he will not abandon a sparrow, or a single child?

⁂

Russet, copper, saffron, rose. Bruised skies, October days, but gleam of berries in the hedgerows, red of hawthorn and wild rose hips, black of sloes. Blood red in the yew trees, treasure trove for hungry birds hidden in the dark leaves, blood red in the poisonous bryony.

Against a blackening sky the autumn leaves glow more fierily than they do in competition with full sunlight, as if they would fend off the coming dark, as if each single leaf were inwardly lit and burnished gold. The birch trees are towers of flame.

Ink-spill in the river, smooth as glass on this windless afternoon and dark as mussel shell. On the still surface fallen willow leaves drift like silvery fish and a floating swan finds a twin in its reflection underwater.

The seasons turn. Winter will soon be upon us.

The eighteenth day of October

The vaulted ceiling of the chantry is in place, and it is a
miracle. Think yourself an ant gazing upwards at a tight
cluster of field mushrooms to observe the interplay of line and
curve and light and shadow, or a dormouse beneath a stalk of
cicely, and then as a woman marvel that stone can be made to
dance. To that constricted space, the Tewkesbury men have
brought an infinity of pattern; angels' wings in palest stone.
Although I saw their drawings beforehand, I never believed that
they could be so beautifully translated or that they could turn
a thing that is solid to the touch into a substance that flows like
honey or like skeins of silk. A ceiling is usually a limit. Here,
in this chapel, above the tomb pit, it soars up into an eternity
of space.

The stone-carvers have gone now, well-rewarded for their
great skill and silent to the last. Today is Saint Luke's Day; they
were true to their promise. A small heap of their pale stone
remains in a corner of the churchyard, flawed pieces, offcuts
and fragments, left behind in case of repairs or should Simm
the mason need it. Now the wall painters are here in their stead,
two men; fitting that they should begin their work on their own
saint's feast, he who made a portrait of the Virgin. Marmion
says that Piero da Fiesole is expected here next week. The red
flowers came this morning, and with them emptiness again,
and pain. My lord my husband's health stays the same. Agnes,
although less tearful, is somewhat distracted, slightly hectic,

and closets herself away for hours in the day. Joan says that it is because she is a woman now and should be dosed with wine and hyssop.

In the month of October, a Friday

William's choir is learning the mass that he has written at my lord's commission for the Lady Agnes; I heard the children singing when I walked past the schoolroom in the village after dinner. I stopped, I hoped to see him, but the door was closed. Their high voices came through the windows, piercingly sweet on cold-clouded air. Preparations are in train for All Souls, but I have no part in them so far. Some mystery surrounds them. There's always a mass for the dead on that special feast, but perhaps this year's is different? The first requiem in the chantry chapel? Yes, indeed the hope that the chapel would be finished before winter's grip took hold in earnest will now be fulfilled. Saint Luke brought his own little summer with the painters; we have had a novena of bright days without rain and the extra hours of daylight have helped greatly. The painting is almost done. And just in time. Yesterday the sun rose from a clear, dewy night onto the field near the house utterly transformed into a glittering sea of spiders' silk, but this morning that same field was shrouded in thick fog.

A midnight hour on the second day of November, All Souls

Where to begin? What to say? Will I lie for all eternity in one bed with my husband's first wife Agnes and her children's bones, jumbled up with mine? I should have known. I am a fool. But what difference would it have made if I had known before? Would it have been otherwise? And will it matter anyway, when all of us are dead?

How shall I tell of these days of reburials and remembering, this unearthing of the dead? How could I have stayed unknowing when all around me knew what would begin with Piero da Fiesole's return two days ago, on All-Hallows Eve? He arrived in the morning, having stopped the night before in Oxford, with two apprentices and three carts heavily laden. My husband was up and waiting in the hall to meet him. They greeted each other warmly. You seem to be in much better health than you were when I left you in the summer, Piero said. Thanks be to God for the miracle of healing and his grace! Do you walk? Have you inspected your chantry and the new works in your church? My alabaster Christ?

Not yet. But I will walk to the church on the feast of All Souls. That will be the right and fitting time. I have waited this long, my husband said, and I can wait for two more days.

I heard what he said but I did not understand it. My lord my husband had said nothing to me of his intentions or of the rites that he must by then have ordered. Such elaborate ceremonies could not have happened on a whim. Surely Piero had long ago been told and Sir Joselin too, and Hugh perhaps, and even Agnes, and it hurts to have been the one kept in the dark. Did they conspire together to hide the matter from me as if I were a child, or still so lacking mental strength that I could not endure their talk of bones, or did they want to take me by surprise? Did they count on that to carry out their plan? Or did I simply fail to see what was before my eyes? Did William know? I cannot bear to think he did.

Only Piero went to the church that day. He said that he and his apprentices had a great deal of work to do if the tomb bed and canopy were to be ready in time for soul mass, and that work would be better done if they were undisturbed. Joan said that no sensible soul should be out today in any case, with those unquiet spirits all roaming about, and it was raining besides. But she trusted that Master Piero would have the place fit for the unburial tomorrow, as she and all the household would wish to be present at it. Meanwhile, we must light all the fires and be glad of warmth and shelter.

When the imager had gone, I asked Joan what she had meant. Oh, it's nothing to fret over, it's just what must be done before that great big tomb is finished, she said. And it will be a blessing when there is no more upsy-downing in our dear church!

All-Hallows Eve. Fire and fleet and candlelight, and Christ receive my soul.

A year ago my daughter was kicking in my womb. I saw her feet, her sharp elbows, pushing through the skin of my belly as milk coming to the boil sends bubbles to the surface.

She did not sin. She was a word of God.

All-Hallows Eve, when the turning world spins into winter.
And then All-Hallows Day.

⁂

Yesterday I went early to mass. It was busy in the church. The
two painters were still there, making new patterns on the roof
beams and finishing off the decoration of the walls. Simm and
the elder Jack were also present, watching the younger Jack and
another man digging up the clay floor about a yard to the left of
the rood screen, and all the covering rushes were swept to one
side in a pile. Behind the open tomb pit in the chantry chapel
was a tumbril with a great stone slab upon it.

Piero was calling to one of the apprentices in his own language; there was a confusion of other voices and commands
being given, a small heap of mortar on a barrow, once more
the smell of earth and stone. Simm's voice was raised, dis-
mayed because he had not been given enough instruction, no
sign yet of Sir Joselin or William Clare. Piero said in answer
to Simm that no, they will not have to dig up the tiled floor
of the chancel, the bodies can be slid in from the north side,
like loaves of bread into an oven. That needs nothing but this
trench besides the tomb. Yes, it is possible to raise the effigies,
but better not, for they are easily damaged. Naturally, it may
be a much longer time until a third burial is... And then the
imager caught sight of me.

By now others were coming in, the villagers arriving for All-
Hallows mass, Hugh, Agnes, Joan and Marmion, even Lambert,
all the household except my lord my husband. Then Joselin,
with William, both robed. The workmen put down their tools.

Sir Joselin called Simm to him and I heard him ask if the bodies had been uncovered. Simm answered that they had, but for the little one in the churchyard, and Joselin said to wait for that until the mass was ended.

The words of the mass were no comfort at all, my stomach churned. The choir did not sing. My heart was spinning and I shivered with cold and was frantic to leave, but the church had turned into a trap. If I had gone, I would have been accused of lacking respect for the dead. And so perforce I stood with the others while young Jack and the gravedigger prised the Lady Agnes's lead coffin out of the ground in which she had lain for six long years, and the bodies of her children with her. John, Edith, Richard, Creature, requiem aeternam dona eis, Domine, Joselin prayed, and Agnes's living daughter Agnes was curiously still. I closed my eyes so that I would not see those fragile little bones. When I opened them again, the coffin and whatever had contained the children's bodies were on a bier at the head of the chancel, draped in black, and William was sprinkling them with holy water.

Then the gravedigger came to me and, bowing, asked if I would witness my little girl unburied. I will kill anyone who dares to touch her grave, I said. Everyone around me gasped, outraged at my response. Pay no heed to her, Joan said, she has not been herself since that baby died, and Agnes slapped my face. I don't know what happened next — it was as if for a moment I was blanketed in dark — but when I came to my senses I was crumpled on the ground and William's arms were round me.

They will never pluck my baby from her crib unless they kill me first. As long as I live she will rest where I left her, at peace beneath her counterpane of grass.

☙

All Souls. The day of remembering, the day of prayer for the holy souls in purgatory, a day of reparation. Candles flickering by the headstones of the dead of the parish in the churchyard, massed candles around the shrouded bier of the Lady Agnes on this the day of her second burial; a spray of flowering ivy on my daughter's untouched grave.

Even in my great turmoil, after a night when if I slept at all, it was only to dream of the corpses of children left out for the crows, I marvelled at the strength of will it took my lord my husband to descend the stairs this morning, to stand in the hall while Lambert cloaked him, to walk unaided out of the house and then to walk the near-mile to the church, step by painful step. He ate nothing and spoke to no one before he went and we, his kinfolk and his servants, followed uncertainly behind. A strange procession it must have seemed to anyone who saw it: a straggle of uneasy men and women led by a tall figure cloaked in green and sable, who moved so slowly that he might have been dragging each foot out of quicksand as he went.

And then he was there, stock-still in the place that his strong will has transformed, with his living daughter on one side and his living wife on the other and his dead wife and children's bodies lying on a bier at the length of an arm away. If he wished, he could have reached out his hand and stroked them through their covering of black cloth. Stone dust on the air, as white as snow, settling lightly on black velvet. The alabaster men were at work only moments before the mass began; the fine dust drifting, mingling with breath-fume and candle-smoke; Sir Joselin in his new vestments of midnight black, more sombre than ever seen before.

Throughout last night, with William Clare, Joselin kept vigil over these five bodies. Candles on the altar in the chantry, an illicit light burning by the image of the dead Christ, the tomb pit empty still, and the stone slab on the tumbril. A bright day, with winter sunlight streaming through the windows, splashing colour on the floor and outdoing the candles; every square inch of wall is painted now, and every image too. Purple of Christ's cloak, blue of Mary's, green for Margaret, golden-haired. Scenes from Christ's life newly painted: his birth in the stable, the wedding feast at Cana, the miracle of loaves and fishes. Blue sea of Galilee in the distance, gleam of a leaping fish. Images in paint link images in glass: it is all here; birth and life and death. And an incandescent Resurrection in the east.

A bewilderment of colour: sapphire, emerald, ruby, gold. Candlelight and sunlight wedded; light on silver chalice and paten, crimson and white chequering on rafters, rainbows for angels' wings. And my lord my husband at my side.

Requiem aeternam dona eis, Domine: et lux perpetua luceat eis, Sir Joselin began. A missa pro defunctis, tallow candles for the dead. The splendour of light and colour set against the dark.

Children's voices: Kyrie eleison, they sang, harmonious and true, Christe eleison, Kyrie eleison, Lord have mercy on us. William's setting of the mass for Agnes's mother; music to break hearts. My lord my husband revealed nothing of what he might or might not feel. Agnes, purged of raw grief by the rage of yesterday, looked almost joyful, transported by the beauty of the music and the presence of her father, here at last surrounded by the bright glass, the stone and paint that he had so desired and which she must have feared he would never see.

William's voice and the good voice of the old clerk who has sung with Joselin for years joined together in the sequence; in a man's voice there lies knowledge that is not in a child's.

> *Dies irae, dies illa,*
> *Solvet saeclum in favilla:*
> *Teste David cum Sibylla*

The world dissolved in ashes on the day of wrath; do we live in fear of dying? Yes.

Sir Joselin climbed the three steps to the new and gleaming pulpit, four winged creatures to support his words.

> *Lacrimosa dies illa,*
> *Qua resurget ex favilla*
> *Iudicandus homo reus:*
> *Huic ergo parce, Deus*

On that day of tears, he said, we must be prepared for judgement, and may the Lord have mercy on our souls. In purgatory the proud are bound to wheels of fire and misers boiled in molten gold; the greedy are forced to sup on venom and the lustful pierced with meathooks through their sinful organs. But do not fear, my brothers and sisters, for there in purgatory, as in heaven, each soul dwells in love. Although the pains be terrible to bear, they do come to an end. And we on earth have power to shorten their duration. We can live a good life and die a good death, having repented fully of our sins. We can bury the dead and feed the hungry, give water to the thirsty and succour to those in need. We can pray. And we can implore the living to pray for us, even after we are dead. That is why we come together this and every soul mass, we who are on earth still, to pray for the souls of our faithful departed, to pray for the Lady Agnes and her children, in sure and certain hope that those who suffer the pains of purgatory will hear us and thereby find relief. Think on this, my brothers and sisters: your dead mothers and fathers, your wives and husbands, your children comforted by the masses that are sung for them, the prayers that you say, all balm to them as cooling water is to burning skin.

I glanced at my lord my husband. He did not return my look. Timor mortis? If he fears — and how could he not? — that fear is still buried deeper than my reach. Kneeling then, I prayed to the merciful Lord Jesus for pity on this sinful man who is investing everything he has in the hope that masses daily sung for him by William in the chapel he has built will save him from the everlasting fires of hell.

Agnus Dei, qui tollis peccata mundi: dona eis requiem, a child sang alone, as clear and brave as a robin; eternal rest give unto them, O Lamb of God. If the music of William Clare can penetrate the sulphurous pit, it will indeed be consolation. His last notes linger on the air, winged by a power that cannot be explained; sempiternam. Each note an arrow to the heart. When I pray in words alone, a fly can distract me, or any passing thought, but these prayers set to music go straight to the ear of God.

The mass is ended. Sir Joselin stepped down from the chancel to the nave and the Lady Agnes's dead body. Oremus, he intoned.

Let us pray. All-powerful and eternal God, creator and redeemer of souls, you who said unto the dry bones in the valley: behold, I will cause breath to enter into you, and ye shall live: and I will lay sinews upon you, and will bring up flesh upon you, and cover you with skin, and put breath in you, and ye shall live; we pray to you for the souls of our dear Agnes and of John, Richard, Edith and Creature, whose bones we now place in their grave.

Piero, his two apprentices, Simm, the gravedigger and both Jacks were waiting in the chantry behind the tomb pit. Two corpse bearers approached from the back of the church and between them picked up the covered bier. The candles guttering and William swinging the censer, sweet-scented smoke floating over the black mound. At a sign from Joselin, the corpse bearers began slowly to move towards the pit, followed by Joselin in his night-black cope, William holding the censer, a boy with a bowl of holy water, my lord my husband and his daughter.

From behind, Joan poked me in the shoulder. You too, she hissed, and unwillingly I joined the small procession behind Agnes. Hugh stayed standing where he was.

The corpse bearers set down the bier beside the stone-walled pit and removed the cloth that hid it. The Lady Agnes lay before our eyes, dressed in a robe of lead, and her children with her, in a row. They were wrapped in cerecloth and trussed with string; three little parcels, one about a yard long, the other two much smaller, three little bodies clearly outlined beneath their layers of waxy swaddling. I could see the shapes of their heads. I suppose that the newborn child who died with Agnes was encoffined with her, or else its bones are lost.

There were two wide bands of woven stuff beneath Agnes's lead-shrouded body, one at her shoulders, the other behind her knees. The corpse bearers lifted her with these and then slowly, slowly, hand over hand, lowered her into the pit. She landed at the side nearest the chancel altar. I looked down at her, a graceful shape in a silvery carapace, like a mermaid, lightly armoured, six years dead. Could she see me, her husband's wife? I thought of her eyes, now lidded with metal and permanently sealed, the shreds of flesh still clinging to her bones. Her open mouth. The children were too small to be hammocked by cloth bands, and they were so light. One of the men crouched at the foot of the pit and the other handed the bundles to him, one by one, to be gently dropped down beside their mother; Richard, Edith, John.

The boy with the holy water offered it to Sir Joselin, who sprinkled it on the bodies with a branch of hyssop. And now it was William's turn to pray over the corpses: absolve O Lord the souls of all the faithful departed from every bond of sins. And by the help of thy grace, may they be enabled to escape the avenging judgement, and enjoy the happiness of everlasting life. Amen.

The Lady Agnes's living child, dry-eyed, composed, knelt then to strew dried flower petals upon her mother, her brothers and her sister. The sight of her still childish hands and her bitten fingernails undid me and I wept but her father did not; he remained on his feet beside the pit, motionless and deathly pale, until Lambert came with a wooden stool and helped him to sit. From where he waited in the chantry chapel, Piero sent him a questioning look, and in response my husband raised his hand and said one word only: yes.

Then the two corpse bearers joined Piero and the others behind the open pit. It took eight men to get the stone lid into position; they hauled the tumbril to the edge of the pit, tilted it and pushed the great slab downwards. It landed on the supporting walls with a thunderous crash but there was silence afterwards; the walls and the arch beneath were holding fast. Simm sighed out loud in satisfaction and Piero shook his hand. A narrow gap along one side remained unsealed, and I could see that there was a shrouded heap on a pallet behind, covered with a piece of sackcloth.

What next? No one seemed to know. I heard Cadd asking Marmion if this was the tomb that all the fuss was made of: this great tabletop of stone? No, no, Marmion said, this is merely the bed of the tomb.

The bed of the tomb. Strange phrase. William Clare made the sign of the cross over the stone lid and thus signalled the end of the ceremony; there was nothing more to do and one by one we left the church. Except for my husband, who stayed behind with Lambert and Piero; I think they must have supported him between them on the way back to the house.

O Lord God have pity on his soul.

The third day of the month of November

The tomb of the bed. Waking before dawn, listening to Agnes breathe and, strangely, to a bird singing in the ivy below the window, I remembered. It was on this same day two years ago, the day after All Souls, when my husband first expressed his desire for a chantry, a cantor and a tomb. The words that he had heard at the mass the day before – the words that we heard Joselin say yesterday, as every year – must have been ringing in his ears still and troubling his soul: Deliver me, O Lord, from death eternal on that fearful day, when thou shalt come to judge the world by fire.

Two whole years he has waited for this day, to witness his wife and children buried again in a tomb of his own design. And now he must wait a while longer to see the tomb completed and his image on it. Can he? Yes, I believe he can, with his iron resolve. Although Marmion, when he thought I could not hear him, did complain to Hugh that time and expense would have been spared if they had left that pit uncovered against the day. But as it is, will that vast slab of stone not have to be removed? he asked.

No, said Hugh, repeating what Piero had promised: he can be shoved in sideways as a pie is shoved into a bake-oven.

With the same sort of wooden peel?

I don't know. But Piero has given Simm a demonstration.

I can only hope that Simm has understood it. If not, I foresee disaster.

In the month of November

Agnes has not said a word to me since All-Hallows Day; at night we lie side by side in silence in our bed. Joan has been kindly, urging me to take aqua mirabilis for mind-healing and to rest, but today at dinner, with my husband absent, she and Marmion, in evident collusion, re-entered the battle ground. They raised the matter by first asking Piero how the work was going and when he answered that it was almost complete, Joan turned to me: as it is your family tomb, is it not entirely fitting that you should all lie there together, you and your daughter too? His youngest daughter, as she was.

Marmion poked in his lance then. Surely it is preferable to be buried under marble than to moulder in the common earth, with no marker to the grave?

Sir Joselin was dining with us, and so was William Clare for once. I sought his eyes across the table and wordlessly begged for help. But before he could say anything, Joselin pronounced that the site of any burial was of no consequence to Our Lord, provided that it was on holy ground. The baby was baptised and her soul will be saved, he said; where she rests until the day of judgement is of no importance.

But it is important to me, I said.

Why, Joan said, why, child?

I did not know how to answer her. I wanted to say that it was because the pale roots of grass befriend her there and flowers grow and nothing weighs her down, but I knew that Joan would think that nonsense. Tears came then instead of words and I struggled to hold them back.

Let her be, said William quickly. As Sir Joselin says, it makes no difference to God.

Well, you are the chantry priest, Sir William, and therefore the baby's soul is your concern, said Marmion. She can always be dug up when her mother…

Uncle Marmion, let us talk of other things, Hugh said.

Marmion's meaning was clear. When it is my turn for burial, then they will ungrave my child and drop us both into the marble tomb. I do not find that a painful prospect; when I am dead it will not matter where we lie, as long as we lie together, and I will not care whether earth is heaped upon me or cold stone.

⁊

My brother died a needless death in France, caught up in some-one else's fight, and was buried where he fell, as far as I know. Our father talked of recovering his body and bringing it home to be buried again in the company of his kin, but nothing was done and after a while the thought was no longer mentioned. My brother was his father's firstborn child, but by the time of his death there were other children, other sons. Perhaps they cushioned my father's grief.

Mine was bitter, though, and it still is. I miss my brother deeply. When we were young, having no mother, and our father being often away from home or distracted by affairs, we were more or less left alone to raise each other. Almost all I know, I owe to him. As there was nothing else to be done with me, I was allowed to share his schooling with our father's chaplain and so

I learned my letters, in English and in Latin. That same chaplain, Sir Alwyn, was a countryman at heart, ever eager to exchange the schoolroom for the fields, and from him we learned the names of trees and flowers, the ways of animals and birds. Later, when my brother had outgrown these nursery lessons and gone away to Oxford, he would come home with scraps of divinity and history and logic; small treasures that otherwise I would never have been given. He taught me much: how a hawk is reared, how to climb a tree, how if you put your thumbs together and clasp your hands in a certain way, you can sound a tune. And he showed me how to swim. No nursemaid or guardian ever found out that he did that, he would have been in trouble if they had, but my brother saw no reason why I should not do what he could. The summer when I was six and he was ten was a summer of blazing heat and in the long, sleepy afternoons we would escape from the house to join the young boys of the town at the river.

The river of my childhood, brought back to mind each time I wander by the river of my married life. That first river widened at a point beyond the town wall to form a little lake or pool, shallow at the edges, deep and greeny in the middle. Bare toes sinking into soft mud, cooling water on sun-baked skin, river-scent, caress of waterweed; it's not difficult to swim, my brother said, and he was right. Remember not to breathe when your nose is underwater, kick your legs as fast as you can, kick them up and down. And trust the water.

My brother, swinging over the water on a branch of willow, wet hair plastered to his head, sleek and happy as an otter; my dead brother, laughing. At least he saw the sea before he died. I think he may have swum in it, in France. The water must be

warm there, I suppose, and a clear blue. Blue water. The rivers
I have known are green or grey.

William, will you pray for my dead brother too?

⁂

Roland has come back and he says that he intends to stay. He is
tired of London and the law.

⁂

The wind blows, the rain pours, from time to time there is a
shiver of pale sunshine, the leaves have fallen from the trees.
Meals are eaten, prayers are said, the grain is threshed, the children of the village gather acorns, Susan moans about the cold.
What else is there to say about these wintry days, these days of
waiting? Titus has a sore leg and is cantankerous; I fear that he
must be suffering from old age. Agnes remains withdrawn and
angry with me; my lord my husband, wearied by his exertion
last week, keeps mainly to his bed. Hugh is making ready for
departure, and I try not to imagine myself clinging to his coat
hem and begging him to stay. Poor Joselin has the ague and,
to my relief, Piero da Fiesole has banished everybody from the
church until he finishes the tomb. He says that with luck he
should be done by Martinmas, and meanwhile William Clare
says the masses in the schoolroom of the village.

I have stayed away from mass this week, but I did go past
the schoolroom at the practice hour of William's choir. It is
possible to stand unobserved beneath the window at the back.
I heard them singing something new; the first words were in a

man's voice, strong and true, and then children's voices rose to meet his, winding round it as honeysuckle winds around a tree trunk, in and out and interweaving, the music lifting and gently falling, like untroubled breathing or the lilt of running water, carrying my soul upon it.

In the month of November, the next day

Hailstones rattling against the window, a day of hard rain after a night of storms and I was alone with my husband in his room. He was wrapped in furs and sitting up for the first time since All Souls; I was on a stool beside him. Through the panelling of the wall came the sound of Agnes at the virginal; it was the hour of her music lesson.

She plays well now, does she not? he said.

She does. She has made astonishingly quick progress.

He must be a good music master, my new chantry priest.

Indeed. Did his choir please you at the mass last week?

Yes. I don't know how he turned that little bunch of urchins into such fine singers.

I am glad that you were pleased, and I hope the music made your sad duty easier to bear?

Sad? Was it? It must have seemed so, but for me there was relief in seeing my late wife and my children laid to rest in a right and fitting place at last, and now I am impatient to see our finished tomb.

I said nothing then. Our tomb? A curious way for a man to speak who until then was used to sole possession. My house. My lands. My wife. Our tomb?

We sat without speaking for a while, listening to the music that Agnes played and the wild weather. My husband's breath comes raspingly these days; the fell disease that is petrifying him slowly has slid its fingers through his bone-cage and is clawing at his lungs; will it choke him next?

Suddenly he reached out to take my hand. It was unexpected; he has not touched me for a long time and I touch him only in passing, when I need to straighten his sheets or help him to sit up. He held my hand, turning it in his and tracing it with his finger, as if to read the future in my palm. Agnes says that you forbade the gravedigger to disinter Catherine before the soulmass, he said. That you flew into a passion and fell to the ground in a faint. She is very angry with you.

Catherine. He spoke his daughter's name. Tears filled my eyes yet again. So will you go against me? I asked him when I found my voice at last.

No, not now, not yet. William Clare's advice is that as you are in mourning, it is too soon to do it.

Thank you.

My poor young wife. You cannot mourn forever.

It has been less than a year.

That's true. Shall we ask William Clare to write a dirge for her, to mark her year's mind, an elegy for Catherine?

The tears were falling fast then and I could only press the hand that held mine in response.

That's enough of graves, he said, let us instead rejoice that the church will soon be finished.

And is it as you wished?

It will be.

The stone vaulting is miraculous.

The painted windows too.

Lambert knocked and entered then, carrying a bowl of water and cloths to wash his master, and so I made to leave. My husband took my wrist and held me back.

I have something to tell you, and now is as good a time as

any, he said quietly. You are young and beautiful and if anything were to befall me, you could marry again. You could bear more children. I do not say that this will happen, I believe all will be well, that I will be well soon. But it is wise to be prepared and therefore you should know that as matters stand, Agnes must be sole heir to my estate. There will be the provision for you that the law demands, and portions for my nephews, but she will have this house and all my lands.

⁂

Joan has had Sir Joselin brought into the house so that she can better nurse him. He will mend, she says. But then she says the same about my husband. I keep turning in my mind the things he said this morning. Does Agnes know? Will she let me stay beneath this roof when I am a widow, or will she turn me out into the cold like a beggar? My only home is here now, and my only tomb. How strange to have a tomb in perpetuity but no warranty of home. And what of the land I brought with me when I was married, the price my father paid to have me taken off his hands? Gone now, subsumed, for on the day that I was married I became one person with my bridegroom, one flesh, one body; that is to say that what had been mine was then wholly his. Widows have rights that wives do not, but what use is there in pondering these questions? I have been a man's possession since the day that I was born. And besides, Joan may be right. He will get well, and he will live for years in right good health. Yes, and the cure that heals him will be brewed from gossamer and moonbeams, I imagine.

꙰

Having come to visit Sir Joselin on his sickbed, William is here
again at dinner today, and Piero. The two men are at the end
of the table, with Roland, and they are talking of the lands that
they have travelled in and their voyages by sea. Hugh and I are
listening, enviously. William, it is true, has only been to France,
and Roland to France and Switzerland, but Piero has been to
both these places and to Spain and the Low Countries besides,
as well as Italy, of course, where he was born. During these long
English winters, Piero says, he is often sick for home, for sunlight
and blue skies. Naturally, it rains in Italy, but not as much as it
does here. The town he comes from is on a height and the light
is clearer there than it is in this damp valley; you can see a long
way over the surrounding towns and hills and there are olive
groves. Oliveti, he says, ulivi, and his tongue caresses the words.

Oliviers, William says, olive trees. They also grow in France,
but only in the south.

Where did you stay, when you were there?

At Cluny in Burgundy and for a time in Paris.

And why did you go?

I went first as a novice and then two years later with some of
my brothers from the abbey after Hugh Faringdon, our abbot,
was hanged on the orders of the king.

What crime had he done? Roland asked.

None. He was accused of treason but sentenced with two
other monks before his trial began. They were drawn and quar-
tered by the abbey gatehouse. I was witness to it.

Roland looked sceptically at him. They could not have been
found guilty if there was no crime, he said.

You don't think so? Not long before his death, Abbot Hugh was in great favour, and he sang the requiem for a queen. Is it not the case that tyrants turn most harshly against those whom they once loved?

Be careful, Roland, Hugh and Marmion said as one, and William laughed.

Why did you return? asked Piero. Having been made to see such a horrible thing? Did you not want to stay a monk in France?

It was not an easy choice. But in the end I wanted to come home. I have a mother living, and brothers and a sister, young nephews and nieces too. It was my lord who tipped the balance by inviting me to be his chantry priest.

How did he know you? Hugh asked. He has never told me why you were appointed.

He knew me through my abbot, when they used to meet at Court. Your uncle was at the funeral of that queen and I wrote the dirge that was sung there. I was still a novice then and studying music.

I understand what you are saying, Piero said. I miss my country too. I miss the food. Nothing in later life ever tastes as fine as the food of childhood. I miss the sound of my native tongue.

Why do you stay here then, if you don't like this country? Marmion asked him crossly.

I do like it. But it is not home. However, where I come from there are many image-makers, that we call scultori, and here there are very few who are worthy of the name. That means there is more work.

You boast, Master Piero! Marmion said.

I only tell the truth. As I have said before, I was asked to make the effigy of a queen. The same queen, I surmise, for whom you wrote your music, Brother William.

That's a pleasing connection, Hugh said.

Yes, and as well she had his music for she never had the tomb.

Which reminds me, Roland said. Are you almost done, Master Piero? And how shall we get my lord my uncle to the chantry when you are? The walk last week almost killed him, he must not do it again.

Agnes, who had said nothing until then, now spoke: he vowed to walk to the burial of my lady mother. But now that he has kept his vow, I think he will agree to go on horseback.

But he cannot ride, he cannot mount a horse.

Well then, by cart.

The king is lifted onto his horse by a crane, Roland observed.

I wish we had such a thing, Hugh said. How quickly could Simm make one?

Not fast enough, Piero said. The monument will be finished by the feast of Saint Martin, as I promised.

The meal was over, the servants bringing clean napkins to the table. When we rose, I moved closer to William Clare. Have you ever swum in the sea? I asked him.

He smiled at me. I don't know how to swim, he said, but I have waded into it, on the coast of Normandy.

And what was it like?

It was very salt and very cold. And stirring. The waves move against you as if they were alive.

It's not difficult to swim, I said.

The tenth day of the month of November

Since All Souls, I have dreaded going to the church. As it has been barred to everyone since the entombment of the Lady Agnes, I have not had to face my fear, but tonight is the eve of Martinmas and tomorrow there will be no escaping from it. It seems that Piero da Fiesole is eager for ceremony and show. No one here had expected a song and dance when the tomb was finished – although can a tomb be truly finished before all the bodies it was built for lie therein? – but he is insisting on it and has asked the whole household formally to assemble in the church after dinner tomorrow to see the work unveiled.

Marmion protested that there was enough to do tomorrow without having to go a-marble-gazing and that he was needed to oversee the first day of the slaughter. Why did the imager choose this day of all days for the uncovering when he could have done it at any other time?

Privately, I think there's a certain rightness to the choice. November is the blood-month and every hog will have his Martinmas, as the saying goes.

࿐

Blow, northern wind,
Blow, blow, blow
Bring back my dear one,
Flower of blood and bone.

Saint Martin's Day

So. It is done. I went to the church this afternoon and into the chantry and I stood there with the others, Agnes, Roland, Hugh, Marmion and Joan, Sir Joselin somewhat recovered, and William was with us too. But not my lord my husband and not Lambert. At the hour chosen by Piero, it was growing dark. There were lighted torches. Where there had been the flat stone, now there was a great mound, like a bed for a giant, and it was draped in sackcloth. Piero had been waiting for us. It was cold. I had walked to the church in the rain and the hem of my cloak had dragged in mud. The earth that the gravedigger disturbed when he unburied the Lady Agnes had been piled back into the place she left but, untrodden, the floor was still uneven. Low light outside had dimmed the painted windows and made the clear ones grey. The church was full of the strange scent of freshly cut stone, the scent of paint and mortar, the smoke of the torches, and the scent of water. They had dampened down the rushes and wiped away the stone dust, but they could not take away the burial smell.

Piero was beaming, as if it were a banquet that he was about to reveal and not the abode of the dead. When he saw that my lord husband was not with us, his smile faded and he asked when he would come. Later, Marmion said. Perhaps tomorrow. He is not strong enough today.

Should we wait? Piero asked. I had intended to leave tomorrow, but if he wishes I can stay.

Agnes answered him: no need. But he will see you to say farewell tomorrow morning.

Che peccato, the sculptor muttered but, making the most of the occasion and recovering his spirits, he said it was honour enough that my lady should be there, and he bowed to me. Then he made a sweeping gesture with both arms and stepped aside as the two apprentices drew back the covering sackcloth.

We lay there, the three of us, my husband, his late wife and me, beneath our stony canopy, sleeping peacefully together in one bed. We did not look like the dead. No, not at all, we looked as we do today, living and breathing – that is to say, I and my lord husband did; I could not speak for the Lady Agnes. But her daughter darted forward as soon as she saw the figure and she cried: ah, you have brought my lady mother back to life.

The Lady Agnes rests nearest the high altar, the holiest position. She is dressed in a white gown, the sleeves turned back to show their coral-coloured lining, the front unlaced over a paler kirtle and chemise. The gown is patterned with roses and green leaves; it may have been the gown she wore when she was married. Her golden hair hangs loose over her shoulders, bound at her head by a garland of flowers; she has a carcanet of gold and pearls about her neck and a gold-beaded rosary laced through the fingers of her upraised hands. Her head rests on a scarlet tasselled pillow and at her feet is Titus, crouching, with a pomegranate in one paw.

Ah look, Agnes joyfully exclaimed, look, here is Titus! And here is Steadfast, my father's hound!

Yes, her father's favourite hound is there, his body curved so that his head is beneath his master's feet and his hindquarters by mine. My feet are shod. I am all in black, a widow's black;

my gown, a gown I do not own, not yet, is plain but for a band
of brocaded silk and pearls at its square neck. Pearls encircle
my throat. My hair is hidden by a black veil, held in place by
a coronet studded with jet and yet more drops of pearl. There
is the faintest flush in Lady Agnes's cheeks but mine are as
white as a swan in a drift of snow. Beneath my head there is
a book, thick, with graven pages, but without words legible
on the spine.

Agnes asked: why does my lady stepmother lie upon a book
and not upon a cushion? Is it because you think that she is
learned? More than my mother was? I don't think she is.

Piero said, I simply thought that she would like a book. See,
here behind the pillow beneath your father's head there is a scroll.

What is written on it?

I do not know.

Roland came up then and said, well, Maestro, it is a wonderful piece of work. I congratulate you. My lord my uncle
will be pleased.

And I suppose he will. He rests between his wives, or his
wife and his future widow – who knows, for I could die tomorrow – in his suit of Greenwich armour, splendid and glittering
silver etched with gold. His hands are ungauntletted and his
face uncovered, his gilt-tipped court sword hanging from a
chain on an embossed belt round his waist. His face is beautiful
in repose. I looked at him then as I have never done in life, I
stared at him, I had a wild impulse to lean over my own effigy
and kiss his mouth.

Roland was examining the end of the tomb and now he called
to Agnes: here, cousin, this is you! She skittered to him, looked
and clasped a hand over her mouth.

It is! she said. Is it? she asked Piero.

Of course.

With my brother?

Yes!

I went to look and there she was, in stone profile, neatly coiffed and kneeling with her hands joined at her heart. Facing Agnes, a young boy dressed in breeches, also kneeling; her dead brother Richard. Then I began to make out other figures emerging in the dim light: carved angels supporting the corners of the bier, each with one golden wing enfolded and the other outstretched to shelter four small children; a baby in swaddling bands and a young child in its gown on Lady Agnes's side of the tomb and on mine two newborn babies, both wrapped in white with chrisom cloths bound about their foreheads.

My little chrisomer. If I had been at her baptism I would have seen Sir Joselin place a grain of salt into her mouth, anoint her head with holy oil and bind the cloth around her. If she had lived, I would have brought the cloth back to Sir Joselin at my churching and he would have burned it, for these are sacred things that none but priest and child may handle. But she did not live, and that chrisom cloth became her shroud. Catherine. There upon her father's tomb, there with Creature, who was baptised when nothing but her head had come forth from her mother, there with Agnes, Richard, John and Edith, eternally in stone.

There is something underneath, Joan said to Piero's apprentices. We cannot see well enough in this light, and it is getting darker, please bring the torches closer. They did, and then we saw that behind the pointed arches there were other bodies,

What lies in there? Hugh asked.

Piero shrugged and mumbled something indistinct that sounded like an apology. It was not a question of choice, he said, but of obedience. He had done exactly as the lord had ordered. To see clearly, you must bend down low or lie against the tomb.

Hugh and I were the first to do as Piero said. The young apprentices lowered the torches for us and by their flickering light I saw something I have only otherwise imagined or seen in my most terrifying dreams. Three bodies, cadavers, not quite skeletal, not quite living, not quite dead, twisted together and entangled, like sticks piled up for kindling. One has an arm thrown over its neighbour, one — the body on the north side that lies directly below my effigy — is arching its neck in mortal pain. Her eyes are wide open and her lips are parted; she is naked but for a cloak of streaming hair. All three are naked under a cloth draped loosely across their loins, except that they wear their rings and bracelets and the central one his sword. Their ribcages and leg bones burst through shredded skin as they fight for their last breaths.

I took this in at a single glance before I recoiled and pulled away. My stomach heaved. William, seeing my expression, bent down to see for himself, and I heard his sharp intake of breath. This is a fearful thing, Hugh said. But Joselin, who all this while had been waiting at a distance, now came to stand beside the tomb. On the contrary, he said, there was nothing to fear in this beautiful representation of our deaths. Eram quod es, eris quod sum, as I am so will you be, but pray for faith and trust in God.

The others crowded round to peer through the narrow gaps, crying out, exclaiming at the liveliness of this wonder-work. Look, Piero said, gesturing to his lads to raise the torches. Have you seen the ceiling?

The canopy above the tomb drapes like the curtains of a bed, and like the bed my lord husband lies in now it is roofed, although with stone, not coffered wood. I looked. It was painted the dark blue of a summer midnight and spangled with silver stars.

※

The words that I did not hear Sir Joselin pray at my daughter's baptism: come, Catherine, into the sanctuary of God, where you will be given a share with Christ in everlasting life.

By the word of the Lord the heavens were made, and by the breath of his mouth all their host.

※

But even a childless mother must be churched, which is to say blessed after her labour by her priest. I had my blessing on the eve of Candlemas, there were snowdrops in the graveyard and children were picking bunches of them to bring into the church. I waited for Joselin to meet me at the threshold of the church, a kneeling woman in a white veil, hollowed out and empty, the blood no longer flowing and my breasts as dry as husks, and when he came he gave me a lit candle, poured holy water on me and he said: The peace of God be with you; come into his house. Adore the Son of the Virgin Mary, and ask him to console and comfort you.

Then he took my right hand and led me inside, to the high altar, and he prayed the psalm levavi oculos meos in montes, I will raise my eyes to the mountains, from whence comes my help, and afterwards the Kyrie and paternoster. Lord, hear my prayer, he said, and I said: and let my cry come unto thee, O Lord, and then he made the sign of the cross upon my forehead. And I did find some comfort there, it's true.

The first Sunday of Advent

The first snow of winter fell last night. I woke to the stillness of a world newly blanketed and the strange and unmatched light that comes with freshly fallen snow. So early in the morning, no one had yet trodden it; only the slight prints of a fox marked it where I looked beneath my window. My white fox in the snow?

It's Advent. Come thou dayspring: another season of fasting and waiting, veni veni Emmanuel, come, thou everlasting light. My lord my husband seems a little better these last weeks and can walk downstairs again, but he has not yet seen his tomb.

The thirteenth day of December

Tonight is the longest night, Saint Lucy's night, whose name belies the darkness, and I am in this heavy-curtained bed with Agnes, who is restless and earlier complained that my wakefulness prevented her from sleeping. So now I am lying as still as a corpse and the dark is pressing down on me like earth upon a coffin. It is said that the living are often buried by mistake and wake when it is much too late and they cannot claw their way through wooden lids nailed tight. I cannot lie here any longer. I have had dreams when the Lady Agnes came and whispered in my ear, more than once I swear I have felt a hand pull at the coverings on my side of the bed. I have felt a body next to mine that was not Agnes my stepdaughter.

I will not lie in this closed space for a second more. It is so dark. Agnes shifts and sighs but even if I disturb her and make her cross again, I must get out of this, this tomb of a bed. A force that will not be resisted impels me to sit up, to slide out from under the counterpane and step down.

Beyond the confines of thick drapery, there is some light even on this, the midnight of the year. The moon is full. Susan snuffles peacefully and if Titus is awake in his sleeping-cage, he does not chatter when I put on my cloak, cross the room and inch open the door.

There are two rooms between this one and my husband's and both tonight are empty. Or empty of sleeping people, yet full of shadows and small sounds that cause me to go through them as swiftly as I can. Lambert is sleeping as usual on a pallet outside my husband's door. His back is turned to me; he is a motionless heap under his wraps but he blocks my entrance, I cannot open the door without stepping over him. I do, and he wakes, of course, and immediately sits bolt upright. It is dark here in this space with only a slit of window, which the moonlight does not reach. I have a sudden fear that Lambert may have a knife. I know he would defend his master's life with his. I am nothing but a shape to him, an intruder in the dark, until he can hear my voice. Lambert, I say quickly, Lambert, it is I and I wish to see my lord my husband. Please open the door.

Lambert scrambles to his feet and makes a strangled sound of protest, putting out his hand to keep me back, but I brush it off. Open the door at once, I order, and he does. He tries to come in with me, but I thrust him away and close the door in his face.

The curtains of the bed are half-drawn and in the unearthly silver-grey light I can make out the figure of my husband. I cannot tell if he is asleep or awake, he is lying very still. I tiptoe closer; he does not move but when I reach the side of the bed, I see that his eyes are open. He is watching me but he does not say a word. The bed is high, our faces are almost at a level but still he does not speak, and then I let my cloak fall from me, mount the steps and slip under the coverlet to lie beside him, very close. We stay like that for a time that is long if measured in heart-beats and there is something terrible in the silence between us, something which is neither love nor the absence of it, something like despair. And also a sense of inevitability: there is death but there is also life and I must do what I have come to do, driven by a force more powerful than fear.

I am crying but I do not sense the tears then, not until much later. I reach for him; he is naked beneath the sheet. I find him and I feel him growing hard. I touch him there and then he does say something but I cannot hear what it is and I do not wait, I climb on top of him and shift myself until he can enter me, clumsily, bluntly, and the resistance that he meets at first gives way.

I will not let him go. I do not know if he can hold but I can hold and I can move and I can ride him. There is no pleasure and there is some pain but we are bound tightly together and it seems that hours go by and yet I have no sense of time or even the limits of myself, it is as if we were in one shared dream, there are no words, no spoken sounds until at last he loudly gasps and then I feel his shudder and his slow release. Before I slither off him, I lean down and for the first time ever I kiss him on the mouth.

We lie together, side by side, and I think I will stay until he sleeps, but after a while he says that I should leave. He says it gently. He will have felt my tears. I want to say something to him but I do not have the words and so, instead, I get down from the bed and put my cloak back on.

Lambert is standing, waiting, on the other side of the door. In the dark, I cannot read his face. As I leave, he moves past me and shuts the door behind him.

It is still the dead of night. The large window in the chamber next to my husband's has clear glass panes and I linger there to watch the moon until a passing cloud obscures it, and then I think I see a falling star. The shortest day, the longest night, but from tomorrow each new day will bring with it one more thin sliver of light.

In the month of December, a Saturday

A dishful of snow.
Take the whites of eight fresh eggs and beat them with a spoon. Add two quarts of thick cream, beaten, with sugar and a saucer of rosewater then beat again, leave in a colander for a little while and place a branch of rosemary therein.

❧

No more lasting snow for now but dismal days of sleet and cold rain, twilit December days, as winter tightens its clamp on earth and even the birds are melancholy. Agnes, however, is glowing with joy, for Henry Martyn has returned and is to stay for Christmas. He came at Roland's urging. I don't know what Roland said to him but to Marmion and Joan, who protested that he had outlived his welcome last time, he said that Henry had no other home or family. On hearing that, Joan softened. Poor boy, she said, to be all alone in the world. Her own sons and their children will be here for the feast day and the house will be full, which is as she likes it. Joan's cure for winter-sadness is to be forever busy and already the kitchens are as lively as a beehive. A great spicing and sugaring and candying is going on, but as we keep the Advent fast, it is the pantry shelves that are growing full and no one's belly.

❧

Every night I dream of babies. They are not my own babies, although I am often answerable for them. And they are not happy dreams. I am forever losing these babies, absent-mindedly leaving them behind, forgetting they need feeding and always, although these babies are very young, they talk. Long before the age when real children say their first words, these dream-children speak whole sentences in clear words and chide me, and I wake up in a wash of guilt and sadness.

※

Sir Joselin is fit again, but diminished in himself. He is getting old and he walks with difficulty now, his knees being painful and swollen. I have never heard him talk about his youth or where his home was; he is not spendthrift with his words but hoards them for his sermons. Roland says that like most priests he lacks scholarship and barely knows his Latin, but that is unfair, I think. Joselin knows enough to serve his parish and, in return, his parish loves him. To be abstemious in speech, to be ungarrulous, is a virtue, not a drawback, in the village. One carefully chosen word weighs more than a purseful of platitudes in the scales of truth. And besides, the first apostles and followers of Christ were not scholars either. As Sir Joselin himself observed at dinner yesterday, when the young men were bickering about new doctrine, Saint Peter was convinced by fish, not logic.

That's true. Peter had witnessed water turned to wine, and miraculous healing, but it was only when his boat began to sink beneath the weight of fish summoned by Christ out of the lake that the fisherman saw God. We must all of us find our truth in plain, familiar things, Sir Joselin said. In pots and pans and hoes and threshing forks.

My lord my husband was at dinner too, having come down-stairs supported, almost carried, on Lambert's shoulder. If per-haps he took Sir Joselin's words as disapproval of the elaborate new finery in the church, he did not say so. Indeed, I do not think any censure was intended. If Joselin can look into men's hearts, as I believe he can, then he will know my husband's truth may lie in the gold leaf and the ruby glass.

Where William stands on ornament is not wholly clear to me. His own habits are austere. I suppose a monkish boyhood leaves its mark; he vowed himself to poverty not many years ago. Even Roland will concede that William is well schooled; he studied at Oxford. While Sir Joselin will never abandon the old ways, William, being younger and better travelled, might be more open to the possibility of change. I am not sure. I should ask him. I once heard him tell Hugh that nothing in the world stays still, and Hugh said: except stone.

Things were simpler once. But then, in this kingdom, there came a babble of voices, each one asserting a claim to righteous-ness. Their noise scarcely reached our secluded fastness here, but I heard it when I was a child in my father's house and now again in the disputes between Roland and his brother, in the occasional unrest in the village and in Marmion's muttered complaints. Is it wrong to pray to the saints for help, to keep their feasts and offer gifts to them, light candles, go on pilgrimages? Should priests be made to marry? And, most pertinently, can it be that all are damned, deservedly so, and it is only by the indiscriminate grace of God that some elect souls will be saved? That the grace of God cannot be earned by prayer or by good works, by acts of spiritual or temporal mercy, that what a man does in this world makes no difference in the end?

There are other questions which can never be asked, unless the questioner is quite alone and talking to the wind. And even then, remember Midas! So whisper to the moon, perhaps: why was it right to liberate the Church from Rome only to enslave it to another throne?

However, as my lord my husband says, the commotion time has passed. The gold and the lands that were seized by the wolves when the friars and monks were driven from their houses has long ago been spent on wars or parcelled out. Indeed, some of it to my father; some is in my portion now. Injunctions come and go with new primers and new prayer books, but for the most part we simply carry on regardless. Let us hope this time of calm will last.

Before William Clare arrived, Joan said Sir Joselin would resent him, but she was wrong; he treats him almost like a son. And William is as gentle with the old one as he would be with a father. When Joselin was lying ill here in the house he came every day to sit with him and shouldered all his duties in the parish. Joan told me in secret that when the miller's wife was enduring a hard labour, William brought Saint Margaret's girdle to her. Now that Joselin is able to go about the parish as before, they have an equitable division of those duties. William says the morrow-mass and Sir Joselin the later ones; William helps Joselin to teach the children in the schoolhouse, trains the choir and, ever since the feast of All Souls, sings a daily mass in the chantry chapel for my lord my husband's dead. The two priests also visit my husband almost every day, separately or together. I pray he takes great comfort from their presence; as is right and fitting, neither he nor they will speak of what transpires between them.

I never went on a pilgrimage and now I never will, for they are forbidden, by order of the king. Sir Alwyn, tutor to my brother and me, used to tell of a place in the Holy Land that is called the Desert of Sin. The faithful travel in their thousands to pray there at the tomb of Saint Catherine in the church where she lies, and once a year a swarm of birds goes too. Doves and crows and sparrows, goldfinches, eagles, hawks – every kind of bird in one great flock together and each bird bearing a branch of olive in its beak as an offering to the shrine. A pilgrimage of birds. What a sight it must be when a million wings darken the desert sky, what a thunderous sound of those wings beating!

In the month of December, a Wednesday

Yesterday my lord my husband announced through his steward Marmion that he intends to enclose a part of the wasteland that borders the near field and turn it into a deer park. As this is common grazing, the villagers will surely be distressed. Life is hard enough for those who have no land of their own, and to seize more of it for private use – will this not give rise to grave unrest?

There was some discussion of this intention at dinner but needless to say no one dared question the rightness of it. William was not present. Henry Martyn was, and I think it was only the fourth or fifth time that he has dined in company with my husband. As there were few of us at the table, Henry was close enough for my husband to engage in conversation. He asked what work he did and how he saw the course of his life. Henry said that he had studied law and hoped to use the knowledge he had of legal process to serve one of the great households, perhaps the Earl of Hertford's. The earl had been good enough to show an interest in him. Are you acquainted with his lordship? he asked my husband, who said yes, but only slightly. Then Henry said that if there were ever any service he could do my lord, he would indeed be honoured. The acquisition of land was something he had studied in much detail. No fees would be required, he added.

My husband looked surprised. I have lawyers already, he said, but thank you for your kindness.

And Agnes said: my lord my father, Henry is very skilled and expert.

Was your father a lawyer? my husband asked, perhaps a pointed question.

No, Henry replied. He died when I was a little child, and my mother too. It was by the generosity of a distant cousin that I was taught at the grammar school in Threadneedle Street. A cousin now also dead, alas.

So, you have no family living?

No, and no home either. But I have ambition and I have friends.

Well done, my husband said.

⁂

Alone in the still-room with Dame Joan this morning, I asked if she shared my concern over Agnes. Her attachment to Henry Martyn grows by the day, and after the time that I found them in the bedchamber, there have been others when they have seemingly disappeared on their own. It is plain to everyone in the household, apart from Agnes's father, that Henry is fanning the coals of her already heated feelings. We thought he had left us at Michaelmas for good, but now that he is here again, Roland has said he can stay as long as he likes. When Henry first arrived, Agnes was a gawky child, but since then she has become a woman and, more to the point, her father's heir apparent. When he dies, she will be rich.

Joan said what she has said before: that girls must have at least one dose of greensickness before they marry. Agnes is at the flibbertigibbety age when girls do lose their hearts, she said, but she will not lose her head. She will buckle down, as she must, in time, and meanwhile it will do her no harm to be a little skittish. Heaven knows, there'll be enough sobriety when she is a wife!

I should accept this counsel; Joan has known Agnes all her life. But I cannot help being anxious about Agnes, this contradictory, bewildering girl. What might cause pain – a marble mother on a tomb, for instance – can appear to give her pleasure, and yet she is moved to tears by the plight of one dead pigeon. Who could blame her for having walled up all the sadness of her childhood in a place so tight it cannot be accessed – death after death and now the prospect of another death – how otherwise could she survive? Yes, but that whereof a child cannot speak, or indeed a man, will not dissolve like salt in water over time but become stony, like a cancer or a gall. Grief left unsaid can calcify a heart.

A prayer for the gift of tears:

> *Almighty and most merciful God,*
> *You who made the rock into a spring of water for your thirsting*
> *   people*
> *Draw tears of sorrow from our stony hearts that we may be able*
> *   to mourn . . .*

The twenty-fourth day of December

Christmas Eve, my baby's birthday, holy day of Eve and Adam. A calm, still night. We shall go to the first mass at midnight, and on the hour, in their stalls, unseen by men, the cattle will kneel to greet the newborn king and sing his praise in human words. A baby. The frailest creature that ever was on earth. Boughs of holly in the hall and mistletoe and ivy, great fires burning, ash and applewood with lovely smell. Eve ate the apple of the tree of knowledge, and to punish her God said: I will multiply thy sorrows, and thy conceptions: in sorrow shalt thou bring forth children, and thou shalt be under thy husband's power, and he shall have dominion over thee. Green leaves in the hall turn it to a forest, there will be a feast tomorrow for all the tenants and the people of the village.

There being a waning moon, my lord my husband has been bled and is continuing to take an infusion of sage and willow bark as Doctor Moreton ordered. It is helping; he is suffering less pain. He is not yet strong enough to walk any distance but he will be at the feast he is giving on Christmas Day. He has not said a word about the night when I came to his bed. I had hoped he might ask me to come back but he has not; over me he has dominion while I live.

Christmas

The hall is packed with trestle tables, men and women squeezed together on stools and benches, fire-glow, torch-light on plate and pitcher, dark wine, civet of hare and boar's head, candied quince and marchpane, my lord my husband in his coat of crimson velvet and I beside him, Agnes to his left. Roland and Hugh are seated with us. Lambert keeps sentry and stands behind. The good health of the lord has been toasted. I can see everyone in the hall from this high table, and the people at the tables on both sides. There is Henry, prised away from Agnes for a while; there are Marmion and Joan, as close as a courting couple in spite of years of marriage; their two sons with their wives; the bailiff and the reeve; there is Sir Joselin. Below them is Susan dallying with Thomas, son of Yatt. There is eating and drinking, there is laughter, a rising tide of noise. And there is William Clare, seated at the far end of the table to my right.

He is next to Ann, wife of Dame Joan's younger son, and she is telling him what seems to be an important and tangled story. I watch him listening to her, nodding from time to time, asking a question that elicits another flood of words. I watch him lift a piece of bread to his mouth. His fingers, long and thin and tense against the white linen of the table. I see him smile at Ann. And suddenly he lifts his head, looks straight across at me and our eyes lock. It is as if I had called him by his name and he had heard me. We stare at each other like two wild things separated by iron bars and for a moment there is no one and nothing else, no sound in the hall. And then I turn my head away and tell myself to stop.

The line of cracked skin on my husband's lower lip is stained with wine, as though it had been stitched with purple thread. He drinks more richly than he eats. Agnes has found the Advent fast small sacrifice, as she is still abjuring meat, but she does like sweet-meats and is amusing herself by feeding choice morsels to Titus, who is underneath the table, tethered to her chair leg. Her father will soon tire, I know, and then she and I will rise and go with him, leaving the rest to feast. But for the present he seems content to stay and to survey his people and his kin. He takes a little of the minced pie and says that we must be sure tomorrow to thank and praise the cooks who have worked so hard to feed so many and so well: it cannot be said in our house, as it is commonly said elsewhere in England, that God sends our meat and the Devil cooks it.

Sir, did you ever meet the bishop whose cook was cooked? asks Roland. Boiled alive in a cauldron, so they say.

I knew him, my husband said. He was the bishop of Rochester then and the cook was put to death at Smithfield because he killed two of the bishop's men through poisoning their pottage. Later the bishop was made a cardinal by the pope, but the king was having none of that and cut off his head forthwith.

Mercifully he did not boil it, Roland said.

But his uncle frowned at that. He was a good and holy man, he said, and he met his death with great dignity and courage. Afterwards some said that he had been preparing for it all his life. He used to dine with a man's skull set before him on his table.

Mercy, what a grisly thing to do, and what grisly talk for Christmas Day! I am glad that we make do with the skull of a dead boar, said Agnes.

The eleventh day of the month of January

And then the whole world turned to ice. So cold that the river froze and the water birds were famished. Hoar frost turning blades of grass to spikes, and crystal casing every twig on branch and bush, so that if they had all fallen to the ground at once they would have chimed like bells. Snow blossoming on bare trees; where there had been dark woods and green fields, now there was only white. White sky, white earth. Too cold for man or beast and neither moved unless it must. Even the mill wheel halted.

Ice inside the windows, in the washbowls, iced milk, iced ale, iced ink. Within the house we huddle by the fireplace in the upper chamber, away from the draughts in the hall. In my husband's chamber, the fire burns night and day and his bed is piled with furs and yet he can never get warm. Ice in the marrow of his bones. He had seemed well at Christmas; now, less than a week after Twelfth Night, he can scarcely lift his head from his pillow. The pitiless cold has laid siege to him and turned his veins to icicles; no longer a man of flesh and blood but a thing as cold and immobile as an effigy in marble. Hoar frost in his silver hair, tangled up in sable.

The stoat in winter grows a white coat and when it sinks its pointed teeth into its prey, that white is flecked with blood. Joan worries that Doctor Moreton will be unable to reach us, if we need him. All the ways into the village are blocked by drifts of snow, we are islanded by winter, and the snow brings with it silence.

Ermine is the fur of kings and princes, but they would not wear a stoat. Where is my white fox? Now is her time, only now can she hunt unseen in daylight, bold under cover of the snow.

The seventeenth day of January

The song for Catherine is written. I had not thought that my lord my husband had remembered to ask William Clare for it but he had, and it is made. It is not the dirge that was commissioned, though, it is a lullaby, a cradle song, instead. Of late there have been too many dirges, William said when he came to us to in my husband's chamber, and I did not have the heart to make another one just yet. She was a little baby, let us wish her peaceful sleep until the day when she awakes in her mother's arms.

He played the music on his lute and it was very beautiful. But there were no words. Why no words? I asked him.

I thought that you might wish to write them, Alice, he replied.

Alice. My name in William's mouth. It is enough.

The one blessing of the hard frost was that it prevented Hugh from travelling to join the Earl of Cumberland, but now there is a thaw, the ways are clearer and he is gone. I held him close, there being no other way to say farewell, and we all stood watching at the gate while he rode away. He knew that it would probably be the last time he saw his uncle. We are all mourning his departure, even Titus.

The twentieth day of January

The eve of Agnes's saint's day and she was flushed and fever-
ish; the outcome of too many hours in the close heat of her
father's sickroom, breathing infected air. He is no better. I cannot
think it will be much longer. To divert Agnes, Joan reminded
her to take rosemary and thyme upstairs with her and dream of
the man she will marry. But Agnes tossed her head. Why should
I dream of what I know when I am awake, she asked, looking at
Henry across the table. Henry did not look up from his broth.
And besides, she said defiantly, as if she thought she might as
well as be hanged for a sheep as a lamb, because perforce I share
my bed with my stepmother, she might get the dream instead.
A dream of her second husband or even her third.

Stop, Agnes, that is enough, Joan said. You know quite well
that the spell will only work for a maid who puts the sprigs in her
own shoes. You are unkind to your good lady stepmother and
in place of herbs I will give you a dose of feverfew and yarrow.

Agnes was not chastened. I smiled – what else could I do? –
pretending to take those cruel words as spoken only in jest. And
I wondered about this winter custom, midsummer's mirror, of
young girls hoping to conjure up their lovers to come. Those
magical plants: rosemary, thyme and the pink orpine that some
call live-forever or midsummer men, and the summer rose-leaves
that elf-shot girls strew round them, saying: he that will love
me, come to me now. Poor instruments for divination, these.
When I was a maid I did as all the others on Agnes's Eve and

lay uncovered on my bed, my hands as pillow beneath my head, shivering in the bitter cold, and dreamt of no one. One midsummer I kept myself awake until the bell struck midnight so that I would see my husband in a glass. No one warned me then that the lovers who visit in dreams are only phantoms. When morning comes, a girl will marry as she is told.

And no one ever said that love would have more thorns than the briar rose. That it might be possible to split a heart in two and love in two directions. That a body may thrill when the will tells it not to, and that a man you married out of duty may stake a claim on your heart. Or your soul. That it hurts to watch a man dying, but you cannot say so if you are forbidden to speak of death. That love and fear are close kin and that it is hard to tell love and pity apart. That you do not know how to be a widow, when you barely know how to be a wife. That the loss of a child leaves an ache that will never heal and that you will grieve for the children who are not born, the ones you might have had and now see in your dreams. That love might come too late, or be misplaced, or never come, no matter whose face you think you see in the small hours of the night.

The second day of February

January is over, it is Candlemas and a year since the illness with no name possessed my lord and husband. I am remembering when it began, with a sudden loss of movement in his left leg and the doctor assuring him that all would be well within a month. Poor man. Like one who stumbling up a steep hill believes that he has reached its summit, only to see an endless range of stony mountains spread before him and barring his passage home, he has endured disappointment after disappointment. Time and again he has seemed to rally, but each reprieve, each stretch of comparative health, has been followed by relapse, and each relapse severer than the last. He was confined to bed from the start of February last year until Ash Wednesday, but between then and now he has been able to get up and walk about. I remember Corpus Christi, how he stood to watch the procession, and it is three months to the day since he walked by himself to the church to see his wife reburied. He could not do that now. He cannot move his arms or legs, he can scarcely swallow any food, and in his eyes there is a look that nobody wants to meet. The extreme effort that he made on the day of All Souls has proved to be his last.

Unless there is a miracle, and that is always possible: the whole household says its prayers for him every morning and every evening and in our quiet devotions in between. At Candlemas the gates of hell are unlocked to let Judas out, so that he might ease the torment of his burning skin in the ice-cold waters of the sea. At all times there is mercy. But then again, at the end of the day, Judas has to go back to the flames.

William Clare is with him now; my lord my husband can still speak, he has time to make confession.

☙

Word has come that the king is dead, and a new one on the throne. Here, we are in dispute. Marmion says that by command every church in the entire land must toll its bell and sing due requiems and dirges all the week, but the latter Sir Joselin refuses. He will have the bell tolled, he says, for the parish must hear of the death, but he will not make his people sing to order for the salvation of so terrible a man. Those who wish to pray for his soul should do so in private, as the priest himself will, for no one is beyond God's mercy and everyone deserves our pity. Marmion's counterargument that the late king was no more sinful than his forebears astonished Sir Joselin. No more sinful? he said. The man who broke his sacred vows and splintered holy Mother Church for nought but lust and then condemned the object of that lust to death upon a scaffold? The man who killed his child's mother and later yet another bride, herself not much older than a child? And sent a thousand more to their grim deaths, some who were his friends? Once there was a commonwealth that stretched from the North Sea coasts to the Levant and we were part of it. What are we now? A little realm adrift, cut off from the right ways of our fathers, scraping saints out of our prayer books!

Be careful, sir, said Roland. If this treason were heard outside these walls, you would be hawk's meat.

Indeed, said Henry. Better by far to knuckle down and sing whatever you're told.

But William, appealed to for arbitration, took Sir Joselin's part. He said that it is right and fitting to pray for every soul departed but hypocrisy to ask for general mourning in this case. Shall we instead sing a mass for the new king, he said, that he may live and prosper and rule well?

Poor lamb! said Joan. A child who only yesterday was still in skirts, who is barely breeched! How can one so young be king? He should be fed warm pap and tucked up in his bed, not perched on a throne!

Vae tibi, terra, cujus rex puer est, et cujus principes mane comedunt, Sir Joselin muttered, mostly to himself, leaving the hall before anyone could answer and taking William with him.

What does that mean? Agnes asked.

Woe to thee, O land, when thy king is a child, and thy princes eat in the morning, Roland told her. And it's nonsense.

Is it not in the Bible?

You should not pay much heed to Joselin, Henry told her. He is an old man and old men can be scatter-witted. He will bring danger on his head if he does not shut his mouth.

He is a good man, Joan said. And he is safe with us.

In the month of February

Beneath the hedgerows and at the edges of the woods, wisps of snow still clinging to the earth, unwilling to relinquish it, and hard frosts in the morning, but winter aconites are scattering warm gold across the hillside and the blackbirds are singing once again. I have had no flow of blood. Susan, noticing the lack of it, asked me today if I were ailing and whether she should go to Mistress Joan for rue and hyssop. If I did not wish to swallow that, Joan would make me a plug of wool steeped in lavender ointment. I told Susan that I was well and she said that I must beware of suffocation.

There are other reasons why a woman's monthly flow should cease, anxiety and an excess of sanctity among them.

The wandering preacher is back in the village and seems to have a following now. He has chosen his moment well; the time is ripe. The king's death has unsettled his people; only the old can remember the days before he reigned, and although the years of his reign have been tumultuous, there are many who say it is better to have the devil you know than the one you don't. In his death, as in his life, the king has caused division. Some are fearful of what may come, others relieved that he has gone, although none of course will speak their thoughts aloud. He may be dead, but his acts live on, and as Roland sharply reminded

Joselin, there is a law of words. But no law can stop the people speaking of the things that they have seen, and it is these that tell the public mood.

Strange lights in the sky, a cloud shaped like the avenging angel, a stag with golden antlers, three-headed lambs, all of these have appeared, and some people are claiming they have witnessed the spirits of those who died on the scaffold or under the executioner's axe, including the beheaded queens and the old lady who bit by bit was hacked to death for owning a tunic painted with some signs of Christ. Others say the banished saints are coming back. In our own church someone unseen drew a cross and placed an offering of coin at the place on the wall where there used to be the altar of Saint Thomas.

Into this fevered mood, the preacher's words have fallen like a drop of fat upon a fire and, according to Marmion, will melt away as fast. Roland, Henry and Agnes went to hear him preach and Roland said that there was no cause for alarm. Yes, a few were stirred by his tirades against idolatry and exhortations to repentance – do you believe that God is merciful, gentle, liberal, protector, refuge and life to all? Then you are wrong! To the monstrous rabblement of heretics and sinners his wrath will be unending. His purpose and his will being eternal, it cannot be moved by temporal works or acts of faith! – but most of those who were gathered there merely jeered and mocked his spluttery voice. Although it has to be admitted that he has a lively turn of phrase, Henry added.

Agnes said the people were more beguiled by Titus than the firebrand. They always love to see him in the village and they come crowding round, begging to see his little hands, to hear his darling chatter. You should be a preacher, she cooed to her pet. Think, Henry, how pretty he would look in a priest's gown, with a jewelled cross around his neck! Titus, you would save so many souls!

No, he is a monk, with that white hood, Henry said.

But no monk or priest has teeth like his, Roland said. Cousin Agnes, you should not let the village children near him, he could bite their fingers off.

In the last week of the month of February

Afterwards it seemed to me as though the last note of the king's death knell had only just ceased sounding on the air when my husband's passing bell began to ring. He took three days to go. We sent for Hugh. It was unnaturally warm all during those three days, a little summer before the start of spring, rare weather for dying. An omen, Joan said, and there had been another: she had heard a barn owl screech outside her bedroom window the night before my lord fell into his final spell of illness.

I knew that death was coming, as we all did. By Saint Valentine's Day the bones of his throat had grown so hard that he could barely swallow and had to be fed water on a spoon. Drop by necessary drop, and even then the water trickled from the corners of his mouth. It is a fearful thing to see a man who was so noble and so strong reduced to this, Joan wept, and we wept with her at his bedside, keeping watch beside him, turn by turn.

Once, but only once, I saw that he cried too, silent tears; I could not tell if he had power over them or not. I held his hand; it was as dry as a dead leaf, and as still. When Agnes was in the room she demanded my place beside him and I let her have it. She was terribly distraught.

By day, the improbable sunshine streamed into the room and warmed it, alighting on the dying man, ash-grey beneath the cruelly bright green of his lily-patterned covers, on his fair-headed daughter, on the bottles of medicine and bowls of salve now rendered pointless. The heat intensified the curiously sweet but festering smell of my husband's body. February reclaimed the night, bringing cold the instant that the sun set, and it was by firelight then, and tapers, that we watched. He could speak, but only with a painful struggle and at the cost of his next breath – a very high cost, as each breath came singly and harshly and, as the hours wore on, with longer intervals between. At dawn, the birds, hearing this rough music, mocked it with the clarity of their song.

Sir Joselin was often there, or William, both by night and day. Constant, the stream of prayer. The priests', Agnes's, Roland's, mine, Lambert's in silence, Joan telling her beads. Sancta Maria, Mater Dei, ora pro nobis peccatoribus, nunc, et in hora mortis nostrae. Amen.

Pray for us sinners

Now and at the hour of our death

Amen

Amen

Amen

On the evening of the third day, Joan told us that the end was very near and we must call for Joselin. While we waited, she made a table ready: a white cloth, two sanctified candles, a branch of hyssop that she had already cut in expectation of these final deathbed hours. Asperges me, Domine, hyssopo, cleanse me of sin with hyssop; wash me, and I shall be whiter than snow.

Sir Joselin came quickly, vested in stole and surplice, and William came with him, holding a wooden crucifix, and the first thing Joselin said was that it was a wonderful thing to die prepared. Your Saviour awaits you, have faith and rue your sins and he will welcome you with open arms, as he does here and now, upon this cross.

The priest took the crucifix from William and held it before my husband's face, so that its embracing shadow fell upon him. Then he asked the seven necessary questions, to all of which my husband answered yes. Yes he believed, yes he was sorry, yes he wished he could make amends, yes he forgave and yes, yes, he knew that it was only by the merit of Christ's passion that he could ever be saved. And for that yes, he did give thanks, for grace, for hope, for comfort, yes.

Sir Joselin, will you now pray for his recovery? Agnes, kneeling at the foot of bed, lifted her clasped hands to him in passionate supplication.

His will be done, Joselin replied, but when he asked my lord my husband if he was ready to receive the viaticum, the fare for his last journey that can only be given once, we knew that the time for miracles was over. Unless you could say that the safe passage of a soul is itself miraculous? Who knows? The Devil schemes for the souls of the dying, lurking in the shadows in the corner of the room, but even he dare not defy the holy candles and the cross.

My husband made a sign that he was ready, yes. And no, as he had been shriven in the morning, he had no urge to confess again in private. So we did not need leave the room but could stay and pray with him.

Joselin opened the pyx he carried, lifted the Sacrament and held it ready to place upon my husband's tongue. Lambert leapt up to halt the priest before he could do so, and I explained: he cannot swallow, Lambert is afraid that he may choke.

The smallest crumb, Joselin said calmly, that will be enough. Lambert, do not fear. Joselin bent over the dying man and gently pressed down on his lower lip until his mouth opened just wide enough to receive a fragment of the sacred bread. Take this, brother, he said, corpus Christi and may he keep you from the malignant foe, and bring you to life everlasting. Amen.

Amen. And yes.

Then Joselin took a phial of holy oil from the silk burse he wore on a cord around his neck and unstoppered it. Please to pull back the covers, he said to Joan. She did as he asked, stripping off the green silk, revealing the naked body of the man. By then he had so little flesh on his bones that he more closely resembled the ghastly figure at the almost-hidden base of his tomb than the proud knight in armour on its bed. I could have traced the path of his veins and his sinews with a finger; his joints were about to burst through his skin.

Per istam sanctam unctionem, by this holy unction I anoint you, and may the Lord forgive you whatever sins you may have done by:

sight

hearing

smell

taste

speech

touch

the power to walk.

Eyelids, ears, nostrils, lips, the palms of his hands, the soles of his feet one by one received the oil from Joselin's fingers. Then Joselin wiped the oil off the man and off himself; no one now should touch the places that it touched but for the priest and the dying man. My chrisom child wore a band across her forehead to keep the oil unprofaned; her father will do likewise with a shroud.

The priest turned to us, all of us kneeling, and bade us pray with him, oremus: Domine, exaudi orationem meam. Et clamor meus ad te veniat. O Lord, hear my prayer. And let my cry come to thee.

And finally he blessed us, the living and the dying: benedicat te omnipotens Deus, Pater et Filius, et Spiritus Sanctus. Amen.

The two priests left then, and after she had settled the bed-cover, Joan said that everybody else should come with her and have some supper before the long vigil of the night. I told her that I was not hungry and would stay. Lambert gestured to say that he would wait with me, but I told him he should go.

It was dark by then, but the candles were still burning and I could see that his eyes were open, I knew he was awake. I am frightened, I said, are you?

He shook his head, and his answer came softly: no, not any more. It is too late.

I climbed onto the bed and lay down beside him, facing him, my mouth to his ear. I am carrying your child, I said, and I know he heard. But then he closed his eyes and said nothing else. I moved so that I was as close to him as I could be, my head against his shoulder, my arm across his waist, and I listened to his laboured breathing until I fell asleep.

A while later Joan woke me, she was standing by the bed with Marmion. Go to your own bed, child, she said, and get some proper sleep. I will wake you immediately if there is any change.

But she did not wake me, for she herself was not there at the moment of his death. Afterwards she did admit to having left the room for a few minutes, in the very early morning. Marmion had been alone with him in the small hours and said that at that time he was still sensate and speaking a few words. The others had come and gone during the night and they all thought he would last beyond the dawn. So when it came to it, he left this world as he had lived in it, essentially alone.

⁂

Remember thou art dust and unto dust thou shalt return.

⁂

Hugh was too late, by a matter of hours. But he is here now, and that helps. He is full of sorrow. That afternoon we went to the river and watched the tall tree trunks and their bare branches casting lattice patterns on the dark-grey water, and the birdsong was so loud it drowned out the tolling bell. He held my hand.

⁂

The bell will toll all through this day and night and then again at noon each day for thirty days to mark his death, to sanctify his passing soul and save him from the fiends that would molest it. Nobody will be able to put him out of mind before the month's end and then, beyond the trental, William Clare will sing for his soul each and every day until William himself is dead and when he is, another priest will take on the charge and so it shall go on until the day of judgement. My lord and husband willed it so, and left gold in trust to guarantee that he and his family will always be remembered in the chantry that he built and in the unending prayers of cantor after cantor. So let us pray that the building stands, that laws permit, that prayer endures and stone will never crumble into dust.

Meanwhile, he must be buried. Marmion and Roland are debating whether to send for the metallist from Woodstock; should he be encoffined in lead like the Lady Agnes or would a shroud suffice? Or cerecloth? He will rest in a stone-lined pit sealed by yet more stone, whereas she was laid in a shallow grave beneath an inch of earth. She would have stunk as she decayed, had she not had a decent casing. But he will stink also, if the burial is delayed. How much time will it take to spread word of his death abroad and make the funeral preparations? And what of the weather? How fortunate that the strange span of unseasonable summer has come to a sudden end; indeed it almost seemed to cease with his last breath. Another omen, some would say, but a blessing also, for the body will not decay as swiftly as it would have done in heat. Lead is very expensive. And, more than that, would render the body as unpliable as a plank of wood. A fine balance, this.

The men do not ask me for my view. If they were to, I would say that he would wish to be buried as naked as he was when he was born and when he died. Like an animal. Why else would he have ordered Piero da Fiesole to make an image of him as a rotting corpse? He wanted those he left behind to know that they were mortal and to live their lives within that apprehension. And in particular he wanted me to contemplate my fate every time I went into the church. And I will, how could I not? On this, the day after the death of my lord my husband I am like one who falls through thin ice and is rendered almost senseless, but I know I am alive still, and that life is in me, and I will not give in to death, not yet.

❧

A funeral requires untold quantities of roasting, baking and brewing, and Joan cannot have sat still for a minute in the last two days. She was in the kitchen issuing more orders and I was with her when Marmion appeared and asked if he might speak to me alone. We walked into the garden; the morning was overcast and threatening rain.

To come straight to the point, he said, in his last hours my lord cousin asked me to promise that his daughter Catherine would be buried with him in his tomb. Needless to say, I agreed. I do know that this may cause you some distress on top of the distress that you must bear already, but you will not have to watch her grave being opened and I will make sure that her shroud is intact before you have to see her.

She is not to be unburied, and my husband said so too.

That's not exact. He agreed that she could be left where she was for the time being but, when he said that, he did not foresee his imminent death.

For sure he did. How could he not?

Ah well, there is none who now can say what he truly thought. I suppose that he continued to place his trust in his doctor and his God. But that is not the question here. What we must do is our duty by the dead. We have no choice but to carry out his wishes.

Were there other witnesses to this request?

No, there were not. Joan was resting. You will remember that I was with him for a short while on my own.

Then I will choose to believe that he never made it.

Are you accusing me of lying?

No. I know you to be honest. But we both know how hard it was for him to speak in those last hours. Is it not possible that you misheard him or misconstrued his meaning?

It is not. And there was more he said concerning you, but perhaps you will not choose to hear it.

Cousin Marmion, you have done all that you could. Let that broken promise be on my head, not on yours. I will ask Sir Joselin for his guidance and then I will abide by it. If he judges that my daughter should be dug up like a dog's bone, then she shall. But I could wish you had not heaped this new sorrow on me at this time.

I am sorry. It is a question of practicalities. We do not want to lift the stone more often than we must.

As I promised, I went in search of the old priest at once, but he was not in the schoolroom, where I would have expected him to be, nor in the priest's house, and no one in the village knew where he could be found. So I went to the church, where I met William Clare on his knees in the graveyard, not praying – at least, that is, not praying aloud – but pulling up some bishop's weed that was sprouting round the gravestones. I was trying to swallow my tears and rage, but I saw that he could read them in my face. He said that Joselin had gone to Finstock at first light, summoned directly to the sickbed of a woman whose own priest was away, and he asked if he could help me instead. I told him what Marmion had said.

When this hurtful matter was raised before, William, you took my part.

And I will again, if it comes to that. Shall we go inside, where we can talk?

This church has become a house of death for me and I would far rather stay outside, here with you in the yard.

But it is raining, William said, and you have no cloak. He was right, I had not noticed the rain beginning to fall. Come, he said, we can sit in the porch, unless you are too cold.

He put a hand beneath my elbow, a tentative hand, a light touch, a touch that may have feared rebuke, and linked like that we went into the shelter that is one of my lord my husband's many gifts to the people of his village. Its new stone is the same stone of the chapel, so clean, so pale in contrast to the old stones of the old walls that it makes me think of bone. This porch beneath its pitched roof is like a little chapel on its own, echoing the outlines of the chantry, except that its entrance has no door but is open to the air, to the daylight and the dark and to the winds. Inside, to left and right, there are wooden benches, silkily planed so that the old and the ailing can rest a while and catch their breath before they lift the latch of the heavy door that gives admittance to the church.

We sat on opposite sides, facing one another; I saw that his fingers were green with grass stains and one of his sleeves was fraying.

Are the living to be bound by the wishes of the dying? I asked him.

That is a question for a lawyer. But if you ask me, I would say it depends on the nature of the wish.

And this wish in particular? What is the nature of this wish?

Deep love for a child, perhaps, or a desire for control beyond the grave? Why do you resist it with such force?

Where are the words that could tell how terrible it was to watch her little body being cast into a grave? To this day I still see it, but now no longer every time I close my eyes. The thinnest of skins has grown over the wound of loss with passing time, but if she were to be ripped out of the sheltering earth like a flower uprooted, that new skin would rip too, and never heal again. It makes me sick to think of her remains, her tiny skull, of what is left behind now that the worms have had their fill, being fetched into the light again and exposed to common view. As it is, I can only just make shift to live my life. It is a sin to wish for death, I know, and yet I do, I did, and the reason I can bear the years ahead is that the seasons change, the old leaves fall and the new leaves come, the blackthorn and the cherry blossom. Consider the violets, emerging now out of the frozen earth.

I did not say these things aloud to William. Instead, I said in answer to his question: I have found some consolation in the flowers that grow where my daughter lies and I do not think that there is a place for them on an alabaster tomb. How could she know that the flowers were for her, if her bones were muddled with the others who died long before she was born?

Mine was a question with no truthful answer, and we sat without speaking for a while. By then the rain had strengthened and was coursing down so hard that it made a sheet of water at the entrance and filled our silence with its noise; we could have been inside a cave in a weir.

We may have to stay here for some time, William said.

I would be glad to.

But you are shivering. Please take my cloak.

Then you will freeze.

Well, shall we take turns and so delay our death by cold? We'll go one after the other that way.

May we not go together? I would rather that than go alone.

If you take my cloak *and* step inside the church, where it is warmer, we may yet live.

For me it would be like stepping into a grave.

It would not. Here, let me show you. He stood up, unfastened his cloak, and wrapped it round me. Heavy, unlined, woollen cloth, smelling of earth and smoke. Come, he said.

Within, a watery grey light, the rain streaming down the windows and drumming on the roof, dimming the coloured glass, and yet the white stone of the dead Christ glowing by the altar, with a candle burning at his head. And the tomb also strangely bright, like something seen by moonshine, drawing my eyes straight to it. Invisible from where William and I were standing but as manifest to me as if they were lit by a hundred torches, the writhing cadavers underneath the bed.

When you look at that tomb you see death, William said, but you could see love instead, the love that binds the living and the dead, which takes the form of memory. Yes, when we sing for the souls of the dead, we are singing for their redemption, but we are remembering them on earth at the same time. We are saying their names. And as long as there is somebody to call you by your name, you are not forgotten. When I was a boy at the monastery school, I happened to meet an old monk, so old he could no longer teach, indeed he could hardly walk, who told me that when each new child entered the school, his name would be given to one of the brothers and that brother would pray for him every day for the rest of his life. Every monk with his own list of names, and often they did not know the child. But that made no difference – known or a stranger, they prayed for that child, and when they died, that child's name would be given to another. So, you see there was a continuous chain of daily prayer: someone praying for you by name, and you would not know who they were, for they did not tell.

And we forge the same chain here – here, and in every place where the living and the dead are bound by love and hope. And faith. Those virtues caused the bright glass to be made and the carved stone, the ceiling that tells the angels that their wings are seen, and they are not vanquished by the grave. Yes, it is true that the breath of every woman, man and child who ever prayed here is held in the stones, their footprints in the clay, but most of them are nameless now or only known by name to God. But as long as we can name the ones we loved, they live in us. We sing for them, we pray for them, we make their likenesses in stone. Pity those who die unremembered and unmourned.

So are you saying that it is right and proper to lay Catherine in that tomb?

No. There is more than one right and proper way to commemorate the dead. Your husband chose to keep his beloved children in memory forever by turning them to angels carved in stone. His daughter Catherine is among them. You choose to keep her in your heart, to leave her grave unmarked and bring her flowers. You are her mother, her body grew in yours, you carried her inside you, and although her mortal remains belong to God, I believe you have the right to say where they should stay until the day of Resurrection. Whenever that may be, the immortal part of Catherine is safe. And she, like her father, his wife and their children, is always in our prayers.

However, the law may carry more weight than my belief and that, I think, is your best argument. It is forbidden to disinter a body that was buried in consecrated ground except with special permission. It may have been illicit to disinter the Lady Agnes. No one, not even Marmion, will want to face the process that might ensue if that unburial is questioned. And if you wish, I will plead so to Sir Joselin.

Sir Joselin is stern on points of doctrine, I said. He may say that a dying man's wish takes precedence over the law. He will not let feeling triumph over what he judges to be right.

He is precise but not severe, he understands the human heart. Because he is plump and often dishevelled, because he listens more than he speaks, he is easily misjudged. I think he is not always seen for what he is: a truly holy man. And even, I would go so far as to say, a saintly one, who never puts his own needs before another's. I have watched him with the sick, the troubled and the dying and I can attest to his tenderness with them.

I love him too, I did not mean to speak against him. Have you ever wondered why saints are never fat?

In images, you mean?

Yes, impossible to imagine Jesus as anything but lean.

That made William laugh.

While we had been talking the rain had slackened and now it was quiet in the church. We looked at each other and I said: I had better go.

I will walk with you, he said.

We left the church, he closed the latch, we walked beneath the dripping yew and took the path that skirts the waterlogged meadow. As often happens after heavy rain, the sun had come out in compensation, and I said it was the sort of day when we might see a rainbow. But we didn't. Where the path forks to the house and the village, we went our separate ways. I gave him back his cloak. As I turned away he said: it grieved your husband terribly to leave you.

❧

When I look back, it seems to me that this, this quarrel over graves, was the beginning of the end. Or, to put it better, it was one cause of our devastation. There were others that had nothing to do with us but were blown here by the winds of change, and yet we might have withstood them had we not been divided. As a flock of sheep will huddle close against a ravening wolf or an icy blizzard, we should have stayed together. But anger, greed and love – yes, even love – sent us scattering and left us open to the storm.

As William Clare had known he would, Sir Joselin ruled that Catherine's grave should not be disturbed. Marmion accepted this judgement with equanimity; after all, he had no stake in this matter of burials and had simply been trying to do his duty. But Agnes was enraged. She should never have learned of her father's wish but Joan had told her by mistake, believing that I would concede to it and intending thereby to comfort the girl. I was not there when Joan had to tell her what Sir Joselin had decided but I heard afterwards that Agnes had hissed with fury, crying and spitting out words like witch and hellcat, screeching that I was no Christian and her father should never have taken me as his wife. She cursed Joselin too, accusing him of impiety to the dead. And she ordered Joan to keep in mind that she was now the mistress of this house.

Joan, recalling that William had managed to soothe Agnes when she was in a sad state before, sent for him and made her go and practise her music in the meantime. I did not hear what he said to her but she was tearless at supper, although she refused to speak to me. Poor child, she must be beside herself with grief, her father barely three days dead and still lying upstairs in his chamber: if anyone deserves compassion it is Agnes. But to my shame I confess that it is hard to feel it. We are all mourning in our different ways.

Lambert is howling like a masterless dog, utterly bereft. What shall we do with him? Joan asked. Shall he be put out of the house to join the fieldmen? He has no wife, no kin, no money of his own. Or, Roland, will you take him as your servant?

Roland said that he would rather not, for Lambert's dumbness makes him less than useful. I will take him, Hugh said at once. I will find a place for him with my Lord Cumberland.

But he has been here so long, Joan said doubtfully. Removing him will be like pulling up a tree by its roots.

Then he must stay where he belongs, I said. This is his home if he still wants it. We should ask him.

⚘

On the day of his death, Mother Wright, the midwife from the village, came to lay him out. Susan helped her. They shaved his face, washed his body with rosewater, scattered thyme and dried lavender upon him and wound him in his shroud. Then Lambert and the other serving men lifted him from his soiled bed and onto the low, narrow table that this family reserves for its corpses to lie on. There he stayed, in his own bedchamber, with a black cloth covering the window and candles burning at his feet and head. And his household took turns to watch with him at night, so that he would not be left unguarded.

At the end of the third day, Cadd brought a length of cere-cloth, and with Lambert's aid the body was wrapped again, from head to toe. Before molten beeswax was dripped onto the cloth to seal the seams, we – his wife, his daughter and his nephews – were invited to look at him for the last time. He had not begun to rot but he would, very soon.

Then it was the final night. I chose to take the last watch and I watched alone. Susan offered to keep me company, but she was tired, having shared the earlier hours with another maid, and I told her to get some sleep instead. Are you not afraid? she asked me.

I said that I was not, but that was not true. I was very afraid at first in that dark room with the candles flickering and the shrouded body and the wind hissing at the shuttered window. Some say that the souls of the dead linger by their bodies in the days between their dying and their burial and I could believe it, then. I felt it. So I spoke to him. I told him I was angry, I asked him why he had gone against my will. I berated him for dying before our child was born. I said that I was sorry, that I wished that I had loved him, that I could have loved him better had he let me, that I thought of the nights when our bodies met. My body felt them still. I asked if he remembered them, I said I wanted more time, I asked him to come back.

And he made no answer. He remained quite still on his narrow board beneath his layer of stiffened cloth and he said nothing. But, strangely – I cannot tell you how – I began to feel a kind of peace. I had said out loud all that I had to, and I had been heard. I knew how cruelly that man had suffered in his illness, and now I understood that the fate that he had battled for a year was not surrender in the end but relief. A pleasure, almost. I also knew that the candles that burned round him, the cross at his head and the bell that would toll again at his burying in the morning protected both of us, him and me. If there were fiends hiding in the black corners of the chamber, they would not dare to touch us beneath the shadow of the cross. And if his spirit were still there, the candlelight would calm it, he need not fear the coming dark. I prayed for him, de profundis and paternosters, and I was sure he listened to the words.

⁂

When they came to fetch the body in the early morning, they found me asleep on the great bed, inches from the board on which he lay. I don't remember getting onto the bed; the stool on which I had been sitting at some distance from him was knocked over on the floor. I don't remember yielding to sleep or even being weary; all I can recall is a deep sense of calm. Later, Roland said that I had stretched out my arm and rested my hand on the dead body.

The funeral bell was already tolling. I did not stay to watch Lambert, Cadd and the gravedigger manhandle the corpse down the spiral stairs. In the great hall, a bier was waiting, and a black velvet pall.

Morning light, rose-flushed, wood pigeons murmuring to one another and dew as thick as rainfall on the grass. The western wind had dropped. Poor Richard, too proud to be carried to the church in life, now left without a choice.

Led by a young crucifer, the household, the tenants and the assembled villagers walked in a straggling long line behind the bier that Roland, Hugh, Marmion, Lambert, Cadd and Henry Martyn carried on their shoulders. Why Henry Martyn? Joan had wondered, and Susan said that Agnes had insisted. Agnes was bearing her father's shield.

A slow procession in keeping with the solemn bell, every one of the household black-gowned and black-hooded. I held a branch of rosemary, deeply scented; rosemary for remembrance, rosemary for weddings and for deaths. At the lychgate, Sir Joselin and William Clare were waiting for us, wearing white albs and black stoles, with incense and lit candles. We followed them through the open door and into the church, where the pall-bearers set down the bier before the chancel. They placed it so that he faced east.

Joselin sprayed holy water on the corpse and prayed: almighty and everlasting God, we humbly entreat thy mercy that thou wouldst commend the soul of thy servant Richard for whose body we perform the due office of burial to be laid in the bosom of thy patriarch Abraham; that when the day of reckoning shall come, he may be raised up among thy saints.

Come in haste to help him, saints of God, come in haste to meet him, angels of the Lord. And may Christ receive you, for it was he who called you, and may the angels lead you into paradise.

Amen. Amen.

As I knelt at my place, the chant of the mass was like the sound of the wind to me or the imagined voices of the sea. The words could not reach me, where I was. But other words rang in my ears, echoed, familiar and remembered words: out of the depths I cry to you, O Lord hear my voice. Timor mortis conturbat me, because in hell there is no redemption but may the angels lead you, hear my voice. The heat of the candles around the bier caused the air to dance and a sudden brightening of the sun through the window to the east caught their rising smoke. The window of the risen Lord. Ego sum resurrectio et vita. Qui credit in me, etiam si mortuus fuerit, vivet: I am the Resurrection and the life; he that believeth in me, yea, though he be dead, he shall live.

When the mass was ended, the gravedigger and Simm walked over to the tomb. They had already lifted the stone that lidded the space and the rectangular trapdoor was gaping. Roland removed the black velvet pall, exposing the yellowy shrouded body, and slid his hands beneath its shoulders. Hugh slid his beneath its knees and together the brothers carried it to the tomb and dropped it straight down into the pit. It landed with a thump like a sack of sodden mortar. Then the gravedigger and Simm took a wooden paddle each and carefully shunted my lord my husband's body sideways into its place beside the Lady Agnes.

A boy server stepped out, holding a small bowl, and led Sir Joselin to the edge of the narrow hole. William, Agnes and I followed him. Now I saw the bowl was full of earth, very fine and dried almost to dust. The old priest took a handful of it and cast it into the grave and, one after the other, William, Agnes, Roland and Hugh did the same. Lastly I put in the rosemary. Requiem aeternam dona ei, Domine, the old priest sang and we responded: et lux perpetua luceat ei.

The sealing stone had been raised by means of a lever and a pulley threaded through the iron ring that was set in it. Simm had judged it nicely. At a signal from Joselin he lowered the stone slowly until it was in position, and then he let it fall. The crash it made resounded round the church: amen, amen, requiescat in pace, amen and fare thee well.

Roland and Hugh draped the black pall over the tomb,

Agnes leant her father's shield against it and we left the church to the clanging of the bell. The poorer villagers were in the yard, expectant, looking forward to their dole of beer, food and money that Marmion had prepared.

At the gate, Sir Joselin said that Richard had been a very lucky man. He was one who had known danger and could have died on the battlefield or at sea, suffering a sudden and unprovided death far away, in the company of strangers, his sins yet unforgiven. Instead he died shriven and anointed in his own bed, with his kinfolk round him. Indeed, he died the kind of death for which we should all pray.

Yes he did, said Agnes simply. And now he is with Christ in paradise.

❧

In paradisum deducant te Angeli; may the choir of angels receive you in paradise and with Lazarus, who once was poor, may you have eternal rest.

❧

On this night I will sleep in the great bed again, beneath the green silk and the lilies. My marriage bed is a deathbed too, but I am not afraid of sleeping with the ghosts. As I must share my alabaster bed with them, why not a wooden one, in a quiet room, alone? Joan had presumed that this bedchamber was to be locked and shuttered up for the time being and was surprised when I said that I would sleep here.

Non timebis a timore nocturno;
You shall not fear the terror of the night,
or the flying arrow,
the thing that stalks the darkness
or the demon at midday.

The second day of the month of March

People who lived near enough travelled here in haste to attend the funeral – kinsmen, friends and colleagues – and some have stayed a while, among them two young cousins who had been at Westminster to see the new king crowned ten days ago. At dinner everyone was eager to hear their tales of the little boy dressed in ermine and velvet, and the streets decorated with cloth of gold. There were cushions on the throne to raise the child high enough and his neck could have snapped beneath the weight of his father's imperial crown. But he bore it bravely and afterwards they gave him a smaller one, made speedily to fit him.

Poor motherless mite! Joan said.

Well, said one of the young men, he has to bear a weight on his shoulders that is heavier than any crown and can never be set aside, for the lad is not only king of England but also God's vice-regent in these lands. That is what the archbishop told him, in his sermon. As if he had not care enough already, the archbishop commanded him to see God truly worshipped and all idolatry and images destroyed. That's quite a burden for a child!

He blasphemes, Sir Joselin said. The archbishop blasphemes. His is the law of Herod. No man – or child – whether crowned or not is sovereign over other men's consciences or the inheritance of shared wisdom that is the Church.

The Londoners smiled at the old priest's fervour but Roland was stern. We have warned you before, Sir Joselin, he said. If you persist in speaking like this you will bring trouble on all our heads.

I speak for myself, Joselin said.

And among friends within these walls, William said. We know how true you are, Sir Joselin. And surely, as we have managed our consciences under the old king, who made himself supreme, we shall do the same under his son.

Henry Martyn, who had been listening in silence until then, looked up from his place next to Agnes and addressed Sir Joselin. You had better be mindful of your images, he said.

I caught William's glance and knew that both of us were seeing the same images in mind-sight: the lights left burning at the sepulchre, the coins and little tokens at the lost altar of Saint Thomas, and at Saint Margaret's feet, the girdle in its casket and the women labouring in childbirth to whom it gave strength and hope.

A western wind is blowing now, flinging birds across the sky like bonfire cinders. Thanks be to God, or to the Earl of Cumberland, that Hugh has leave to stay here until Lady Day at least, and maybe a while longer.

❧

Prayers to be said by my mourners on the first, third, seventh and thirtieth day after my death:

At their uprising five paternosters, five Aves and a creed in Latin. Then to go to the church of Saint Margaret and there hear the mass in the new chapel. When the mass is ended, those that can to read Dirige and De Profundis at my tomb. At night-time, on their knees, Our Lady's Psalter.

And may the Lord God bless you and keep you in faith, now and forever, amen.

In the month of March, a Sunday

Roland, Hugh and I were leaving the church together with Marmion after this morning's mass when Cadd the warden stopped us. He wanted to know if there was money in the will for an almshouse, as he believed had been promised years ago. Marmion said that he did not think so but the funeral doles had been extremely generous and there would always be help for the poorest in the parish, as there had been in the lifetime of the lord. Cadd agreed that the lord had indeed been a charitable man and that Dame Joan had never left a sickbed unvisited in the village. But, as we must have heard, the enclosure of the common wasteland for a deer park had aroused much anger, and some in the village were calling it theft. In truth, it had already made for hardship – the widow of the swineherd John, left with four mouths to feed when he died at Christmas, had been seen in Church Street begging for bread. And this at a time when the visiting preacher was drawing an ever-larger crowd to hear him inveighing against rich folk who build themselves great tombs and would have lavish funerals, with pomp and finery, which, to his mind at least, go against the nature of death.

William Clare joined us while Cadd was speaking and listened to what he said. Cadd told us that of all the villagers Goodge the wheelwright was the most persuaded by the preacher, whom he was now sheltering in his own house, and in consequence was liable to stir up further trouble. Besides, although we were distant from London and the doings of kings, yet we were not deaf to rumour. He would even go so far as to say that rumour could be truth and grow as loud as thunder, especially if, as it was said, the country once again was going to war.

War against which foe? Hugh asked, but Cadd did not know. All he did know was that some voices were raised and he felt we should be warned.

Marmion thanked him for his forethought, promising aid to John's widow, and Cadd left us. When he was out of ear-shot, Marmion said: I predicted this would happen. I told my lord cousin that the times were out of joint for his endeavour. Nowadays, it is the poor box that counts, not airy prayers for the dead.

But, surely both? said William. When I spoke to the lord before he died, he did say that he had made provision for poor relief.

Yes he had, Marmion said, but not for almshouses or perpetual support. His sole bequest in perpetuity will go to you. Or, rather, to you and to your ilk, in saecula saeculorum.

Let us pray, Hugh said.

William said to Marmion: there is one thing I know. And that is that we cannot judge the dead. What was in his soul was in his soul and only God can read it clearly. If he believed he was in need of perpetual intercession, then that was his belief.

But would you be his intercessor if he did not pay you?

Yes. I would pray for anyone in need.

Then why should he have spent so much money on his masses? Roland asked.

Because he was a worldly man and he knew that priests must eat. Think of it as a form of charity, if you wish. And remember that in the works he caused to be done in the church, he meant

to give a lasting gift to the poor and the rich alike. When he paid
for all that costly glass, it was not simply for his sake but for ours.

Uncle Marmion, Hugh burst out, why do you doubt him?
When he brought William here, he did not merely bring his own
cantor but also a second teacher for the children in the parish,
a choirmaster, a music master for Agnes and a much-needed
assistant for Sir Joselin. Would you do without all these?

Of course not, Marmion said. That's a foolish question. But
the fact remains that the times are on the march and it behoves
us to listen to the drumbeat.

⁂

Five works of mercy: to feed the hungry, to give drink to the
thirsty, to visit the sick, to ransom the captive, to bury the dead.

The twenty-fifth day of March, the first day of the year of Our Lord 1547

I am watching Agnes now while we sit with Joan in the upper chamber; she is singing softly to Titus and rocking him like a baby in her arms. Like a doll. She seems like a child with her plaything, an innocent child, but she is a grown woman and at other times I think I see the look in her eyes and the dreamy satisfied half-smile that women sometimes have when they remember pleasure.

Yesterday was the month's mind, the thirtieth day, the removal of the black pall, the final tolling of the bell. Today is Lady's Day and we are in suspension here, as if there were a wall of glass between us and the outside world, as if we were forgotten, as if we were neither quick nor dead but encased in ice like the carp in the fishpond in the winter. Waiting for what? I do not know. Hugh has had a letter ordering him to return to Lord Cumberland in the first week of April, and William has gone to Hereford, where his mother lies with a badly broken hip. The blackthorn is in flower once more, and the blackbird singing, but these signs of spring are at odds with a household looking backwards and uncertain of the future. Black-gowned lawyers come and go and cluster in conclave with Marmion like a murder of crows, and no one talks to anyone except in whispers.

When a great tree falls, the saplings that surrounded it are shocked by new exposure to the sun. In time, with grace, they too will flourish and grow tall. But meanwhile we are like mistletoe that dies when its host is felled, or like sailors, uncaptained and navigating in the starless dark.

Who is the head of this household? I was in the room with Joan when she told Marmion that Henry had received more than enough bed and board gratis and should be asked to leave. Besides, she was beginning to fear that she might have been wrong about the little game between Henry and Agnes; she should have paid more heed to Lady Alice, who had warned months ago that it was getting out of hand. But she had dismissed it as harmless dallying and had trusted Henry to be honourable, as befits a guest. Of late, Joan said, I have had reason to be doubtful.

Marmion agreed with her but reminded us both that Henry was here at Roland's pleasure and Roland had promised he could stay. What is Henry's hold over Roland, Joan wondered, but Marmion did not know.

I should be the one to tell Henry to leave, I thought, and was ashamed I did not say so.

Rose Sunday

Laetamini cum Jerusalem, et exsultate in ea, rejoice and all that love her: be joyful, you who mourned, that you may suck, and be filled at her consoling breasts, and now the baby begins to show; I shall not be able to hide it for much longer. Susan is already making sly remarks. I mystify myself by my desire to keep it secret; among my reasons, apart from shyness, may be that the thread that binds the baby to me is still as fine as gossamer and if it breaks, I will want to be alone with my loss. When I feel the child quicken, I shall know that it has a chance to live. Meanwhile, I scarcely dare to breathe. New life is as frail as an eggshell, as contingent as dandelion seeds on the wind.

⁂

Today's gospel tells of the woman taken in adultery, in the very act, said the scribes and the Pharisees who would have stoned her to death. Where was the man caught in the act with her? Children and apprentice boys shy stones at cocks in Shrovetide; a cruel way for fowl or woman to die.

I asked Sir Joselin if he knew what words Christ wrote on the ground that day, and he said that no one knew, it was a mystery, although some doctors of the Church believe he made a list of the accusers' sins, so that they would read them and be shamed. That sounds too lawyerly to me; I would rather think he wrote the woman's name in his book of dust.

I am missing Hugh. And William Clare, who is still in Hereford helping his sister to tend their injured mother, the other brothers living at a distance. Joselin told us that the sister was weak from recent childbirth, and with five more children needed William's help. The parish was the poorer without him, especially on the brink of Holy Week, Joselin also said.

·❧·

Agnes was complaining that she could not have new clothes for Easter because so much has been spent on our gowns of mourning black that they must be worn at least another month. Shall I be married in a midnight gown? she whined, and Joan scolded her for talking nonsense. She should not be thinking such ridiculous thoughts and her father less than two months in the grave. And Agnes opened her eyes wide and said she was not talking nonsense but the truth. I must be married soon, she said, mustn't I, little Titus?

Nonsense or not, this bold declaration spurred me to seek Sir Joselin's advice. Knowing that he would have to be in church for most of every day this week, to hear the annual confessions of the parish before Easter, I went in the late afternoon. The last of the day's penitents, Ann Brakespeare, the blacksmith's wife, was still sitting with him and so I stayed where I could not hear what she was saying, near the altar of Saint Margaret. On it were a posy of primroses and a silver penny. No one else was there.

As Ann left, the old priest rose stiffly from his seat to greet me; of late he has been limping badly. Have you come to confess? he asked crossly. It is almost time for supper.

No. Well, maybe yes. But first to ask you about Agnes.

You know I cannot tell you what she tells me as her confessor.

No, no, I only want to know what to do about Henry Martyn, with whom she is besotted.

Love is a gift from God.

But I do not think that he loves her. I think he plays with her, as she plays with her pet. And besides, we both know that her father would have forbidden their marriage.

Well, that's out of his hands now, I must say.

Then in whose hands should the matter be?

Yours, I suppose. But can you be sure that the young man does not love her? Love can take strange forms.

I can't be sure. I can only trust my feelings and they tell me that there is something wrong.

You should pray for better guidance. It would be quite wrong to sunder a couple who love in goodness and faith. But you could also talk to Roland. It seems to me that he and Master Martyn are very close.

I will do so. But good faith is exactly the question. Is Henry acting in it or for a baser motive? Will you talk to him?

He will not talk to me. Have you ever seen Henry at mass here, apart from your husband's funeral?

Is that not another reason why he should go?

If it were my feelings that carried weight, I would rather see the back of him. But my feelings are beside the point. There are other considerations here. Speak to Roland. Now, are you confessing or not?

I will come back tomorrow.

Dominus te benedicat, child, he said. I know you have a loving heart.

Eastertide

Passion Week. Sheaves of willow sanctified and blessed for the procession of the palms, a wooden cross in the sunlit churchyard, the children of the choir, gloria, laus et honor, a rush for scattered singing-cakes and flowers. The painted veil over the rood that was strung up on Ash Wednesday, torn down to show the suffering Lord. Maundy Thursday, the altars stripped and washed with wine and water, swept with a broom of birch twigs. On Good Friday we crawled up the nave on hands and knees to kiss the foot of the cross. Every one of us bare-legged and unshod on the clay. When he died, Christ gave a loud cry; at the sixth hour there was darkness over the whole land.

Then Sir Joselin, divested, wearing nothing but a surplice, fetching Thursday's reserved host from the tabernacle, shrouding it in white linen, carrying it reverently to the alabaster statue of the dead Christ, placing it in the heart-shaped hollow in the bier, locking it there behind its iron grille. The real presence in the stone, the living God in his white tomb. Over it the servers draped the same black velvet pall that had covered my lord my husband's tomb for the thirty days after he was buried. The sepulchre now surrounded by lit candles that will burn there until Easter morning, and a continual watch kept on it.

❧

After the mass on Friday, Joan asked me outright: why is your belly swelling when you appear so pale and sickly? Are you ill?

I am not ill, I am with child, I said. I knew that to dissemble would be useless, Joan could not be fooled, and anyway, when I spoke the words out loud, I liked their sound.

She gasped and her hands flew to her mouth. O Heavens above! O merciful God! I would never have thought it of you, Lady Alice. What shall we do? Poor girl! Artemisia, tansy, pennyroyal in cinnamon water. I could prepare the draught for you but be warned that if the babe is quickening already and you drink it, you will be in mortal sin.

What are you saying, Joan?

How much more open must I be? Do not make me spell it out.

I stared at her in disbelief. Do you think I wish to be rid of the child? I asked. How could you think that, Joan?

Stop there and say nothing more. If I conspire wittingly with you, I too will put my soul in mortal danger. But if I honestly believe that all you need is a dose to bring on your late courses and there is no new heartbeat in you, my conscience will be clear. So tell me if you want the draught or no, but tell me nothing else.

Joan, you do not hear me and I will not stay to hear you any longer.

I left her in the still-room and went straight out to the river, in my thin shoes and uncloaked, needing to get as far from Joan's foul suspicions as I could. Even in my early bridal days I had never felt so much alone. What had I expected? That Joan, who was the nearest I had to woman-friend, would share my joy and help me to get ready for the birth? Yes, I had hoped for that. I would have told her soon, in any case, before she asked me, for now the child is stirring in my womb. It lives.

The river calmed me a little with its quiet song and cleared a place in my mind for wiser thought. I saw that in her own way Joan had been trying to help and that I should not have been so angry with her. But I was still deeply puzzled by her supposition. I am not a child; I am aware that some maids do resort to desperate remedies for a plight not of their choosing, but a married woman who longs for a child is surely not among them. Rather she should be prescribed the cordials and the delicate foods that will nurture the baby and help it to grow strong.

Well, I may not be a child but I certainly was a fool. It had never crossed my mind till then that anyone would question the baby's fatherhood. I am a woman who has only known one man, and the question cut me to the core. I thought the family would be glad, but as it turned out, for differing reasons, most of them were not.

The days are becoming lighter and each is longer than the last. Every tree is in green leaf and there are swallows in the sky. This Easter Saturday was warm and bright. I walked to the river again and stopped at the weir before the mill to watch the tumbling water, and in my womb the baby leapt like a little fish. Greetings, I said. I love you. I will look after you. We shall be two and I not alone, you have changed my mourning into dancing.

I am sorry for my anger yesterday, I later said to Joan. She said she understood that I must be in dreadful agitation and forgave me. But afterwards she took me aside and whispered in my ear: so tell me then, who is the father? And when I said who should it be but my lord my husband, she still looked doubtful. How could it be? she asked.

Must I tell her – tell all – what we did on Saint Lucy's Eve, how I lay with him in the dark?

He was, I said, and you must believe me. I swear I speak the truth. But I do not need to share my privateness with you or anybody else.

She was not convinced. I think it wiser that no one but my husband Marmion should know about the baby for the present, she said. Let us keep it as our secret.

⁂

The sun dances for joy when it rises on Easter Sunday morning, Christus resurrexit, alleluia, alleluia, how was it that the soldiers guarding the sepulchre lost the King, when the stone was there? Our church is ablaze with light, sunlight streaming through the windows onto the heads of the faithful kneeling side by side before the rood screen to receive their rights, and light from candles at the altars and the tombs. Hoc est enim corpus meum, solace in this vale of tears, journey-money for the pilgrims, alleluia and amen.

It is never easy to find Roland on his own, but I obeyed Sir Joselin when at last I did. He was in the stable yard, leading out his beautiful black horse. Blood brothers – man and animal – with their shining hair and the proud lines of their mouths.

Henry's intentions towards Agnes, he asked, in response to my question, who knows? What does love mean, anyway? Does any man love anyone better than he loves himself? We must all look out for ourselves, and the Devil take the hindmost.

But Roland!

I hear what you say. Perhaps Henry has trespassed somewhat on our generosity, but is it not an act of mercy to shelter the homeless? At this Eastertide, may we not do so a little longer? At least till Pentecost, to give him time to find somewhere else to go?

In the month of April

What happened in the days that followed Easter eclipsed even the matter of my baby, at least as far as Joan and Marmion were concerned. The first was that Titus died. Gradually he lost the power of his limbs and then the light in his eyes; in his final days he lay crumpled on a pillow, shivering but otherwise barely moving. Agnes nursed him with a fierce devotion. She had wanted to keep him in her bedchamber but, accepting that he needed the warmth of a steadily burning fire at night, allowed him to be moved to the hall. Joan made her leave him there when it grew late, and go upstairs to sleep, but nevertheless she would still creep back in the middle of the night. So when she found him stiff and dead one morning, after a night that she had slept through by mistake, she blamed herself and would not be consoled. We'll buy you another monkey, Roland said, but his offer made her weep the harder. If it were a child who died, she said, would you replace it with another at once and grieve no longer?

Then it came to the question of burial. When the dogs die they are thrown on the midden, but this would not do for Titus. A little pit dug in a corner of the orchard seemed the right place for the corpse, but Agnes had other plans. Telling no one – except for Henry, as I later learned – she sought out the gravedigger in the village and ordered him to lift the stone that sealed the opening to her parents' tomb. The gravedigger, John Verney, went to Simm, and Simm, knowing that this command could not be fulfilled, came straight to me.

I tried to soften the message. I promised a ceremony at a grave in the orchard and flowers to strew on it. But Agnes was immovable, and I asked Sir Joselin to talk to her. He explained that an animal, however deeply loved, could not be laid in holy ground.

But Titus is carved on my mother's tomb, she argued, so why should he not be in it?

Because, unlike yours, his soul is not immortal. And unlike you, he will not rise again. To your mother – to all of us when we die – the grave is like a bed in which our bodies rest until the voice of the archangel calls them on the last day, just as the cock crow wakes us now while we are living.

But I believe that I will see Titus in heaven.

Well, God loves his entire creation and, as his is the law of the kingdom of heaven, who are we to say what we shall find there? But on earth it is against the law to bury an animal in a consecrated church.

Do you not know that the law is changing? Are you too old and blind to see that?

That law will not change.

William will disagree with you when he comes back, Agnes said.

I do not think he will.

When the priest had left us, I rebuked Agnes for her discourtesy to him. I had to; it could not go unremarked. She did not care. You forget that this is my house, she said, and I am mistress of it. And he is a stupid old man.

I let that pass. And as the creature's body was beginning to decay, the next day she allowed it to be placed in a hole dug hard beside the wall of the churchyard. When William comes, I will rebury him, she vowed.

The next disturbance was instigated by the wandering preacher. Or, since he has ceased to wander, it would seem, perhaps he should be called the new incomer to the village. No longer satisfied with his daily pulpit by the water pump, he took his gospel of dissent to the very door of the church. While Sir Joselin was saying the morning mass of Thursday, when the willow was still green in every house and the candles were still burning at the sepulchre day and night, the preacher took up a position in the porch to denounce what he termed the idolatry within. Images are lewd lessons painted by the Devil, in his words. Poor Joselin came out to find a band of his own parishioners clustered at the open entrance, cheering on the firebrand. The people soon dispersed when they saw the priest, but later in the day someone unseen daubed a streak of pitch on the white marble bier of the dead Christ. For now, that sacrilege has united the most part of the village in outrage – and the transgressor must have been either half-hearted or a coward to have spared the image and only marked its bed – but how long will that last? Marmion has heard that all the churches in the land are to receive visitations to confirm that their proceedings keep within the letter of the law. Whose law? As Agnes rudely but rightly said: the laws are changing now.

These are confusing and unfathomable times. When I asked Roland for his opinion, he said: Jesus was a rabble-rouser too. That's why Herod feared him.

I see that could be true. I wish that Hugh were here, with his untrammelled vision.

The monkey and the turbulent preacher had fewer immediate consequences for the household than the third event. Yesterday,

Saturday, Agnes did not come down to breakfast and Joan, ever motherly and mindful of her, went up to her bedchamber to see if all was well. It was quiet and dark within, Susan having risen hours ago, and Joan was worried. Afterwards she told me she had been afraid that Agnes might have taken poison. If her seeming composure since her father's death had been deceptive, the loss of Titus could have tipped her over the edge into despair. So it was with caution that Joan drew back the bed-curtains, to be met by the sight of Agnes fast asleep in the embrace of Henry Martyn. The lovers woke, of course, and Henry scuttled shamefacedly away with his shirt clutched to him, and Joan berated Agnes roundly. But what is done is done; Agnes is undone and must be betrothed at once. Now Henry is firmly lodged here, like a burr in the fur of a dog.

Do you sleep like the dead? Joan railed at Susan. So soundly that this knave could steal into a maiden's bed unbeknownst to you? Did you not hear them at their unlawful business?

It seems that she did. Susan wept and protested that she had only been obeying the young mistress's instructions and indeed was trying to save her from doing herself worse harm. Joan was not the only one to fear for Agnes, and the girl had insisted that Henry alone could save her sanity. But Susan's good intentions were not enough to save her and now she is dismissed. And Joan is beside herself because she fears that Agnes may be pregnant.

William Clare returned to the village this evening, straight into this commotion. I have not seen him yet. I don't know what he can do to help, but we are all glad to have him back. Sir Joselin has not yet recovered completely from his illness of the winter and I know he has been struggling to carry out his duties on his own.

The first day of the month of May

It is May morning once again but this year it is perishingly cold, and in any case there is no one in the household with a mind for dancing. Except perhaps for Agnes, who remains in a strange and hectic mood, seesawing between troughs of sorrow and heights of giddy rapture. And no wonder: such ups and downs that she has endured would upset the most evenly balanced of girls. Mourning robes one day, and a bridal gown the next. She is mad with the first flush of love and now that her passion is licit by default, she cannot help but flaunt it. Last night she laughed as she recalled that a year ago she might have risen at dawn to gather the morning dew but that nothing now would drag her early out of bed!

What Henry feels is still a riddle to me. He and Agnes have made their contract of betrothal, the timing of the marriage itself conditional on when she formally inherits her estate. That day should not be long in coming now – Joan tells me that Marmion is near to concluding his difficult affairs with the lawyers. Meanwhile Agnes and Henry may live as man and wife. And I, with no knowing what may lie ahead, daily loosen my laces and sing to my dancing baby where no one else can hear.

❧

William backed Sir Joselin on the question of Titus's burial, to no one's surprise but Agnes's, and now she is up in arms against

225

him too. I suspect that in the end she will prevail on somebody to lift the heavy stone and help her deposit the dug-up remains of her beloved pet in secret. Good luck to her; what does it matter if an animal's bones rattle around with the bones of her brothers and sisters? What the eye does not see, the heart does not grieve, as the saying goes.

In the month of May, a Tuesday

There was a great storm last night and the wind is still howling like a soul in grief this morning. It has stripped the apple trees of their sweet blossom and the air is full of whirling petals, the ground as thickly covered in them as if it had snowed.

In the village the preacher's following grows. So too does a rumour that my lord my husband committed a sin in his youth that was so grave it could never be forgiven, a sin that cried to heaven for vengeance – the murder of his brother, even. A lifetime since of attempted penance – witness all that almsgiving and that chapel-building – was entirely fruitless, for the wages of sin are death. Instead of salvation, what did he get? A sickness such as no one had ever known before, that slowly turned a living man to stone. Condign punishment for a mortal sin!

William, preaching at mass on Sunday in place of Sir Joselin, tried to suppress this slander elliptically, rather than risk heaping coals upon it with a direct challenge. Remember the blind man Jesus healed, he said. What did Jesus say when they asked him if it were the man's own sins or the sins of his fathers that had made him blind from birth? Do you remember his answer? It was that neither the man nor his parents had sinned but that in him the works of God should be made manifest. Insofar as the works of God are beyond man's understanding, they are also beyond question, but what is not in question is the boundlessness of God's mercy. Is there a sin beyond forgiveness? Yes. But only one, and that is the sin against the Holy Ghost: dying stubbornly unrepentant. That is, deliberately to harden one's heart against God's mercy and in despair reject the promise of salvation. And even then – who knows but that our compassionate God may choose to keep the miraculous gates of heaven open?

You would think there could be no dissenting from this gentle message. I thought so then, but afterwards I saw that some in the now-divided parish did take deadly note of William's words and used them as a weapon.

※

The king of France is dead and war again is rumoured. On Thursday, a letter came from Hugh that sent a splinter of fear right through me. He said we must be careful, and I could tell that he had been careful himself in what he wrote, having no way of knowing whether the letter might be intercepted and unsealed on its way, but the closeness between us made it easy for me to read between the lines and see what he had left unsaid. Having been in London at the king's Court, and afterwards in Winchester, he observed that both places were quieter of a Sunday than he had expected, for bell-ringing has mainly been outlawed. *We have grown so used to bells pealing at all hours in our village that in those towns the silence was unnerving. Processions are soon to be forbidden too, in churches on Sundays and everywhere on feast days, so as kindly to spare the people from being jostled or annoyed or competing with each other who should lead them. So, Alice, you need no longer muddy your shoes in the fields at Rogationtide or on any other holy day – and nor need you bother with your rosary, for beads are also superstitious nonsense. And moreover so are any painted or carved images abused by ignorant worship.*

THE BOOK OF DAYS

I knew that Hugh would never dismiss the old ways as fit only for the ignorant and foolish, for he has always loved them as the heartbeat of our lives. All our days are measured in our prayers, our years in the feasts and the seasons. What do those who would ban them know of the ever-turning wheel – Advent, Christmas, Lent, Easter, Whitsun, spring, summer, autumn, winter, the new grain and the old leaf, the moonlight and the falling snow? Does the wind blow through palaces and throne rooms as it does through the hovels of the village, do the rains fall alike on the poor and the rich? The women of this village will never own necklaces of rubies; they will only ever have their precious rosary beads. I want to ask the kings and the princes of the Church, who have never known a day of hunger, why they should begrudge the joys of the humble, when they are so rare. A sheep roasted after harvest, a goose at Christmas, flowers strewn along the way at Corpus Christi, meet reward for faith and arduous labour. Why would those whose walls are hung with cloth of gold deny the pleasures of an image to men and women who otherwise would only see the ordinary things of everyday before their eyes? People who cannot read must learn their Scripture from their own church walls and in that way find the stable at Bethlehem and the cross at Calvary as familiar as their own homes and their fields, while never straying more than five miles from their doors. You who take so much for granted, with your sound walls, rich food and fine jewels – and books, especially books – do you truly begrudge the people of this or any other lowly parish their little scraps of coloured glass, their painted saints, their confidence in prayer? How cruel you are, if you do.

Needing time to consider the contents of this letter on my own, I did not show it to Hugh's brother at once, or to anyone else in the household. Might the new laws be enforced with rigour in the large towns but not in out-of-the-way villages like this one – out of sight and therefore out of mind – or were we in immediate danger? It was not yet Rogation Sunday, and besides Hugh had said processions would be interdicted, not that they had been prohibited already. As for bells, well, who would ever hear them apart from those who lived nearby? But then I remembered Marmion talking of promised visitations, and I foresaw a brood of prying officers snaking out across the kingdom to hunt down every misplaced candle, every meagre offering of brass button or copper coin in order to condemn the ones who put them there and the priests who led them.

And then my fear was great. I had to speak to William Clare, and speak to him alone. There was nobody apart from him and Joselin in whom I could wholly trust – and Joselin was tired and infirm. But to find William on his own was hard. Agnes has refused to have her music lessons ever since she quarrelled with him over Titus and so he no longer visits the house every day and seldom comes to dine. The villagers are glad to feed him, especially the women, the mothers of the children whom he helps to teach, and he is often in their company or, if not with them, then with Sir Joselin in the house they share. Whatever time of day he sings his mass of remembrance in the chantry, there will be people there to see him elevate the host. But in the church was my only hope of finding him without calling attention to myself.

I went there early this morning. For a while I had the church to myself and I knelt in its stillness, watching the daylight colouring the painted windows by degrees, listening to the small sounds of scuttling things and creaking wood, breathing in the smell that is only of this one place: damp and clay and rushes, incense, tallow, stone. I said the mandatory prayers for my dead husband but as far as it was possible I stopped my mind from straying to the image of his decomposing body barely yards away from me, under our shared tomb. Someone had placed a candle near it, as if it were an altar. By its companion, Christ's tomb, on the other side of the chancel, there were three candles guttering, slowly dripping down to stubs, and with them a wreath of hazel. Then Cadd's wife came with Ann Brakespeare to sweep and tidy, and soon afterwards Cadd himself to make ready for the masses. We talked about the wintry weather, some lambs of Cadd's that had been lost to crows, and Ann's daughter, whose baby was expected any minute now. I saw the women eyeing my belly but neither spoke of it. Cadd's wife, Marjorie, told me my maid Susan was angry that she had been put out of her wages, protesting that she had done nothing to deserve it. I suppose she has told the whole village the reason why. I said that I missed her, which is true.

More people came. Cadd said that Sir William would be singing the early mass, Sir Joselin the mass at noon. Not long to wait. A deep unease was in me.

William at the altar in the chantry, the music of his voice, the sacred presence incarnate in his raised hand, a sudden ray of sunshine from the east; ite missa est, a blessing on the bowed heads in dismissal. The worshippers were slow to go, lingering to speak to William or to pray for their intentions at the altars. Ann was the last of them, having spent a long time on her knees before Saint Margaret, begging her to aid the safe delivery of her daughter's baby, lighting candles. She placed a scrap of scarlet ribbon on the altar when she left. I stayed leaning against the arch of the chantry until William had said goodbye to her and turned to me.

He said: I am glad to see that you are warmly dressed today and have not forgotten your cloak.

I showed him the letter. He does not know Hugh as well as I do, but they have spent enough time in each other's company for William to be sure of his good faith. He was not surprised by what he read.

This pulling and pushing, this ebbing and flowing has been going on for years now, he said, but when I heard that our arch-bishop had named himself the messenger of Christ, I knew the direction of the tide was fixed.

What does it mean for us?

It means that we should mend our ways or else risk breach-ing the new laws. It means no candles, no offerings, no images, no bells, no palms, no processions, no holy water, no psalters, no rosaries, and although Hugh does not say so – and may not know – in the end it will mean no sacramental bread, no altars and no more prayers for the souls of the dead.

Then what shall we do? No singing for our dead? Must they go down into silence without us? But what can be done except abide by the edicts of the Crown? Everybody knows what hap-pens to those who dare to question power.

Well, if we obeyed all the king's decrees, most parishioners would grumble at first, but then as time went by they would accept that things do change. They would find other ways to be mindful of the dead and then they would forget what went before. Others would rejoice to see old customs overthrown – indeed some would want reform to go much further – but the one person who will never allow the old rites to be suppressed is Sir Joselin.

Because he is too ancient and too stubborn to see the benefits of change?

No, because he believes in the unchanging law of God. And because he holds that it is only by long-established usage that men escape the dangers of delusion. Or, to put it another way, authority comes with centuries of practice, not with changing fashions. Because he believes in the unity of Christendom – one people, of many kinds and many nations, joined together in one commonwealth with God. And, above all, because he knows that the imposition of new creeds by fear and force is evil in itself. A man cannot trim his own conscience to suit the whims of another, even if that other is a king. Sir Joselin has lived his life in the assurance that his practices and his beliefs were sanctioned by a thousand years or more of shared tradition. Why would he now bow down before a handful of reformers, whose care may be more for their pockets than their souls, and a boy-king who is their puppet?

Shush. You must not speak like this.

You see? That goes straight to the heart of the matter. I must not speak my mind – or my conscience or my heart – because a single word may be heard as treason and the speaker sent to the stake.

I don't want you to die.

I have no intention of dying. Probably we will find a middle way that will satisfy the parish and still stay within the law. But Joselin truly believes in the power of signs and emblems. He says that God is like a mountain so steep that none can take its measure and so we must have handholds on our way.

Like stepping stones, maybe?

Yes, like that. So every candle flame, every note of music, every flower left as an offering at an altar is a step or a rung on a ladder as tall as the sky. And every inch walked in pilgrimage or procession is a token of that long, long journey.

Do you believe this too?

Well. Sir Joselin has the questionless faith of a saint. No, that's not how to say it, he has won that sure faith step by step, testing each along the way.

It is true what he says about vastness. Trying to understand God is harder than numbering each star in the sky.

That is why he gives us saints, go-betweens with human faces.

Or a baby in a manger in a stable?

Exactly.

Then without warning William sank to his knees before me. Like that baby, all babies are the words of God, he said. Will you let me bless the one that you are carrying? He lifted his hands and laid them lightly on my belly, cupping the swelling within. O Lord, guard the life that is yours; defend it from all the craft and spite of the pitiless foe, he prayed, and watch over it from Sion.

> O Lord heed my prayer
> And let my cry come unto you,
> in nomine Patris, et Filii,
> et Spiritus Sancti.
> Amen.

The seventh Sunday after Easter

It is Whitsun, but we do not have the trapdoor in the ceiling of the church that my husband promised and we did not have a flock of snowy doves at mass. Last week someone unknown left a dead rat on the floor of the church beside the alabaster tomb. Or perhaps the creature died a natural death there or was dragged in by a cat? Marmion is taking no chances. Already on guard after the damage done to the sepulchre – and no one in the village will say who made that black streak – he has told Brakespeare to fit an iron grille or gate at the entrance of the chantry. It will be kept locked.

William counselled against it. To bar the people from entering the new chapel would be to pile fuel on the anger simmering in the village, he said, but Marmion argued that it was his bounden duty to protect the tomb. Otherwise, how else can we prevent some madman from taking a hammer to it or coating the whole thing in pitch?

These are the honeysuckle-scented days of June, steeped in golden sunlight, and yet I am shivering from a fear yet unbodied, like a storm cloud in the distance, and I know that others sense it too.

The eleventh day of the month of June

It sickens me to write of what was said to me this afternoon. Lawyers were here, and when they had left in a whisk of black gowns after dinner, Marmion called Roland, Agnes and me to the upper chamber. Henry came as well, unbidden. Marmion said that the business of inheritance was settled now at last, insofar as possible, given unknown outcomes.

You speak in riddles, Roland said.

No, I speak quite plain. The argument between the lawyers and trustees has been about remainders – contingent remainders, that is to say people not yet born. My lord cousin's will, made upon the death of his first wife the Lady Agnes, left his estate entailed on the true heirs of his own body begotten or, if none such survived, to his two close nephews, the elder taking precedence, and this was tail general, inclusive of daughters, if there were no living sons. He did not revise the will in the remainder of his lifetime. Therefore, the estate will pass to his legitimate children in the following order: male, and thereafter female. Upon the death of the last surviving child, if that child has no issue, then to Roland and the issue of his line.

Henry interrupted. What need is there to spell this out, when we know that my betrothed Agnes is his only living child?

Indeed, Marmion agreed. And she would inherit if, as I said, there were no sons. But a son there still may be.

Three pairs of eyes flashed to my swelling belly. None but William and Joan have yet remarked on it aloud to me but anyone with eyes must have observed it, for it grows now like a summer melon.

Agnes, who had been sitting, stood then. Yes, so, she is a whore, she spat, and Henry laughed. Roland remained still.

Agnes, your father knew that Alice was with child, said Marmion. He told me so in his last words upon his deathbed and he bade me then remember the provisions of his will.

But that is preposterous, for he was sick and cannot have been the father of her child, Henry objected.

They looked at me again, this time Marmion too.

He was, I said, but anything else that I might have tried to say was drowned by Agnes screeching.

That whore's child is William Clare's, and everybody knows it.

There was utter silence then, as if we had been turned to stone. Then Agnes began to cry and Henry put his arms around her. Trying, I suppose, to pour the oil of reason on the tempestuous scene, Marmion said: if the child is a girl, Agnes, you will be the sole heir as you expected, and it will make no difference then who is the baby's father.

But if it is a boy?

Ah, well then.

Then I will be disinherited by a bastard?

I left that room and went to my own, where I will stay alone. The late sunlight is streaming through the window onto the green silk coverlet, turning the air to dust-flecked gold, making mock of my wintry mourning and my prayers. Prayers for a daughter; let her be.

Be very careful, Joan said tonight when she brought me food. If it should happen that Agnes gets nothing but a daughter's portion, Henry may yet renege on his betrothal vow. You know yourself that he is ambitious and I daresay he finds little Agnes's expected fortune fairer than her face. And she will be a hellcat if he leaves her. Dangerous to you. Should I fetch my gold ring and dangle it over your belly? Or Mother Wright the midwife may be able to foretell?

The sixteenth day of the month of June

Corpus Christi. On this same feast day a year ago, my lord my husband walked upon his own two legs to the great gate of his demesne and beheld the flesh of God. Today his own flesh is flaking off his stiffened bones. Can he now see the face of God or does he burn still in the cleansing fire? Requiescat in pace, you have been dead four months now but still there are nights when I wake in the dark hours and hear you breathing quietly beside me. Then I dare not stretch out my hand lest it should meet your stone-cold body. Can you shield me from your grave? As well ask if you can bind the cluster of the Pleiades. Or who pours water on the sea?

I shall not walk in the procession this morning, I shall keep to this room, our room, I and the child who is your child and who will be born in less time than you have been lying dead. There is a measure of safety for the two of us here, behind a locked door, although a confusion of raised voices reaches me through the open window; shouts and loud protesting from the direction of the boundary wall.

The last days of the month of June

It was fire that drove me from our bedchamber after my days of solitude, on the night of that day of remembering, the night of Corpus Christi, flames leaping where they should not be, at the edge of the near field, competing with the lingering twilight of the season. From the window I watched the fire spreading as fast as a running deer. Then there came a loud banging at the door, so urgent that it could not be ignored. I unlocked the door to Lambert who beckoned me to follow him, and because it was him and his look was so afraid, I went with him to the upper chamber.

They were all there: Roland, Marmion and Joan, Agnes and Henry, with anxious faces and the remains of their supper on the table. I had seen none of them but Joan since the day the lawyers left and I retreated to my room. She rose to embrace me but Agnes neither greeted me nor met my eyes.

What is it that is burning? I asked.

The processional cross, Marmion replied. And all the wooden fencing round the new park.

Where are the priests?

We don't know. In the church perhaps. We have sent men to search for them but it is not safe for us to leave the house ourselves.

Then was it not an accident, the fire?

It was deliberate, Roland said. They are saying that somebody stole the holy cross from the churchyard where it was standing after this morning's procession, set it alight and used it as a torch to burn our fences down.

That's sacrilege.

Yes, and more than that, it is a crime. When the thief and his accomplices are caught, they will be hanged. The wheelwright and his sons are the ones under suspicion.

And Susan with them, added Joan.

No, not my faithful Susan? That cannot be.

Well, ever since her banishment she has held a grudge against this house. Which I must say I can understand. You remember that Goodge's family took her in when we sent her packing? And now she is to marry the elder son. Those hotheads have fried her brains and left the poor girl addled. Who knows how many others are on their side? Lord, what is to become of us if our own household should rise against us, shall we be burned to death in our beds?

Be more cheerful, Henry said. Now that they have made their protest against the enclosure, they will quieten down. And if you hang one or two as examples, the rest will fall back in line soon enough.

But was it the cross or the fence that was their object? I asked.

Both, Roland and Marmion said with one voice, and Joan covered her face with her hands, praying through her closed fingers: Good Lord have mercy on us all.

But no, Henry argued, surely it was the fence they wished to burn. I believe that the cross was nothing more to them than kindling wood. Besides, by destroying it they were keeping rightly to the letter of the law. For that they might reasonably expect praise not punishment.

What can you mean? asked Joan.

The Act against images and signs. I wonder that you need to ask.

There is no such Act.

Indeed there is, Dame Joan.

No, there is not, not yet. For now there is nothing but the babbling request of an infant king.

The requests of kings are orders in disguise, Marmion said, which made her cry the harder.

So then I stayed in the chamber with them, in a temporary truce. What else could I have done, what should anyone have done that evening? We spent the rest of it in a troubled state of forced inaction: a family divided, at our familiar table, each one alone with our thoughts and fears, and the clamour of voices in the distance as neighbour fought with neighbour or perhaps, as I hoped, helped one another to put out the fire. That was a forlorn hope, as it turned out; in the morning there was nothing left of the new fences, and the deer that had been penned within had all fled into the fields and woods.

If my Lord Richard had been here, Joan said after a long silence, he would have put an end to this insurgence.

Would he though? Henry asked. How would he have done that?

They would never have defied him in the first place, Agnes said.

Henry smiled a strange little smile of private satisfaction. No man will be able to hold back the coming tide, he said.

His words were met with silence. I saw the warning look that Roland gave him but could not read what was in Roland's mind. What is the nature of the contract between these two young men? Or indeed the new contract between Roland and

Marmion? Who is now the master of the household and why should Henry's voice carry weight?

The baby hiccoughed inside me then, perpetual reminder of what there is to live for, how much I could lose. In the tumult, Joan had forgotten to send supper up to me earlier in the evening and suddenly I was hungry. I still wonder that I could think of food at such a time, but there it was: the instinct of a mother to survive, and when I hoped no one was looking, I took a piece of bread from the table. Joan had stopped wailing and was beginning to make an inventory of stores, in case of siege, until Marmion said: wife, there is no call for that.

No word came of the priests that night and all through it fear throbbed in the deep core of my being. If William had been in the churchyard and had seen the men who seized the cross, he would have intervened, and so would have Sir Joselin. They are not cowardly men. Was Henry right? Was the cross nothing to the ones who took it but a piece of seasoned wood? But if he were wrong? If a new tide of righteousness had swept up with it men who owned little but their dreams, and those dreams of equality and freedom, would the priests seem like a barrier to be rode over roughshod? O God, I prayed, save William from the fire. I thought of Anne Askew burning at the stake, sniffing her own flesh roasting, as feasters prick their nostrils at a suckling pig. The stench of burning hair. O William, beautiful, good William, may the Lord preserve you from the fire.

Dawn of the following day, rose-misted, smoke still scenting the air. During the night the others had drifted away to their

beds but I went down to the hall, with the restive dogs, to wait
for the morning and a message from the world beyond. When
it came, with Rafe, one of the serving men, it brought infinite
relief. William was alive. The man said that Sir Joselin had been
in the churchyard after the noon mass of the feast day and had
indeed tried to stop Goodge from pulling down the cross. But
he had been no match for the wheelwright and his sons. In the
tug of war between them, the priest had been easily conquered
and sent sprawling, the poor limping old man. Cadd had arrived
then, with the blacksmith Brakespeare and some others alerted to
Joselin's plight, but too late to rescue the cross and, besides, the
wheelwright's band had been armed with sticks and cudgels. No
one had the stomach for an all-out fight. Consequently, there was
nothing Cadd could do but let the rebellers take the cross they
had uprooted, and help the priest rise from the mud in which he
lay. Naturally Cadd's men had wanted to carry the bruised and
shocked priest to his house, but Sir Joselin would have none of
that and insisted that he must stay in the church. So they had left
him. Sir William, in the meantime, had gone with the children
after the procession and was dining with their families in the
village while the uproar in the churchyard was going on but as
soon as he was told about it, he went directly to the old priest's
aid and now both men were locked inside the church. That is,
they had locked themselves inside it; it must have been hard to
shove the great bolt into its iron hasp, so seldom was it used.

But why did they barricade themselves inside? To save
themselves?

No, in the village they are saying that they did so to save the
tomb. But there are no sure answers yet, for no one knows what
is going on, or who is friend or foe.

I saw them in my mind's eye: the young man and the old, waiting out the evening and the long night in the church. Sunset would have turned the west window fiery gold, but even in midsummer, nights are cold. What might they have found to cover them? Nothing but the altar frontal, and that they would never have defiled. Would there be meat and drink for them? No, unless it had been smuggled in; there would be nothing but the sacred body in the tabernacle and the holy wine. Where did they rest, on the damp ground or on the wooden bench along the wall? Did they speak of earthly things in hushed voices in the dark hours or did they pray their silent prayers alone? At least when night fell they would have had the sanctuary lamp to light them and candles in storage there to burn. Then did they watch the small flames flicker on my husband's effigy and mine during their dark vigil as they listened for angry voices outside their refuge, or for stones thrown through fragile windows or fire leaping at the wooden door, hungry as a lion, seeking ingress?

What now?

Rafe repeated that he did not know for certain, but rumour was that the wheelwright's band meant to hold the two priests hostage. And then it would be for the Lord Roland to pay the ransom they demanded.

This makes no sense. Why? What is it that Goodge wants? The priests have done him no wrong that I know of, not him, nor anyone else. Why Roland?

He shrugged. O Rafe, I cried, what shall we do, how can we save them?

Lady, he said, you must ask that question of my masters.

※

And now it is midsummer's eve, Saint John's eve, the night of fire and magic, a night when this world and the next world meet. These past seven days have been deeply clouded in every way, days of chaos and confusion, days of rain. Rafe was right; it had been the rebels' plan to hold the priests to ransom but Marmion, clear-eyed, hard-headed Marmion, mustered just enough men to drive them away from the churchyard, for a while at least, and they are in retreat, albeit angry still, their fire not quenched but smothered. Sir Joselin and William let themselves out but refused Marmion's exhortation to stay here safely in the house, saying that they had to be in the village with the parishioners who need them. I have not seen either of them yet. Guards are posted at the church, loyal to the household for the moment but perhaps not for much longer. The ground beneath our feet is tilting, as the deck of a ship must do on the high seas in a storm. If we cannot find a rail to cling to, we will all be swept away on a tide of cold salt water.

In the midst of this turmoil Agnes informed the whole household that she was expecting a baby. She said it at dinner, sweetly, in an almost childlike way, as if it meant little more to her than the arrival of a kitten, and as the serving men were there, the news is everywhere already. Joan told me afterwards that Agnes is scarcely more than ten days late and could easily be mistaken. Even so, it makes her solemn marriage more urgent; her child must be born in wedlock to be a rightful heir. That child will be my child's niece or nephew; how strange they are, these new bonds and these shifting times.

And into this disorder Hugh has come, suddenly and unannounced, riding fast and straight up to the door, having travelled through the night from Windsor. I heard the sound of horse's hooves and looked out of the window, saw that it was him and felt a great lift of the heart, my dearest Hugh, bringing, as I thought, a fresh view to our troubles. But my delight became alarm when I heard what he had come to say.

What should we do?

Where is Roland? We must tell him too.

Yes, and Marmion? Marmion is the one who is making the decisions, it seems to me.

But whose side would Marmion take?

The side of law and order?

Well, then he must not know.

I saw them as serpents, those visiting commissioners, winding their menacing way through the counties, forked tongues aflicker, eyes on the prize. Yesterday at Dorchester, this morning at Oxford, tomorrow or the next day they will get to us. And, like serpents, or like kings, they will transfix the hapless creatures they encounter in their path. Lawyers, landlords, priests and farmers, wheelwrights and stewards, all rendered immobile by the power of their scrutiny and the mandate that they hold. And then compelled by those powers to do as the serpents order: to fulfil the requests of a king. Images shattered, reliquaries ground underfoot, splinters of glass scattered across floors, like a hard frost, like stars that have fallen from the skies.

All of us mortals helpless, without agency of our own. Worms to the ploughshare, dandelion heads in the teeth of the wind. We who are subject to rule by fellow mortals must expect the arbitrary, rather than wisdom or mercy, for those are the gifts of the gods.

Roland was nowhere to be found. His groom said that he had ridden out early in the morning, with Master Henry, and had not said where they were going.

Will they be back by dinner?

The boy did not know.

Can we wait till then?

No, we cannot delay, Hugh said. I will go right away to Sir Joselin.

Marmion would say it is dangerous for us to leave the grounds.

Well, but I must. Alice, you stay here.

I want to go with you.

You cannot. Think of the child.

Did Roland tell you?

No, but I have eyes to see.

I wished then that I had written to him about the baby and I said so, but he smiled at me.

It is a marvel, he said. I only wish that my uncle could have known you were with child.

He did know. I told him on the night he died.

He must have been glad.

I hope he was. But no one else is, and your cousin Agnes will not accept that he was the father.

That's absurd! Who does she think the father was?

I cannot repeat her accusation but I have no doubt that she will, as soon as she sees you, and I beg you not to hear her out.

Alice, have I ever doubted you?

Hugh's kindness and trust undid me. All these weeks I had held my head up high, but now I could not help the tears welling.

I must go, he said. There'll be time to talk after I have seen Sir Joselin.

And William Clare?

Yes, if I find them both together.

How long can you stay?

I think only until the day after tomorrow. Meet me in an hour by the great beech. If I find William Clare, I will bring him with me.

I watched him running from the stable yard. Taller and thinner than he was when he left home two months ago; a man now, not a boy, my Hugh. An hour to wait. Far too long but not long enough: what if Hugh were to return with William, if I had to face him in the knowledge that his name and mine had been so shamefully linked? But what if he did not come? Wished never to see me again? O merciful God, how foolish to imagine that I might enter his mind in any way at all. I pictured him meeting Hugh, on the street outside the schoolroom perhaps, with children clustered round him, or in the priests' house, alone; the greetings they would exchange, his dark head bowed to Hugh's fair one, and his hearing Hugh out gravely. It is a pity their lives were not more entwined; they would have loved each other.

Marmion's interdiction on leaving the grounds put the river out of reach or else I would have gone there and let its indifferent waters calm my beating thoughts. Rain began to fall, but I could not return to the house in case I encountered Agnes or Joan, for both would have heard by now that Hugh had come. Where had Roland gone? In the village, people would be gathering green boughs for their doorways; fresh leaves and scented herbs. Kindling for their bonfires too. Fires again tonight. Might these midsummer fires burn away the bitter rage and leave us purged? Yes, but only by a miracle, or magic.

❧

William at the purple beech, no anger in his regard at all but only tenderness; warmth in his greeting: Alice, how do you fare? And the baby? Calm too, despite the danger he was in, steadying Hugh, assuring me that there was nothing to fear now that matters were in hand. Hugh, so tired from riding through the night, mud-stained but standing tall, brave; both men strong and determined. Such comfort to be had from their strength; we are here together and together we will do what must be done. And we will do it tonight. Smoke from Saint John's fires making pillars in the air, midsummer lark-song, raindrops on the beech leaves, raindrops on William's hair.

❦

John Verney the gravedigger has almost finished his work. It is still some hours before midnight and there is a whisper of light in the sky, but the merciful rain that came in the day has thickened it for our sakes and we are no more visible than shadows. Moon-dapple, and the worm-tilled earth gives out its damp rich smell; a tangle of roots gleams white in the murk; nearby, a woodcock startles with a raucous call, and drops of water fall gently from the dark needles of the yew. Hugh is holding my hand. We are at the edge of my daughter's grave, and in the early evening I cut down the moon daisies and cornflowers that grew there. Cadd and Verney know the boundaries of the graves and I believe their promise that hers will stay untouched.

The field fires have been dowsed by the rain but the great bonfire in the village burns still and most people will be by it, drinking and dancing and revelling through the feast-night, careless of happenings in the churchyard. Or so it is hoped. And it is true that few would dare in any case to venture near it on midsummer's eve, for fear of meeting themselves or the ones they love in the ranks of the year's dead to come. I myself am afraid of seeing over my shoulder the silent procession of faint shapes passing one by one into the church – what if my unborn child were there among them? – and I keep my eyes fixed on the ground. We are as safe as we can be at this time, which is to say that we are in danger but ready of necessity to take this chance. Well, I say that *we* are ready. But are we united in our purpose? I am here because of Hugh and William. And they are here for Joselin. I cannot speak for the rest; who can say what a man holds dear but that man himself? Or woman. All I know is that for some, like Joselin, faith is as firm as a rock, and for others – and yes, now perhaps I speak for myself – it is a candle flame borne unshielded in a wind.

Simm is here, with Jack the younger, and John Brakespeare and Cadd, and Lambert too. Lest they were missed at the fires, Marjorie Cadd, forewarned, told her neighbours her husband was sick and Ann Brakespeare, her dear friend, would stay with her to nurse him. John Brakespeare and Jack made sure to be seen at the earlier feasting and John Verney, a widower, is known to be a curmudgeon. In the merriment, who will take the trouble to count heads? And who will ever know what courage these men and their wives have; courage and steadfast faith?

This muster is under Sir Joselin's command. Old and infirm though he may be, he is showing that he can be steely. When he heard what Hugh had come to say, he decided at once what had to be done before the visitation, and he sent immediately for Simm, whom he knew that he could trust. Simm, like Cadd and Brakespeare, is one who holds to the old ways and dismisses the new. Whether they are right or wrong is not a question with a single answer, in my view, and nor is tonight the time to ask it. What is at stake are the beliefs of people who cannot survive in the valley of the shadow of death without hope. The people whose trust lies in things immemorial: places of pilgrimage, relics of saints, and images graven in stone. By what authority can any man say that they are mistaken and that their beliefs are sinful? When the Lord God speaks, man hears what he wants to hear and disregards the Word. Diliges proximum tuum tamquam te ipsum; if we must love our neighbours as we love ourselves, then we should judge them just as gently.

Verney steps up from the shallow pit and plants his spade in the earth. It is agreed that a depth of three feet is enough. At John Verney's signal all the men but Joselin move quietly away and, braving the apparitions, go through the porch into the church. The old priest and I are left alone. This is no place for a woman, he says, you should go home. But he does not argue when I say that I must stay.

Saint Stephen, the patron saint of stonemasons, must have lent a hand himself, for otherwise eight mortal men could not have done what they do in so short a time today. All eight are Christ's pall-bearers now, and even so they struggle with a weight that is greater than any human body. Together they push him onto a makeshift frame, drag him through the church with ropes, lever him over the threshold and haul him over the soft ground of the churchyard on makeshift rollers, until he is balanced at the edge of the pit. In the half-light his stone flesh glows whitely, his eyes are still closed and the fingers of his right hand still shield the wound in his side. For the length of a heartbeat he hangs there, then he falls. And we all look down

at him, in his new grave, our Christ who died and was buried
and now is buried again.

Make haste, says Simm. It will soon be too dark to see.

Wait, I say, and on an impulse break off a spray of yew to
drop into the grave. The scarlet of the incipient berries is lost
in the darkling, but under the ground they will lie with him,
these bright beads of blood and the evergreen leaves of the tree
of the dead.

Verney, Brakespeare and Jack are piling earth back into
the hole as fast as they can and soon the ground is level again,
although the fresh cut will be evident tomorrow. But that is the
intention, and the great task is done.

Come, Hugh says to me, we cannot go back to the village in
a troop, you and I should go before the others. We turn to leave
but Joselin stops us. Alice, he says, I know that you are brave.
I would not ask this of you if there were a choice, but there is
not. Please step into the church with me. Yes, Hugh, you may
come too.

We follow him, and William with us. A ghost light in the
church, the last trace of this longest day – with the window
glass become the grey of moth wings. William lifts a lantern
that was left by the doorway and lights it from a candle by the
rood screen with a spill. Now there are deep shadows thrown;
darkness made profounder by the small flame William holds.
I can see that the great cross and the figures of Our Lady and
the beloved disciple are still upright on the rood beam and that
nothing has been removed but the stone Christ and his bier.
Where he was is now an open tomb chest filled with rubble, the
upper edges ragged where Simm, Jack, William and Brakespeare
hacked hurriedly through the mortar this afternoon.

Can we be sure that the commissioners will not see what has been done? I ask Sir Joselin. I want the assurance of this wise old man. Yes, he says, yes, Simm and Verney will come back at first light tomorrow with a tiny coffin and a slab of limestone that has been cut to fit the base exactly and the sepulchre will then seem like a new-made tomb.

A child's tomb?

Yes, if the commissioners cause it to be unsealed, they will find the coffin but they will not commit the sacrilege of opening it. They will not know that it is empty, and the disturbed earth next to your daughter's grave will convince anyone who cares to ask that you have finally yielded to your lord husband's will and buried the child within the church for the time being.

We must go now, Hugh reminds us, and Joselin says: so to the urgent matter, Lady Alice. I would not ask this of you if there were a choice, but there is not. Will you take the Saint's girdle for safekeeping?

Before I can answer, both Hugh and William protest. William is the louder. Dearest Father, he says, you cannot ask that, you cannot put her in such danger.

She will be in less danger than anybody else, the old priest says calmly. No one will know that she has it, apart from the three of us. Not even Simm. My house may be searched, and I cannot hide the holy relic there, it would be discovered quickly. But I strongly doubt that the king's surveyors will be so bold as to ransack the manor house, and besides there surely must be hiding places there.

Could we not put it in the empty chest tonight, before it is sealed? Hugh asks.

No, because the visitation may ask for that to be opened. Moreover, it must be kept somewhere where I can retrieve it in a hurry, which I could not do if it were under a heavy stone. Women in childbirth seldom have time to wait.

In the flickering light the three men look at me. I will gladly take it and keep it safe, I tell them.

※

And now I have it here, the girdle in its gilt casket, resting beneath a fold of the green silk on my bed. I carried it home, concealed by my cloak, held close against the child in my belly. A promise of a kind, or a pledge. I walked home with Hugh, in the one dark hour between midnight and the precocious dawn, and the rain was falling again. If only we had fern seed, we would be invisible, I said. But even without it we were not seen, and the serving men still awake in the house let us in without question, thinking that we had been at the fire in the village. The priests and the other men had gone their separate ways, padding silently like foxes in the night.

I already knew that the inner panel of one bedpost is loose. It is simple to prise it free with the knife I have borrowed from Hugh, and within is a little space that could have been made to house the casket. I slide it in and push the panel back into place, where obligingly it stays. No one would ever know that the panel had been disturbed. Saint Margaret preserve your holy relic, for I may have need of it soon, I say out loud, and perhaps she hears me.

The last hour of night before the longest day, Saint John's day; it is time to sleep. It was on the longest night that this baby was conceived. Saint Lucy's night; midwinter; midsummer now, the world turns; we are born and then we die. Sanctus Ioannes ora pro nobis, Sancta Lucia ora pro nobis, Sancta Margareta pray for us, nunc et in ora mortis nostra, now and at the hour of our death, sleep now, amen.

⁂

Early on midsummer morning, we met in the garden, Hugh, Roland and I, the three of us alone. Roland was pale and angry – or frightened perhaps and hiding fear with harshness. Why did you not tell me before? was the question he asked first.

Hugh said that he would have done and had wanted to, but Roland could not be found and time had been of the essence.

But why the dead Christ in particular, not the rest?

Because it is an object of love. Because in a matter of months, the people have taken it to their hearts and made it theirs, they kneel to say their prayers beside it and leave their gifts. You have heard the ranter and others of his ilk. You know that they accuse Sir Joselin of breaking a commandment and that such a charge can spread like wildfire. Already, the village is bitterly divided. Left alone and given time, the people would have forgotten their differences, for in the end what do they – or most of them, most of us – truly care about? Food in the belly and a roof above the head. Few of us have time to spare for doctrine. But the preacher, like a gadfly, has provoked them, and like maggots come to feed on bleeding sores, the king's men will come riding here in judgement. Or, rather, in prejudgement. Roland, my beloved brother, you know better than I do what this means.

The people worship other images – the painted saints, for instance.

Yes they do, if worship is the word, but we can do nothing to protect the pictures. If the edict is that they must be destroyed, they can be made again, in safer times. But how could we hope to replace the marble Christ?

And the rood?

Joselin and William believe that it is licit. The injunction that forbade burning candles at the altars made exception of the roods.

And how do you suppose Sir Joselin will account to the commissioners for the missing Christ?

He will say that having seen the error of his ways, which if left unchecked could have led his parish into sin, he had caused the image to be broken into rubble and the base used as a tomb.

A tomb? And who is to be buried in it?

Catherine, your infant cousin.

Roland looked at me in utter disbelief.

A temporary resting place, I said. I have had second thoughts about your uncle's will. I do wish her to lie with her father in the fullness of time, but it is a pity to disturb his tomb again so soon. So arduous to insert even the smallest coffin.

I do not think that I convinced him, but he let this pass. I could see how deeply it pained Hugh to keep the whole truth from his brother. And there was worse.

What about the Saint's girdle, where have the priests put that?

Hugh and I looked at each other and I shrugged. We don't know.

Well, at least I was the only one of us to lie outright. Hugh never knew where I had hidden the relic, no one did.

And more interrogation came soon afterwards, at dinner. What brings you here unheralded, Cousin Hugh? Agnes asked.

My Lord Cumberland is in Oxford and gave me leave to visit.

But where did you go yesterday? Dame Joan says you arrived in the morning.

And so you did, Joan added. The grooms told me. They had your horse. We expected you at table.

Hugh was a poor dissembler and his confusion showed. I had business with Sir Joselin, he stammered. Of a spiritual and private kind. And then he and William bade me stay and eat. Afterwards, I sought you out, but perhaps you had all gone to the revels?

Not I, said Agnes. Nor Alice, I daresay. But you knew that, for I heard that you and she were seen together.

As ever she spoke as if I were not there at the same table with her, or as if I were mute and deaf.

I did meet Lady Alice, Hugh said quickly, and we went walking to the church.

And William with you too? Agnes's voice was sharp as a needle.

Before Hugh could find an answer, Marmion said sternly that he should not have gone to the church, or indeed beyond the gates with the Lady Alice. Did Hugh not know about the fire and the danger we were in? Surely the priests had informed him?

As they talked of the fire and the revolt, I could see that no one at the table except Roland knew that the Christ had vanished in the night. But very soon they would. Both Marmion and

Roland had been warned about the approaching visitation and were expecting it at any hour. Joan wanted to hear what they thought would be the outcome and said that she was fearful, but Marmion assured her that all would be well. The rule was that anything deemed idolatrous would be removed. Idolatry, however, was a matter of opinion. Sir Joselin need simply swear that nothing in the church was worshipped in its own right, as that of course would be abuse, for such reverence is due only unto God.

But then Sir Joselin would swear falsely, Henry said. And perjury is against the law.

Hugh protested. You cannot say that any image in the church is actually worshipped. When the people leave offerings before them, they merely do what they have always done, they do not confuse the emblem with the truth.

Oh no? You think not? I wonder if you are right, Henry replied. But, turning to other things, they left the question smouldering there.

As it was, the commissioners were delayed by a day and so we spent this longest day of the year, this day full of light, in ordinary ways – or in the pretence of them. Dame Joan's kind heart and fondness for children had vanquished any qualms she might have had about my baby's parentage, and she said we should make use of the fine weather to air some infant clothes. Together we unpacked the chest in which she herself had folded Catherine's linen and spread the clothes on the rosemary: a crop of lacy white, as fine as butterfly wings. Again she asked if I wanted her to divine the baby's sex; she was sure I would be praying to Saint Margaret for a boy. Ah no, I said, I am praying for a girl. Yes, she said, I suppose a daughter would be safer, although Lord knows what would become of you. I think that Agnes would drive you from the house.

From the grass on which we were kneeling, I looked up at the house before us. So familiar to me now, its chimneys and tiled roof, its walls, its mullioned windows and their diamond-shaped panes. A child of mine was born here and another is coming soon. Is it home? I don't know. No, wait, perhaps I do – it is where I am, and there is nowhere else to go.

Later came the inevitable word of the vanished Christ, and by the time we met together for prayers, the household was aquiver. The talk was all of where it could be, and who had taken it, and why. Beyond my hearing, there must also have been talk about the newly stripped grave of my baby daughter, but no one confronted me. All evening I tried to avoid Hugh's eye, in case his reddening skin betrayed his lack of guile. He said nothing about the image, but anyone who knew him could have seen how he wrestled with concealment of the truth. Roland said nothing either, while I was in the room at least. Afterwards, I came to see that he must have said something to Henry, although I never knew how much. I have forgiven him for that. No man alive can keep a secret wholly to himself – remember the barber of Midas? – and we all turn in the first place to the one we love. Yes, I could wish that Roland had whispered to the ground instead, but would that have made much difference? As Midas found, even the wind has voices.

Agnes misconstrued the state of things. Somehow she conceived the notion that a tomb lay half empty, with room for bodies, in the place where the marble Christ had been, and she said in high excitement: now Titus can be buried as he should be, with my kin. And Henry said, why not?

Roland looked to me for an answer, but I gave none. Cousin, as you know, the Church forbids the burial of animals in consecrated ground, he began to say, as gently as he could, but Agnes interrupted.

You are such fools, she said. All of you. You two brothers and my dead father's wife. Do you not see? How do you not see that change is coming? You prose on and on about the rules, about what is right and what is wrong, about who has a soul and who does not, and you do not see that those rules are only so much chaff! These are the days of change. Soon are the days when we will find that every man and woman must make their own contract with God. No intercessors, no saints, no priests, no rules. If I believe that Titus has a soul as good as mine, then so be it and no one will gainsay me.

And then she turned to me, face to face at last.

Alice, she hissed. Of all of us, you should see this. No longer the old rules. The old rules that were fetters. You can marry your lover! Even while he remains a priest and takes my father's money! Go on, make haste, before you deliver your bastard!

A stunned silence followed. And then, to my astonishment, Marmion rose to my defence. No, Agnes. The Lady Alice's child is not a bastard. It is brother to you, or sister, your father its father too. You should beg pardon of your stepmother and do penance for your slander!

I shall not, for it is no slander! Why would you take her word?

I took your father's word, he said, as I have already told you. His last words, on his deathbed. And Lambert also knows it to be true, for he was there the night that Lady Alice came to the lord's bedchamber.

I will not believe you, Agnes cried. My father cannot have been in his right mind. And Lambert is dumb, so how could he tell you what was truth or falsehood?

Marmion began to say that even without speech Lambert had understanding, but Agnes did not stay to hear him.

The end of days

Immediately after the tribulation of those days shall the sun be
darkened, and the moon shall not give her light, and the stars shall
fall from heaven, and the powers of the heavens shall be shaken;
And the brother shall deliver up the brother to death,
There shall not be left here one stone upon another, not one stone.
All these are the beginning of sorrows.

꙳

It was not like that. If there had been any pity in heaven, the
stars would have fallen from the skies and darkness mantled
the whole land but as it was, the end of days began with birdsong, the scent of linden and the blessing of the sun. And, in
the morning after the feast day of Saint John, the arrival of a
royal commissioner and his secretary. Courteously, they called
at the house before proceeding to the church. Neither man was
snake-like in the least: one was as round as a barrel and laughed
readily; the other was more solemn, with watering eyes and the
rapid blink of a cornered rabbit.

I was in the hall with Marmion, Hugh and Roland when they
came. They accepted ale and sat a while, explaining their business
to us. There was no cause for concern, the fat visitor promised;
their purpose was not to censure but advise. This visitation was
a preliminary one. Our parish, with every other parish in the

bishopric, was now required by law to meet certain conditions:
to have, to use and to make available the Holy Bible in English,
and additionally the book of the revered Archbishop Cranmer's
sermons; prayers and masses to be said in English, and all clerics
to preach four times a year against the usurped powers of Rome.
Hinderers of worship and supporters of Rome to be detected
and reported. Graces at meals to be prayed in English, not in
Latin. From this day onwards, there must be no candles burning
anywhere but on the altar before the Sacrament, and then two
candles only, and all images and monuments that are accessories
to idolatry to be taken down. Parishioners to be exhorted to do
the same. Clerics to preach at least once each quarter against
fantasies such as idols and pilgrimages. A ban on ringing bells and
lighting tapers and any other intercession or ceremony where
the intention is to imply discharge of the burden of sin.

We listened to them in silence. In my head was Joselin's voice,
chanting the Kyries and Glorias, and William's too, and the voices
of the children singing the old words in the old ways; would
the new rules be acceptable to them all? I knew that the others
shared my doubts. I knew that in their minds the brothers and
Marmion were picturing the faithful lighting tapers at the altar of
the dead Christ, and the women on their knees before the Saint.

Well, it is a fine thing to pray in the native tongue, together
with the Latin, Roland said at last. So it is, Hugh agreed, and
no doubt to have the Gospel accessible to everyone, although
few in our parish can read.

This parish has a chantry priest, according to our intelligence,
the rheumy-eyed secretary said. As His Majesty demands that
cantors must teach the youths of their parishes to read and write,
all will be literate soon.

If the parishes can keep their chantries, Roland said quietly. And that may depend on the king's will too.

The visitors said nothing to this but only asked Marmion for the total of the benefice. And while the steward was at his ledgers, would the young gentlemen care to go with them to the church?

Hugh said yes at once, but Roland hesitated. Poor boy, speared on two horns; at the time I did not understand how near he was at his wits' end, how torn between competing loyalties and creeds. If only he had exercised his right as elder brother to keep the younger within the safe bounds of the house. But instead he made his excuses and let Hugh go without him. And I went too, before Marmion or Roland could hold me back. I knew that William Clare would be there, waiting for the visitation.

⁂

We heard the voice before we rounded the corner and saw him. He was in the churchyard, standing on an upturned pail, and a small throng was gathered about him, gazing upwards, adoring, sucking in his words. It was the first time I had seen him for myself – the wandering preacher. I had imagined him as gaunt and hollow-eyed, but in the flesh he was tall and burly. The two visitors stopped at the lychgate to hear what he was saying, and Hugh and I waited with them.

Their idols are the work of human hands! Idols of silver and stone. They have mouths, but they cannot speak, they have eyes, but they cannot see, with their ears they cannot hear, with their hands they cannot feel, with their feet they cannot walk, no sound comes from their throats. And their makers will come to be like them – things without speech or

*sight, deaf and paralytical – dead things – and so will all who worship
at their altars…*

Stamping, shouting, clapping in response; the people were
as far gone as they would have been at the midsummer revels
two nights ago: the licence of the dark carried over into daylight, a strange new wildness in them. I saw faces that I knew:
Goodge, his sons, Mobey the father of the red-haired child,
our own man Rafe, and Susan. O Susan, who was a child of
my own home and travelled here with me when I was a bride,
Susan my trusted friend. And the sun poured down upon us on
this summer morning.

These travelling preachers, they always call to my mind Saint
John the Baptist, the secretary said.

The commissioner laughed. This one manifestly does not
live on a diet of locusts! Look at him, he is as broad as an ox.

It was true, and he did have a way of lowering his brow and
thrusting his shaved head forward as he spoke that, with the
folds of flesh at his neck, increased his ox-resemblance. But there
never was an ox with such fire in the eyes, and everybody saw
that the sparks had caught.

We were observed as we came closer, and the preacher halted
in mid-torrent. It seemed he had also been expecting the visitation. Both the priests were at the entrance to the porch, framing
it on either side, Sir Joselin leaning on a stick, looking frail and
very old; and my baby made a sudden, violent lurch, as if impul-
sively to reach him. William raised a hand in greeting. It was a
greeting for me, I felt, and not for the two visitors, whom Sir
Joselin saluted more formally when they had made their way
through the press. The blessing of Our Lord be upon you, he
said. You are welcome to our church.

Ask him where he hid the graven image, a man's voice roared from the crowd. Idolater that he is! Idolater and Roman, traitor to the Crown and worshipper of sinful gods!

If the preacher had struck the spark, that man heaped on the fuel that set the fire blazing. Other voices took up his cry: idolaters, idolaters, idolaters and Romans! – and Hugh said urgently to me, how shall they be saved?

It is only Joselin that they accuse. Not William.

William will not leave Sir Joselin's side.

As if in a dream, I watched, entirely calm. I could have been looking at a painting on a wall that was wholly remote from me. Four sets of figures: the old man and the young one in the doorway, like statues carved on the jambs; the men and women grouped around the preacher; the king's commissioner and his minion; and at a little distance, Hugh and me. And as in a dream, there fell a sudden hush when the commissioner took a step back and turned to speak to the crowd.

Romans? Traitors? Why do you say this?

An uproar of competing voices answered him, each one keen to stoke the flames and none there present to protest against the charges. In no court of justice should there ever be a trial without witnesses for the defence, as there was in our village that June morning. Or as there was lifetimes ago, in the court of Pontius Pilate. I could not comprehend it then, and still cannot: how could the people whom he had christened, shriven, married, turn against their priest? A man whom they had loved? The one who had come to their sickbeds, their childbeds, their deathbeds, with his prayers and blessings? A man who had loved them, equally, without judgement or favour.

Now there was nothing familiar in the faces of the crowd, for each was changed into a furious, hissing mask. Single words rang out of the clamour: commandment, graven, chantry, deer park, stone. Chantry, chantry, chantry; singing for the dead. And then out of the corner of my eye, I saw Henry Martyn. He was under the yew tree, half-hidden in the shadow of its branches, but his pale hair shone out as bright against the dark leaves as the wings of an owl in the night. Even from where I stood, I sensed his absorption, and the thought came to me that in some mysterious way he had foretold this scene and was waiting for it.

The yew spread out its darkness like a curtain. It was hard to see what was beneath but when I looked, I made out Agnes, cradling something in her arms. A small shape swaddled in white like a baby, or like the body of a baby wrapped in cerecloth. Like a chrisom child. Titus? Or Catherine? No, not possibly, how could she?

Then it was as if the world slowed down or as if I saw it through a veil, the scene before me wavering, as when the rising heat of a blazing fire makes the air to shimmer. I did not see who cast the first stone or the stone itself as it struck William, but I did see him fall to the ground. No, not fall but slide, quite slowly, along the side of the doorway, as if he had grown tired of standing and simply wanted to rest. He stayed where he was, slumped against the wall.

Someone also unknown to me grabbed Sir Joselin and pulled him away from the porch. I saw him struggling to escape his restraint and get back to William, but he could not. The commissioner ducked down and disappeared into the crowd. There was another suspended moment: everybody still, everybody quiet, everybody waiting for what would happen next, but it lasted less than an indrawn breath before the frenzy took unbreakable hold.

I tell it now, so many days later, as if there had been a clear sequence of events – a stone, a hush, a shout and bedlam – but that is not truly how it was. There were all those things, but in contradiction: time stopped and time speeded; sound and silence; I saw it and I took it in and yet I did not; it happened slowly and in a flash; after the first stone standstill, then the hail. Shattering glass as the next stones found their mark on the west window. And Hugh dashing through it towards William, and reaching him, and trying to pull him clear of the bombardment and being hit by a jagged stone and his blood flowering round him like a halo.

Hugh's blood stemmed the rain of stones, and again a silence fell as the people saw what they had done. But such elemental fury could not be held back long and they knew – I knew – that what had begun must be brought to an end, as a raging storm must run its course or lust reach its own quietus. Some of the throng were already melting away, but others surged forward past the fallen bodies into the church. And all the time Henry Martyn and Agnes were watching, beneath the cover of the yew.

I remember little after that. A warm gush of water between my legs, water or maybe blood. A startling wrench of pain. And Susan leading me gently away from the churchyard and the men I loved.

🐉

Sunlight on the green silk, moonlight on the lilies, days becoming nights and nights becoming days in fever dreams with neither end nor clear beginning; through the hours the women come and go with columbine and belladonna, hot rags and wine and scent of cloves. Mother Wright the midwife binds my belly and Joan prays, and Susan too, bidding the child to stay a while and bloom in darkness like a snowdrop, not to seek daylight too soon. Wild thyme and oil of musk. The baby listens to the spells: Agios, Agios, Agios, Cross of Christ protect you, Cross of Christ defend you; but not for long, not long enough, a week at most; the little thing lacks the gift of patience, and so Joan must bring white linen for my bed, a birthing sheet or shroud.

So small a thing, although so perfect, hands and feet, so small he cannot live. Or so Joan says, but I can hear him cry, thin and high and weak as a fledgling, and Mother Wright puts her finger in his mouth; he breathes, she says, and she wraps him swiftly and carries him from the room. He must be baptised at once, Joan warns, but there is no priest to do it. No priest is needed; if he be alive still, there is no time to lose, and Mother Wright will do instead, Susan replies, and the two of them hurry away and leave me alone to beg the saint whose scrap of girdle I have hidden by me for her prayers. Margaret of Antioch, you survived the dragon. You whose aid brought forth this child, now let him live.

They told me later that William died quickly, from a hard blow to his heart. It took Hugh more time to die. The stone that hit him fractured the back of his skull and the wound became infected. Doctor Moreton came, and Dame Joan did her best, but they could not save him. He died awake and in pain. Why did you not take me to him, I cried bitterly, but they only shook their heads and tried to soothe me, patting me with their ineffectual hands, softly, softly: quiet now, hush.

Poor Joan, her sickroom skills were severely tested during those terrible days. Moreover, she had her own sore grief to bear, for Hugh was like another son to her, she who had looked after him since he was a child. When I was strong enough to hear it, she described his dying and the anguish that Roland has suffered ever since. He blames himself, she said, for letting Hugh go to the church and for bringing Henry Martyn to this house.

Henry was a witness at Sir Joselin's hearing in the Consistory Court. As in Pilate's court, none were present who loved the defendant; only Marmion attended, and he was not allowed to see Henry's deposition. But, as he said afterwards, it needed little imagination – the charges had been made often enough before. And also as in Pilate's court, the accused stayed silent and refused to plead his case. Whereas Marmion had hoped that Sir Joselin would escape with nothing but a fine, now it seemed that he would no longer have the benefit of clergy but might stand trial for treason. Henry Martyn would not be the only one who remembered what the priest had said about the law of Herod; he had never made a secret of his firm belief that God alone could claim sovereignty over a man's conscience. A dangerous thing to say aloud, when earthly sovereigns make themselves the arbiters of truth. In the meantime, while the matter was undecided, the old man was in the bishop's keeping and rumoured to be ill.

What of the stone-throwers – would they be tried for murder? Ah no, for there were none to testify who threw any one particular stone among the several that were intended only to break windows, never heads. In that affray, errant aim was understandable, no one in the crowd had meant to kill. Their first target was the west window, branded sinful by the preacher for its likeness of things in heaven and on earth.

If that was so, which I can believe, they admirably succeeded. Not one pane of bright glass remained when they were done. I did not see the destruction then, but Joan described it vividly: the floor of the church abristle with fragments of glass, all three holy images on the rood torn down, and every painting scratched out; nothing left undamaged except the marble tomb behind its iron grille. And the vaulted ceiling. It was mainly the stones left behind by the carvers from Tewkesbury that formed the crowd's artillery, those flawed cuts of beautiful pale stone.

No thirty-day bells were tolled for Hugh and William; no one dared defy the new ruling. I do not know who said their funeral masses, for I was high with fever then, but Joan told me that both were buried in the churchyard. That's good, that's how it should be: I think of William on his knees on the grass, attending to the weeds; he will love the flowers that grow above him, and so will Hugh. Blood streamed from Hugh's head that morning, but the Lord will change it into golden rays, as gold encircles the head of the lost god in the corner of Yatt's field; why not? He died a godlike death.

Today, the twenty-fifth day of the month of June, the day after Midsummer's Day

If no month's mind, well then a year's mind: the world has turned a full circle; it is midsummer again and high time to remember. A whole year gone. Death's calendar is not simple; or is it the conjugation of the verb that is so difficult: they died yesterday, last week, last month, a year ago? And the permanence of the past tense also; yes, hard to believe, even now, when they have been dead a summer, an autumn, a winter and a spring, a harvest and a great storm, Michaelmas, Advent, Christmas, Lent, snow and sleet and sunshine, new growth and falling leaves. Four deaths, two births; not quite a fair exchange, but when were the scales equal? Four deaths if I count my husband's, more than a year ago, soon after the feast of Valentine, an unnaturally warm time, I remember. Death should come on cold days, when icicles hang from the trees and nothing stirs, not in the full bloom of June, as it did for Hugh and William Clare.

It was cold here in the parish when Sir Joselin died, and it must have been colder yet where he lay, in London, in a prison cell. Word came to us in November, but the exact day of his death is unknown. Roland had been with him a fortnight or so earlier, and now reproaches himself cruelly for not having stayed, for leaving him to die on his own. But Joselin would not have been alone, I think; not if there is a God. No man was ever more steadfast in his faith than the old priest and consequently less afraid of dying. His death was, as Joan said, a blessed mercy – far better in a bed, albeit in a cell, than upon the scaffold or the bonfire. She is right; even if the angels had swooped straight away to rescue his soul at the moment of his dying, those dreadful means of exit would have been a prospect to confound the very bravest.

Roland should not be full of remorse, for he fought to save Sir Joselin, at grave risk to himself. What we have learned in these last years is that anyone who wants a long life must lie as low as a vole in a hedgerow: sticking out one's neck is asking for the blade. Nonetheless my nephew Roland wrote letters to clerics and patrons at court protesting Joselin's innocence, he rode up and down to London with the testimonies of the warden Cadd and other parishioners, he appeared at the trial and swore that the priest was no papist but instead a loyal subject of the king. In the end, though, it was Henry Martyn's evidence that prevailed, being more to the taste of the times. Although they reject the images that were as books for those who cannot read, these henchmen of the young Josiah, they are very fond of exemplars that serve as warnings. And poor Sir Joselin was one such – strung up like a dead bird as deterrent. It was the girdle of Saint Margaret that undid him finally. Charged with superstitious practices and, contrarily, of stealing valuable possessions of the church, he refused to deny the power of the relic or to reveal where it was hidden. His accusers must have felt deprived when the old man had the effrontery to die a natural death of ague before he could be burned or hanged, but in truth they should be glad that there was one less martyr for the annals.

I have not seen Agnes's son and will never see him, I suppose, although he is half-brother to my own. Agnes has severed all bonds with me despite my promise that this house would be hers too, for as long as she wanted to live here, alone or married to Henry. She will not forgive me for bearing her father's lawful heir. However, the liberal sum my lord left her as her portion in his will was enough, it seems, to bind Henry Martyn to his troth, against Joan's fears. Or was it Roland who held him to it? I hear that Henry prospers and am pleased by that for Agnes's sake. Does any woman freely choose whom to love? Having lost her mother, her two brothers and her sisters, is it any wonder that Agnes adored her monkey Titus with as fierce a passion as a mother's for her child? I suppose that she got what she wanted in the end – the creature's burial in the church – but I have not asked if that was indeed what happened, and I do not care. On that day in June, a year ago today, there was such havoc in the church that the levering up of stones would not have been remarked. Nor do I know if the king's commissioner ever caused the tomb chest where the Christ had lain to be unsealed: the limestone lid that Simm made is in place still, with nothing written on it.

As drunks are sheepish when they come to their senses, the makers of mayhem are hangdog these days but calm again, their fury spent. When they woke from their madness and saw what they had done, most of the rioters were very sorry for it, but it was too late by then; the dead stay dead, no matter how fervent their murderers' repentance. A public avowal of culpability, and due legal process, might have been tidier but would not have brought Hugh or William back. As it was, the half-hearted enquiries into the killings came to nothing – Goodge the wheelwright's brother is the constable of this parish. As it is, the perpetrators will have to square their consciences with God.

The wandering preacher has moved on. There's no need to fear, though, that his next stopping place will catch fire, for his is no longer the voice in the wilderness but the voice of the orthodox. What had been a call to arms against the superstitious old ways is doctrine now, imposed, inspected, controlled and regulated, and woe betide the dissenter. The little king has signed an Act that shuts down every chantry in the land and converts all their assets to his use. Well, it is widely known that his father left an empty treasury and a pile of debts. Poor boy, he had to get his money somewhere, and the dead are less likely to complain than the living over the loss of their bequests. If they believed that they could buy songs for their souls in perpetuity, then they were fools, according to the law. Fools anyway to expect that anything could be done for them when they were dead and beyond hope. It's only their tombs that are safe still, left standing when all else is torn apart. Marmion says the reason for that is the general respect for the dead, but why the stones that house their corpses should be sacrosanct, if their souls are not, remains a puzzle to me.

Joan and I went to mass this morning to pray for William, dead this day last year. Our prayers were of necessity unvoiced; the new priest teaches that salvation comes through faith alone, not through our own deserving, and is anyway predestined; therefore prayers for the dead are prayers in vain. This new priest is temporary, only here until the bishop – likewise newly installed – decides what should become of this parish. To this day the commissioner is seeking to discover where the relic of Saint Margaret and the marble Christ are hidden, but no one will tell him, and because he is ashamed of having fled precipitously when William was killed and Hugh mortally wounded, without even trying to use his powers to enforce order, he dislikes returning to this village and his investigation is as cursory as the one into the murders. It is enough for the Commission that they have confiscated all the silver and the vestments that the church owned, with the money my lord my husband left in trust as provision for his chantry and perpetual prayers for his soul. With my heart I give thanks that the dead Christ lies with Catherine, Hugh and William, the book of their lives written in air and birdsong, not in stone. Let the earth rest lightly on them, requiescant in pace, you who were beloved.

The church is a white space now, clean and white like bone, and empty of almost everything but pews and font and pulpit, and the tomb in its idle chantry. The altars have gone, with the rood screen and the images of Jesus, Mary and Saint John; all the walls are bare, except for one. On the east wall, beneath the window which used to show the risen Christ, a careful hand has lettered the Ten Commandments of Moses in pitch-black paint, for the benefit of the three or four here who can read. Another kind of doom. Eleven imperatives; eight times thou shalt not. Words shall be our coinage now, in place of pictures; one day people shall learn to read them, but will that bring them closer to the Word that was in the beginning, the Word that was with God? Perhaps, if our letters, like the alphabet of the Armenians, were shaped like birds.

Listening, half-listening, to the priest reading from a letter to the Romans – *Let every soul be subject unto the higher powers* – I remember William telling of those bird-forms, moving his fingers like wings. I remember William singing. My son, William Hugh, sings all day long, from the time he opens his eyes in the morning until he closes them at night; he cannot talk, but he can make the sound of words in music. His eyes are sloe-dark, like his father's.

Sunlight is dancing through the clear glass of the windows and alighting on the white stone of my tomb. Hands raised in prayer, pearls round my neck, my black-veiled head resting on its book of stone. That tomb can wait, I think. I don't entirely miss the painted windows, although they were beautiful, for the plainness of the crown glass in their place is pleasing in the way it lets the light in; whiteness and clarity, they have their own truth too. This is a peaceful place, but something has been stolen from it — not solely the candles, the colours and the pictures on the walls. The saints have gone, they who were ambassadors of a power beyond all understanding, stepping stones to God. And it was here where the living and the dead met, where the living had faith that their songs would reach the ones they had lost and give them comfort. A place where the dead, although invisible and speechless, were present in prayer and imagination, a place of covenant between us. Now it is simply where the bones lie, nothing but a tomb, for the bridge of prayer has been condemned and the dead shall only be remembered in graven stone and in the short span of a heart. Safe they may be, in the gentle night, but what of us who mourn them in this silence; how shall we sing for our dead?

A song for my daughter

Lullay, lully, lulla, lullay,
Now close your eyes and sleep
Sleep, my little one, sleep,
Your ceiling is the sky above
Lully my love, the stars your light
Fear not the dangers of the night,
But close your eyes and do not weep,
Sleep peacefully, my dove.
Lullay, lully, my little child
In your soft bed of leaves,
Rose petals for your counterpane,
Lullabied by gentle rain
And I who for you ever mourn
Will cradle you again.

In memoriam
Catherine
William
Hugh
Richard
Joselin
Agnes
John
Richard
Edith
Creature
dona eis requiem,
sempiterna requiem
eternal peace give unto them,
Amen
Amen
Amen

Acknowledgements

My thanks to Mark Richards and Swift Press, Alex Billington and Alex Middleton at Tetragon, Sarah Terry, Madeleine Rogers, Anna Webber, Mark Alexander, Martin Jennings, Keith Kirby, Simon Miller, Aidan Mortimer and, always, to Susannah, Arabella and Joseph.

William Clare's words on page 95 are taken from a sermon preached by Lancelot Andrewes on Christmas Day in 1611.